Praise for Cracks in the Foundation

"It's hard to think about real estate without crying...Well, try laughing, instead. In *Cracks in the Foundation*, Erica Ferencik convinces us that comic reality is more hysterical than we ever imagined. This is a fun read, as if Ferencik were to the (mini-) manor born."

Alex Beam, *Boston Globe* Columnist

"Erica Ferencik is one of our podcast's most popular contributors, a triple-threat humorist and fiction writer with the heart of an angel, the wit of a first rate satirist, and the zaniness of John Cleese..."

Tony Kahn, Creator and Producer of National Public Radio's "Morning Stories" Podcast

"Ginger Kanadoo is outrageous and ridiculous. I loved her from page one. What a delightful book!"

Barbara Corcoran, Founder of the Corcoran Group

"Seldom have I loved a heroine with more abandon than the ever-optimistic Ginger Kanadoo, washed up realtor with an outhouse to sell and a daughter from hell. Erica Ferencik's big-hearted debut is very fresh and very funny, full of flawed characters with feet of clay and hearts of gold. Like a scrappy dandelion struggling through a crack in the pavement, Ginger Kanadoo grapples valiantly with love, work, parenthood, her mother, even a ghost or two. Will she succeed in blooming in her beloved Squamskootnocket? In the capable hands of the talented Ferencik, Ginger's journey over the hill is a hoot with a heart. *Cracks in the Foundation* is a winner of a novel, an enjoyable reminder that the grass is always greener on the other side of the outhouse."

Mary E. Mitchell, author of *Starting Out Sideways*, St. Martin's Press

"Get ready for a bumpy, surprise-filled ride as Ginger Kanadoo—covered in donut crumbs and pond scum—lurches toward realtor immortality, middle-aged romance, and reconciliation with both her cantankerous mother and her sullen Wiccan daughter. A successful concoction of broad comedy, finely observed detail, and real emotion, *Cracks in the Foundation* is a compelling read."

Holly Chamberlin, author of *The Friends We Keep*, 2007, and the upcoming *Tuscan Holiday*, Kensington, August, 2008

"The most ridiculous, hilarious romp I've ever been on! This book is entertaining, silly, and wonderful!"

Katrin Schumann, co-author of *Mothers Need Time-Outs, Too,* McGraw-Hill, 2008

"Erica Ferencik's comic novel should be required reading for anyone buying or selling a house, or just anyone who wants a good laugh. There are so many funny things in this book, it makes me want to sell my house. Well, not really. But if there is such a thing as real estate fiction, Ferencik is the queen of it. Read and enjoy!"

Becky Motew, author of *Coupon Girl,* Dorchester Publishing

"Disastrously compelling and exceptionally funny! *Cracks in the Foundation* is a page-turning romp seasoned with unique, eccentric characters. Ginger 'Another Zin, please' Kanadoo is a loveable lush who crashes through life with the reckless abandon of a frat house social director. I'm already jonesing for the sequel!"

Rick D'Elia, Comedian and co-author of *How to Talk to a Yankee Fan,* Seven Locks Press

"Ferencik's *Cracks in the Foundation* is a hoot! Ginger is simply irresistible even as she fumbles from one disaster to the next. Her big heart prevails with the help of her fleet of nutty relatives and friends who are equally endearing. I was gripped (and laughing!) right to the very last sentence."

Cindy Pierce, Comic Storyteller and co-author of *Finding the Doorbell, Sexual Satisfaction for the Long Haul,* 2008, Nomad Press

"How much of Erica Ferencik's portrait of a real-estate agent as an aging caricature is wickedly funny satire and how much is reporting from the front lines? Each reader can draw that line. If I were a licensed real estate agent, Ginger would make me squirm...and laugh...and squirm...and laugh..."

Curtis Seltzer, author of *How to be a Dirt-Smart Buyer of Country Property,* Infinity Publishing

From Readers in the Real Estate Community

"This book is drop dead hilarious. Ginger is the Lucy Ricardo of realtors! I couldn't wait to see what she got herself into/out of next! File under fiction...but this is a day in the life of Real Estate. I was supposed to be reading another book for my book club, but I could not put this down!!!"

Susan Gonnella, Realtor

"A rip roaring ride through the hills and valleys of real estate!"

Scott Adamson, Realtor

"Erica Ferencik has masterfully captured the very essence of the stereotypical realtor in her creation of Ginger Kanadoo. Ginger epitomizes the very worst qualities of her profession, yet she still manages to capture our hearts. Anyone in a "commission-only" profession will probably see a little bit of Ginger in themselves...and hopefully have enough of a sense of humor to laugh it off. Erica is a very, very funny writer and I can't wait till her next book!"

Debbie Greenlaw, Realtor

"A cover-to-cover delight! The hilarious misadventures of Ginger Kanadoo is a must read. Janet Evanovich, make room for Erica!"

Tom Fama, Realtor

"There are two kinds of books for me: the red light book, which is where you are so excited about it you read it at red lights, and the open house book, which is what you read when you are stuck in someone's house for two hours with nothing to do. This was a red light book, no question. I was reading this book in the car and actually blew off business until I finished it on Sunday. I loved it!"

Beth Byrne, Realtor

"Oh, my God...when I wasn't smiling I was laughing, and when I wasn't laughing I was smiling my face off! I will certainly never look at a bottle of white zin the same way ever again. Laugh out loud funny!"

Cat Strahan, Realtor

"Witty and entertaining, this book will hit a nerve with anyone who's ever bought or sold a house, while realtors will relate to every wild adventure Ginger has—this book is a scream!"

Mike Hunter, Realtor

"I couldn't put it down and wanted to keep going after the last page!"

Marji Ford, Realtor

"Because I am the #1 Realtor in my own mind, and have also followed my Mom's footprints, I could really relate to Ginger. Easy reading that puts life into perspective...and you thought you had it bad...Ginger's simplistic solutions make you want to turn the page to see what disaster is waiting right around the corner for her to somehow wriggle out of!"

Kathy Gatos, Realtor

"I couldn't stop laughing, and I couldn't stop loving these characters! What a great story. Now I'll never be able to recruit!"

Barbara Epstein, Broker

"Great read! This really nails the crazy world of real estate."

Dave Banks, President, On the Level Home Inspection

CRACKS IN THE FOUNDATION

* * *

A NOVEL BY

ERICA FERENCIK

waking dream press

waking dream press
Framingham, Massachusetts

Cracks in the Foundation

Publisher's Note: This is a work of fiction. Names, characters, places and incidents either are the product of the author's imagination or are used fictitiously, and any resemblance to actual persons, living or dead, business establishments, products, events or locales is entirely coincidental.

LCCN: 2008924584

Printed in the United States of America

Cover design by Henry Sene Yee
Cover illustration by Victor Juhasz
Map drawn by Valerie Spain

Publisher's Cataloging-in-Publication Data
Ferencik, Erica.
Cracks in the foundation : a novel / by Erica Ferencik.
p. : map ; cm.
ISBN-13: 978-0-9815741-0-3
ISBN-10: 0-9815741-0-6
1. Real estate agents--New York (State)--Fiction. 2. Real estate business--New York (State)--Fiction. 3. Wiccans--New York (State)--Fiction. 4. New York (State)--Fiction. 5. Humorous fiction. I. Title.
PS3606.E746 C73 2008
813/.6 2008924584

For George

⁂ ⁂ ⁂

LAKE SQUAMSKOOTNOCKET

dancing wiccans

Billy Higgins' house

Ginger's outhouse

The Jones' house

old Man Higgins' 35 acres

OLDE TOWNE

the MALL at VANDERSKLEET-ON-HUDSON home of the original CHESS KING

A Map of Squamskootnocket New York

COXSACKIE NECK

MAIN STREET

old Gummy Be[illegible] Factory

Voorheesvrankinville Farms House of Freshwater Taffy

warm pretty places

Boo!

Vandersloot and the Haunted House

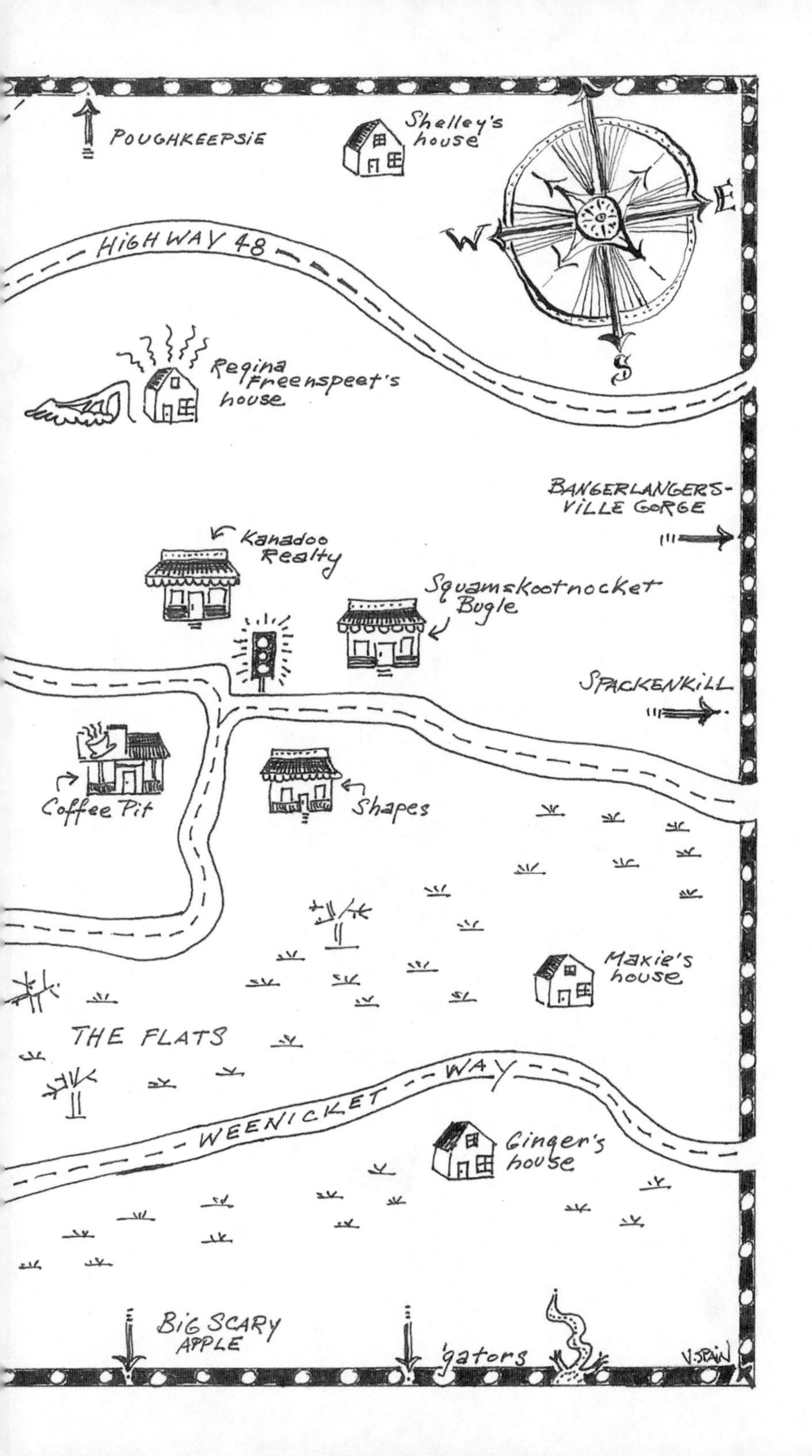
POUGHKEEPSIE
Shelley's house
E
W
S
HIGHWAY 48
Regina Freenspeet's house
BANGERLANGERS-VILLE GORGE
Kanadoo Realty
Squamskootnocket Bugle
SPACKENKILL
Coffee Pit
Shapes
Maxie's house
THE FLATS
WEENICKET WAY
Ginger's house
BIG SCARY APPLE
'gators
V. SPAIN

GINGER KANADOO

A life-long resident of Squamskootnocket, New York, Ginger Kanadoo is the end result of an unbroken line of Kanadoo realtors that stretches back to the legendary Myles Cornish Kanadoo, 18th century fur-trader and real estate magnate whose untimely death by stoning in an unrelated sheep incident is mourned to this day.

A proud graduate of Squamskootnocket High, Ginger was first alternate on the "Skooter Cheetahs" cheerleading squad during her 1964-65 academic year, when she was also voted "Most Likely to Never Leave Town." According to the Squamskootnocket yearbook — "The 'Nocket" — Ginger's goals included helming the Gummy Bear Factory float in the 'Squam Parade, and not getting pregnant. After a brief stint in the performing arts as "Second Alternate Crowd Member" during the 'Skootnocket Players production of "Brigadoon," Ginger got down to business. Following in her mom "Big Jean" Kanadoo's footprints, as well as those of her Aunt Maxie Kanadoo, Ginger has become a real estate legend of sorts in the white-hot Lower to Mid Eastern NY regional real estate niche!

Chapter 1

Jim Steele, photojournalist from *The Squamskootnocket Bugle*, wiped the sweat from his forehead, then fluttered a hand through his clammy comb-over. It was only mid-May but the air hung still and swampy smelling, heavy with spring rain that threatened but never seemed to arrive. Mosquitoes hummed and whined; dragonflies zoomed by like small aircraft, landing and debarking from Jim's camera and tripod set at a cockeyed angle in the muddy ground.

On his left, a great clattering erupted from behind the upraised trunk of a 1966 mustard-colored Pontiac.

"You need some—" he started.

"Nope, I'm good..." came a woman's voice from behind the rusted metal. "Why dontcha just hold on a sec." More scuttling, a random crash, a muffled curse. "It'd look so damned good...it's gotta be in here someplace."

"Sure would be a nice touch." Jim hiked up his oversized aviators with a squinch of his nose and started toward her car.

"It's just that it's been a while since I've had a" —grunt— "listing."

At that moment Ginger Kanadoo, of Kanadoo Real Estate, emerged, triumphant. She marched around to the front of her car holding a banged-up orange and black For Sale sign straight out in front of her like a shield. On it was a photo of her—circa thirty-five years ago—with a smile, a wink, and a jaunty thumbs up. Now cresting sixty and cotton-haired, she took a step back in her low-to-the-ground, bowlegged way, and looked quizzically at the sign.

She leaned it against a tree and disappeared again into the bowels of the trunk. Out flew a measuring tape, some tattered maps, a broken compass, the gnawed-on heel of a shoe, a half-eaten Ring Ding.

"Watcha doin', Ginger?"

"Just, y'know, wanted to wipe it off a bit. Best face forward and all that."

She trundled back around and rubbed hard at the sign with a piece of old newspaper. "Bit of elbow grease'll fix this right up."

Leaning back on his car, Jim watched as she bent to her task.

"Pretty exciting, huh?" She spit on the newspaper and began to work at something that looked like bubble gum.

"What?" he said, gazing at her.

She gestured with the fistful of *Bugle* at a decayed lump of a structure behind her. "Whaddya mean, 'what'? The new listing! Whadja think I meant?"

"Right." He shook his head. "Jeez, a' course. I'm a dope." He pushed himself off the car and gathered his photography equipment, moving his tripod out a few feet into the road.

"So when's your deadline for tomorrow?"

"An hour ago."

"No sweat. We'll make it." She put her hands on her hips, one foot at an angle, like a dancer. "Now, where do you want me?"

He regarded her. Through the eyes of a still-crushing high school boy, Jim looked at Ginger and saw a copper-haired beauty with an hour-glass figure tossing a baton skyward and leaping up to catch it; the sun glinting off her flashing white teeth, the pleats of her skirt opening and lifting with the wind to reveal inch after inch of creamy, nubile thigh... He blinked hard, then cleared his throat. "Ah! I know."

But she hadn't been waiting for instruction. He watched as she turned and clambered up the slight, bramble-gnarled hill to the door of the hovel, struggling for purchase in her sensible realtor walking shoes. He scrambled up after her, thorns ripping at the bare flesh of his forearms. "Do you need any help...?"

Ginger whacked at a vine or two with her handbag, reached the shack and grabbed the crumbling door handle, yanking herself up with surprising strength.

"Nope, I'm all set." She turned and brushed herself off. "Everything's A-OK up here." She took a deep breath and exhaled mightily, standing tall and stretching her neck as if she stood at the top of an awe-inspiring peak. "What a view, Jim! What. A. View. I tell ya, this puppy's gonna fly off the market. Better bring me an offer and fast if you want a piece of this action!"

She gazed at the sumpy muck of Lake Squamskootnocket which lay like a brown diaper stain to the west, while next to her the tiny building listed forty-five degrees to the east, as if reaching toward the road or whatever happened to be the quickest way out of town.

"So," she said, clapping her hands together once. "How do you want me to do this?"

"Well, you could—"

"I know! I can be opening the door, sort of a welcome-home kind of thing. How does that sound?"

"Sounds fine. I'm ready when you are." Jim took his position behind the camera, squinting into the lens and framing Ginger next to the hut which loomed stark and warty against the troubled sky.

All smiles, Ginger grabbed the doorknob with a practiced flourish and turned it.

Nothing. It was stuck shut. Still mugging for the camera, she yanked on it again, rattling the knob harder in its loose casement. Nada. Grin pasted on, she shook it again, this time with both hands, then gave it one last mighty heave.

With this, the door burst open, releasing a torrent of bees that poured out like the spewing guts of Satan. Screeching and flailing in the dark cone of buzzing fury, Ginger plunged down the mound toward the camera, face red and arms windmilling as Jim snapped away.

⁂ ⁂ ⁂

Later, ensconced in a turquoise booth at Squamskootnocket's Coffee Pit, Jim took a sip of Sanka then dug around in an old leather satchel by his side. He pulled out a tiny tape recorder.

"Fightin' off bees gives a girl an appetite, I gotta say," Ginger remarked, tucking into her grilled cheese and tomato on white. "We'll get that nest removed before we have any showings, don't you worry. You can even put that in your story if you want," she added, gesturing at his recorder with half a sandwich. "Like a selling point, y'know? 'Bee-free sanctuary-flexible close!'"

"Hey, you're the expert." He pressed Record. "OK, let's get started."

Ginger pushed her sandwich away and bellied up to the recorder. She lowered her head, her lips almost touching the machine. "This is Ginger Kanadoo, your kana-doo realtor."

"OK, we know that."

"Just warming up."

"Why don't you tell us about the market—you know, what we discussed."

"Then can I talk about my new listing?"

"Sure."

"First of all, there's no bubble here in Squamskootnocket. Sales are healthy and I'm always ready to list your home. How's that?"

"Maybe a few more...details."

"You got it, Jimmy." She inflated a bit, continued. "Squamskootnocket has finally been discovered as New York City's hottest new getaway community. No longer known as simply the former 'Home of the Gummy Bear,' Squamskootnocket's other charms are rocking the charts: the haunting beauty of Lake Squamskootnocket, the hopping downtown which features a very accessible gas station and town hall—not to mention the town's amenities which include Squamskootnocket's lax 'hunt anywhere you want' policy—no hunting licenses needed! Just start shootin'! Kill at will! Very family friendly. To sum up: sales for single-families up TWO PERCENT in the past year alone! I tell you, things are just nutty!"

"Good, good—"

"Now can I talk about my listing?"

"Shoot."

"112 Lakeside Way is a charming circa 1885 outhouse—"

"That was an outhouse?"

"Heck, whaddya want? It's a two seater!" She cozied up to her decaf. "Y'know, Jim, a lot of people in town don't know that—they think it's a one-seater. Problem! But easily rectified when I advertise all the great features this place has. Room for a mirror. Heck, ya could even toss in a sink. Plumbing's there too, in a way. And why not pop in a window—can't beat the view! People don't think about possibilities like that. They got no vision."

Jim worried a bee sting lumping up on his wrist. "How much land?"

"A tenth of an acre, give or take. But Jim, it's waterfront!"

"Isn't that protected land? Part of the historic district, I mean?"

"Yeah, true. I mean, sure, you have to keep the outhouse part but you could add on. You can go back two feet, and three feet on either side, with a variance. But think about it, you're holding on to a piece of Squamskootnocket history right in the middle of your own little...house. Trust me, everybody wants that."

"Wasn't that a for-sale-by-owner?"

"For sixteen years. Been workin' on him, you know."

"Isn't the seller...what's his name..."

"Old Man Higgins!"

Jim brightened. "Billy Higgins!"

"Yeah, our old Sunday school teacher, remember him?"

"He owns half of Squamskootnocket, doesn't he?"

"And most of Bangerlangersville, the old coot."

"No kidding. Wow, you know all the ins and outs, dontcha Ginger." He snapped off the recorder.

She blushed a bit as she polished off her sandwich. "Well, you know a fair amount about this old town, too, Jimmy, I know ya do."

He gave her a shy smile. "I suppose. Listen, you know I'll do the best I can with this."

"I know it's no castle, Jimmy. But I got lemons. I gotta make lemonade."

"I admire you, Gin. You just never give up, do you—"

"Well, I got Harvest, you know. She's not up and out yet."

"True, true. Well, I'll be burning the midnight oil on this one, so I better take off." He tucked the recorder in his satchel and reached back for his wallet, but Ginger held out her hand.

"Hold on there, Mr. Steele—your money's no good here at the Pit. I really appreciate you writing this."

"Goes both ways, you know. The empty page is a hungry thing."

"You always had a way with words."

"Thanks, Ginger." He gathered himself, leaned forward to hug her, realized in that second how awkward it is to hug a seated person, went to kiss her on the cheek, but as he did she turned slightly so he kissed her ear, which was as cool as a shell.

"Bye now," he said.

"Bye—oh—did you get stung a lot?"

"Oh, fifteen, twenty times. No big deal. I have my antidote with me all the time anyway." He patted his meaty hip.

"Oh, darn. Can I pick you up some salve or something?"

"I'm all set. See you in the papers!"

Chapter 2

The next morning Ginger turned over, opened one eye and stared through the murky remains of a half finished bottle of pink zinfandel on her coffee-ringed dresser, then rolled away. The alarm clock had already blasted off several times and each time she'd slammed down the helpless little button and gone back to sleep. She just wasn't ready yet for the world and all its worldly demands. Make money! Be a nice person! Eat well and exercise! Get a mammogram and a pap smear! Fix your car! Be a good mother! Make something of your life before it's over! The silent screams of daily life were already howling in her ears.

She jammed a pillow over her head and curled into a tight ball. Thus situated, she successfully revisited a thrilling dream about her new listing.

She sat at her kitchen counter reading the *Bugle*, her photo (circa 1969) smiling up from the front page. As she sipped her coffee and read about how she was the new face of real estate, her fax machine whirred to life behind her. She turned and stared. Multiple offers on the crapper poured forth, gathering in frothy heaps on the floor. She reached down and grabbed one.

"Ten thousand over asking with no contingencies? We'll take it!" she muttered in her sleep, slapping at the night table and knocking over the bottle of wine that dribbled out onto a splayed-open copy of Tomorrow's Realtor magazine and an article entitled: "It's All Up to YOU! All of It!! So Get Started Now, You Big Loser!!" The plastic smile of the model nearly filled the page, her French nails clutching a Sold sign in a death grip.

"Godammit to freakin' hell," Ginger said, sputtering awake and wiping away stray drops of sweet wine that had landed on her face. She sat up in her twisted, sweaty night-gown and reached for her glasses. What in God's name will I do with myself today, she thought, then suddenly remembered her article in the *Bugle*! At least that was no dream. She pushed herself to her flat, wide feet and padded across the creaky pine boards of her tiny, second-floor bedroom to the bathroom, where she splashed cold water on her face and stared at her reflection in the cracked mirror.

She blinked. Me again, she thought, every damned day. Never a break with that. Why can't I be somebody else for a second? Instead of an over-the-hill single mother with forty pounds to spare, a dead husband, no listings for nine months (except an outhouse) and a teenage daughter who hates my guts? What happened to the glory days? Days of poly-blend power suits, brooches, being Squamskootnocket's most sought-after realtor with the top producer husband, a beautiful baby girl, a brand new bungalow and our whole lives ahead of us...?

Ah, well, she thought, no use wallowing in it, especially when I've got an article featuring yours truly waiting on the front steps!

She stabbed some clips in her matted hair, tossed on a fluffy pink robe, and headed to the stairs. A few steps down, she stopped short and held her breath. Had Harvest gone to school? What the hell time was it, anyway?

She tiptoed to Harvest's door. A poster of Marilyn Manson covered it, eyes dripping blood, middle finger with its black-enameled nail outstretched. Ginger gave the door a weak shove. It opened a few inches with a horror-movie-sound-effect creak. A waft of closed-up air, clove cigarettes and teen girl-hair product snaked out. She nudged it open a bit more and peered into the darkness. Under a deep purple satin comforter, a small form dreamed the unknowable.

Ginger glanced at Harvest's clock. 10:07. "Oh, piss," she said. Tightening her robe, she shoved the door all the way open. It moved stiffly across the high-pile shag rug. Harvest's screen saver, a bat ceaselessly flapping across a starlit sky, glowed in neon colors from her desk. Ginger pulled open heavy curtains sewn from scraps of dark velvet gleaned from the remnants pile at the Squamskootnocket Bee. Midmorning sun filtered through grungy windows, landing halfheartedly on the sleeping lump.

"Wake up, Harvest. You're late for school."

The form rearranged itself, a puff of smoke inexplicably escaping the covers. Ginger folded her arms under heavy breasts.

"Harvest, it's past ten."

"Go away."

Ginger reached for the foot of the coverlet and started to pull.

"I hate it when you do that!!"

Ginger let go of the spread. "Then get up, Harv. I'm waiting."

A sigh from beneath the eggplant-colored quilt. "I can't get up, cuz I'm dead." The covers flew violently back. A small, slim girl with dyed black hair lay with one arm melodramatically flung over her eyes. "People die in their sleep, don't they?"

"Oh, please—"

"Put that on my tardy slip. 'Harvest died this morning, sorry to say.'"

"You're bleak today."

Harvest lifted her arm from across her face, raised herself on her elbows and looked at her mother with moss green eyes. "And what if I were dead? Would you care?"

"Geez, Harv, what the hell is your problem this morning?" Ginger said, randomly gathering empty soda cans and dirty ash trays.

Harvest shook her head, whipped her covers all the way off and got to her feet, ankles jingling with belled Indian bracelets as she stepped on layers of ripped black clothing. "You wouldn't get it even if I explained it to you, which I have, like a thousand times." She rummaged among the clothing, picking up and smelling a T-shirt, fishnets, a skirt.

Ginger sighed and headed for the door.

"You could have woken me up," Harvest said.

"You have an alarm clock."

"You are my mother."

Ginger turned to face her. "Meaning?"

"You're supposed to wake me in the morning. You're supposed to care enough about me and my education to at least do that. If you didn't drink so much maybe you could—"

"I was celebrating."

"You're always celebrating."

"I can't help it. Life is a thrilling, wonderful experience to be constantly savored and enjoyed."

Harvest brushed by her toward the bathroom. "You're such a dork."

"Get dressed, and I'll take you to school."

⁂ ⁂ ⁂

As soon as she heard the plumbing squeak and bang to life and she could be sure Harvest was in the shower, Ginger ran out across the hoary stone walk and grabbed the *Bugle*. She kept it tucked under her arm and laid it face down on the table when she got back inside. She wouldn't let herself look at it until her Nescafé was hot and her English muffin popped.

With great ceremony, she opened the newspaper on the sticky kitchen table. Filling the front page was a photo of her in mid-air as she leapt from the swarm of bees which darkened most of the photo just above her right ear. A string of spittle flew back from her mouth and her hair fluffed out like a cloud. A look of terror widened her eyes.

The headline read: "Local Realtor Ginger Kanadoo Kicks Off the Spring Season With a Bang!"

She lunged for the phone and dialed the *Bugle*.

"Jim Steele here."

"It's me."

His voice warmed when he recognized hers. "So, do you like it?"

"Well, it's not exactly the most flattering shot in the world."

"But it's got action! Movement! Heart!"

She took another look. "Ya think?"

"Course I do, Ginger. Your phone'll be ringing off the hook."

Ginger glanced back at the slumbering lump that was her fax machine—green light on, unmistakable hum of 'ready when you are,' but, as usual, no paper spitting out. "I don't know, Jim."

"Come on, Gin, you know what they say! Any publicity's good publicity."

"Is that what they say?"

"Trust me, this'll kick-start your season, big time."

"..."

"You'll see."

"I guess so."

"Just read it. You'll love it."

"Movement, huh?"

"Yeah, action! The other shots were so typical. Bor-ing."

"OK, well, thanks again for your help." With a sigh, Ginger hung up the phone, opened the paper and read all about her outhouse.

⁂ ⁂ ⁂

"I'll get the cocksucker fired!" Dickie Kanadoo raged, slamming down a statue of St. Joseph on his heavy mahogany desk.

Ginger shut the office door behind her. "Come on, Dickie, it's just one photograph. Besides, it's an action shot."

"Action shot?" he said, his voice syrupy with sarcasm. "What does he think this is, film school? Artsy fartsy time? You look like a friggin' maniac in that picture. He hasn't got the common sense God gave a stone. Never has." He tossed a copy of the paper in the trash. Ginger's saucer eyes stared skyward from the front page.

Ginger eased herself into the chair opposite his desk. "Hey, it's publicity. Has the phone rung today or not?"

"Hmmm, let me think. Oh yeah." He jabbed a finger in her direction. "No."

"The phone hasn't rung?"

"Not once."

"Oh."

"Nope." He looked at the big-faced watch on his thick wrist. "No calls on the shitter. But hey, it's only two o'clock."

"So it's still early."

Dickie reached back and pulled at the tight collar of his shirt. "Look, Ginger, you know I like you, you know I care about you. I have no choice. You're my sister."

"We're Kanadoos!" Ginger erupted brightly.

He stared at her a moment, then lit up a half-smoked cigar from a dusty marble ashtray. "Yes, we're Kanadoos, all right."

"And nothing gets us down, right, bro?"

He sucked at the tired stump until the end glowed red. "...Right."

"And how long we been selling real estate?"

"Between you and me? Seventy years."

"Wow," she said, misty-eyed. "Seventy years. We're number one in the Squamskootnocket Valley, right?"

"No, Ginger, we're number seven out of eight companies here in the valley."

"So we're better than...which one?"

"Well, there's that brand new company that's come to the valley, Vanderskleet Real Estate. They haven't even moved into their storefront yet, so they have no sales."

"So we're better than them, right?"

"Yes, Ginger, we're better than them. We've had one sale this year. Maxie's pig farm on Highway 8."

"Well, there ya go."

"Whaddya mean, 'there ya go'?! Ginger, we're dying over here!"

"Oh, come on, Dickie! It was a tough winter!"

He blew cigar smoke out of his nose like a cartoon bull about to charge. "It was the warmest winter on record! With the lowest interest rates since 1958! With 35% higher sales in all the other towns in the valley but the ones we serve! The problem is us, here, Kanadoo Realty!"

Ginger played with a button on her sweater. "Wow, if Mom heard you say that..."

"If Mom heard me say that, and if she had all her marbles and understood what the hell's been going on, she'd fire every single one of us, Kanadoos or not!"

"She's got all her—"

"Yeah, yeah," he said, stabbing out the cigar and getting up to pace. Ginger watched him as he circled his desk, looking beyond him and through the window of his door at a form that strode quickly past. Ginger sat up straight and peered out.

A tall, whip-slim woman with cropped black hair stood at the coffee station making herself a cup of tea. She wore a sharply tailored suit with patterned stockings and black boots that zipped up to her knees.

"Um, Dick."

He joined her staring contest.

"What's that?"

"That, my dear," he said, hiking up his pants past his belly, "is the future of Kanadoo Real Estate."

Chapter 3

Ginger followed Dick out of his office and into the tiny conference room where she made her way to her chair at the back left-hand side. The chair she had occupied for thirty-nine years of weekly office meetings. She knew every coffee stain, every rip and pen mark on its mustardy leather arms, every wad of gum she'd stuck to its forgiving undersides, every creak and groan it made as it lovingly accommodated the heft and haw of her haunches over all these long years.

To find that it was taken by the thing with the boots.

Occupado.

Ginger, slack-jawed, stood staring a long moment at the fishnetted knees before she could gather herself enough to hustle on over to the upholstered chair nearer the door, the one redolent with memories of Kiki, the office cat who died years ago, famous for its inability to keep food down, ever, yet remain alive, and who'd left orangish memories of cat gack everywhere.

Maxie Kanadoo, ninety-three years old and in the Guinness Book of World Records as the oldest living realtor, snored loudly in her armchair next to Ginger, a shapeless bundle of rust-colored knitting loose in her gnarled hands. Maxie was Ginger's aunt, and also a Kanadoo. These days she could only sell slab ranches and land since her knees were shot and she couldn't handle stairs.

Ginger elbowed her gently. Maxie stirred and began to knit before she even opened her eyes. "Where am I..." she turned to Ginger. "Oh, hello, Ginger. This is a surprise—"

"It's time for the meeting," Ginger whispered.

"Oh! The meeting," she tittered. "Wouldn't want to miss that now, would I?"

Dickie blushed hotly as he arranged papers on the table.

The thing in the boots unzipped a sleek leather bag and pulled out a small handheld device. From it she produced a tiny pen and made some quick taps on its face. She turned to Ginger and Maxie, smiled with her mouth, not her eyes, then turned her attention forward.

"OK, we may as well get started," Dickie said, clapping his hands once. "We've got a lot to cover today." He stood in front of the office blackboard, rocking back and forth on his heels. "The first thing I want to do is welcome the newest realtor here at Kanadoo Real Estate, Miss Tandy Brickenhausen." Tandy tapped some more into her device. "Tandy brings with her ten years of experience in real estate from the trenches of Manhattan, where she's been a top producer for eight of those years. Let's give her a warm welcome."

Ginger clapped a few times while Maxie ticked her knitting needles together just before kicking into a long coughing spasm.

"You OK there, Max?" Dickie asked.

"Oh, sure," she sputtered phlegmily. "Just one too many Pall Malls."

"Well, I'm sure we'll accept Tandy warmly into the Kanadoo family," Dickie said, staring hard at Ginger who looked like she'd turned to stone. "And that we'll all enjoy and profit by learning from each other."

He reached under the conference table, pulled out a laptop bag and unzipped it. "And to that end, I've decided to make a major change here at Kanadoo Realty. We need to put Kanadoo back on the map. We've got to join the twenty-first century. And the only way to do that, ladies, is to finally go online." He pulled a sleek PC from the bag and plugged it in.

"What the hell are you talking about, son?" Maxie said, dropping her knitting to her lap.

Tandy tucked her head down. Her shoulders shook as she gagged a laugh.

Ginger looked at Tandy, then back to Dick. "But you said we'd never do that! That all that online stuff was hogwash, 'just old hooey' you said. You said it would pass, 'like gas in the night.' You said Kanadoo was above fads, that our books were just fine for customers to look through, that people have bought houses with us for forty years without this all this hocus po—"

"And I was wrong, Ginger." He cleared his throat, his face flaring an even brighter red above the white of his shirt collar. More gently, "I was wrong."

"Now hold on there, Dickie," Maxie said, hiking her small frame a little taller in the chair. "Ginger has a point. We've gotten along fine here for over fifty years without all that newfangled nonsense. Why, I've been selling houses since before you were born without all this zee-mail and this www.kissmyass and hey, I'll cyberspace you and blog you and log you and all 'a that. Frankly, it doesn't sound above-board. It almost sounds kinda dirty. I even heard you can get free porno twenty-four hours a day on them things," she said, casting an arthritic paw in the direction of the now humming laptop. "And people get possessed by it and go insane. Now, why do we need that here at Kanadoo?"

Tears were streaming down Tandy's face. She delicately wiped her cheeks with a tissue, then passed a fine-boned hand through sleek hair.

"We need this here at Kanadoo," Dickie said, staring down Maxie, "because our revenue is down. Way down. We are competing with other brokerages who have gone ahead with this technology—"

"But Dickie," Ginger began, "we've always bucked the trends. Always. And we always came out on top. We're trend buckers!"

Dickie held his hands up, palms at the veterans. "Look, ladies, I know change is difficult. Heck, it's painful sometimes, even a little scary. I think we felt this way when fax machines came around. And now we all feel fine about them, right?"

"I hate goddamned fax machines," Maxie snarled. "Paper always catching in 'em. Can't read 'em anyway—"

"The point is, now we don't have to drive offers over to the other brokers. We can fax—"

Ginger folded her arms tight. "Oh, I still drive them over. I don't trust any old machine to—"

"OK, enough!" Dickie roared.

Ginger and Maxie fell silent. Tandy dropped her stylus and leaned gracefully over to pick it up. Everyone stared helplessly at her cleavage.

"With all due respect, ladies, you have no choice. The company is going online. Tandy here," he gestured, as if no one knew which one was Tandy, "has generously offered to design our website, using some very cutting-edge ideas from her former company. Frankly, I'm more positive about Kanadoo's future than I have been in years."

Tandy smiled at him, then returned to pecking at her eentsy keyboard. The tinny sound of a popular tune filled the room. Tandy reached into a slim leather case, pulled out a cell phone and hit a button, silencing the phone, then slipped it back in its case. Ginger and Maxie stared.

"Cell phones will also be mandatory for all Kanadoo realtors."

"Not for this Kanadoo realtor," Ginger said. Maxie rolled her eyes and returned to her knitting.

"Let's move on. How's the market, ladies? Any new listings besides...Ginger's?"

"Well," Maxie said, "I'm hot on the trail of a parking lot back of the old Merit station on Route 80. Practically got the paperwork in hand."

"Very good," Dickie said. "Anything else?"

Tandy spoke in a deep, honeyed voice. "I've been introducing myself around town, just in casual but I believe effective ways: attending town meetings, having lunch at the local coffee shop, meeting vendors such as mortgage lenders, local tradesman and the like. I've been by the schools to check them out, as well as the planning board to see if there's anything new in the works. In fact, I've already met with some local builders—"

"Whore." Maxie mumbled, then coughed.

"Excuse me?"

"Nothing, nothing. Go on with your list," she said, a fully formed sock hanging almost obscenely off her needles.

"Well, that was it, really. No listings or sales yet, but we all know this takes time."

"Tandy," Dickie said, smiling warmly, "you've only been in Squamskootnocket a week. You should be commended for all you've done in such a short time."

"Well, thank you, Dickie. I'm honored to be here."

Maxie looked up from her lap. "Did I miss the doughnuts?"

Dickie pointed to the far end of the table. "There's some holes, right next to Ginger."

"Ginger, could you get me some powdered, and some plain if there's any—"

Ginger somberly handed Maxie the box.

"Why, thank you, dear."

"Oookay," Dickie said, gripping the back of the chair in front of him. "Let's get through this, shall we? One more announcement. I'm sponsoring a contest for our spring market. Whoever has the highest gross sales by August thirty-first wins an all-expense-paid trip to...Hawaii!"

"Well, aloha to that," Maxie said, racking up the other sock.

"So if there are no further questions, I'll leave you ladies to your work."

Chapter 4

Ginger sat under her desk, sobbing pitifully.

"Get up off the floor, Gin," Dickie said, leaning against a copy machine.

"I don' wanna get up."

"Ginger, I have to meet with someone in a few minutes. You can't be on the fl—"

"I don't care. You hate me. You hate Maxie. You hired that...that—"

"Realtor?"

"She's not even a Kanadoo!! I mean, what are you gonna call us now? Kanadoo 'and Tandy' Real Estate?! That's so stupid!"

"Yes, that would be stupid."

She blew a wet wad into a flimsy piece of Kleenex. "You're my own brother and you don't even care—"

Dickie grabbed her by her forearms and yanked her to her feet. For a moment she was too shocked to cry and just stared at him, hiccupping.

"Ginger, you're fifty-six, not six, OK?"

"I'm fifty-nine."

Dickie let her go and held his head as if his brain hurt. "Grow up. Face change. You'll be happy you did."

"I will not I will not I will not!" A fresh round of tears.

"Holy crap. You're an infant."

Ginger sniffled, then squared her shoulders. "I'm gonna go see Big Jean."

"Go ahead. Mom doesn't have a clue about what's going on in this business, kind of like you."

"Yeah, but she lubs me."

"Oh my God."

"And she hates computers too."

"Fine. Have a party. A poverty party."

"I will! I will have a party! Without you!!" Ginger said, and stomped out of the office into the chilly spring morning.

⁂ ⁂ ⁂

As Ginger got settled in her car it occurred to her she could have handled that whole thing a teensy bit better. Maybe curling up in a ball under her desk and sobbing her eyes out wasn't the best all-around tactic, strategy-wise, although it certainly felt good at the time. But heck, who cared, anyway? He could never fire her. She was a Kanadoo!

Or could he....? She recalled the clickity clack of Tandy's handheld, her neat stylus, the boots!! and ran a shaking hand through her kinky grey hair.

Her heart fluttered as she fired up the Pontiac. It roared to life, then sputtered and choked, settling at last on a low rumble as if she sat in the guts of some giant, ailing mammal.

She patted her dashboard lovingly, then blasted herself with "heat" which rolled out icy for the first fifteen minutes of the drive. This breeze was joined by brisk blasts from various rusted-out holes in the bottom of her car. Spring had taken its typical fickle turn toward cold again.

Shivering, she glanced at the floor. There lay her dirty little secret. A cell phone. She had actually gone out and bought one a few months ago, brought it home, and with Harvest's help, set it up. She had never, however, mastered the art of gathering messages from it, or even recharging it, for that matter. It also seemed to randomly change ring tones on her. More than once, she had run home to Harvest saying the damn thing was broken again, only to learn that in all her spastic button pushing she had unwittingly reset it to "silent" and just never heard her calls. In addition, it had taken a picture of the inside of her mouth, probably on the one occasion she had succeeded in using its photo function, and in its efficient, demonic way, saved this shot of her silver-patched molars and lumbering tongue as a screen saver.

She hated the godforsaken thing. Its shiny, silvery sleekness, its mocking tony tiny-ness, its smug and unknowable nanotechnology, its whirring, clicking microchips, its tiresome multitaskiness. It was the thing that got in the way of the thing. The thing of talking to people, helping them sell or buy houses, something she'd taken great pride in for as long as she could remember.

As she drove along toward The Final Rest to see Big Jean, she started to well up again. It was at times like these that she sorely missed her husband, Carl Kanadoo (he'd taken her name when they married, to become an official Kanadoo) who died during an unfortunate septic tank incident years ago. He'd fallen in during an inspection and, well, there was just nothing anyone could do. Evidently there were bystanders but no one volunteered to jump in and save him. The rest of the septic guys said that though they had noticed that "the realtor had disappeared," they hadn't done anything about it because they figured "another one would show up soon enough." Ginger never could figure out what the guys at We Scoop It meant by that.

Ginger would think of Carl down there, how he'd been just hours away from a commission check he would never receive. She'd hope it had been quick, and would try to take some comfort in the fact that he died doing what he loved: selling real estate. In fact, she liked to think of Carl as everywhere, as just part of the soil (especially the soil at 129 Timberleaf Way), and sometimes, if the wind was right and she listened with her heart, she could hear him whisper, "List, Ginger, list...list...list..."

It was like he was comforting her from the beyond, fortifying her.

As if to show him she was listening, she took a detour past her outhouse listing, slowing for a few moments as she passed to admire her sign planted rakishly in the moss, the brilliant way the sun glinted off the bronze latch on the front door, and the pure nobility of the building's silhouette against the brittle blue sky.

Chapter 5

Big Jean raced down the hall in her wheelchair, her oxygen tank clanging against the back of it as she careened into other residents shuffling or wheeling alongside her.

"Get outta my way! I'm tryin' ta get to bingo!!" she shrieked, arms flailing, causing one old gent to fall backwards, luckily into an easy chair.

"Ma, come on," Ginger said, jogging alongside her. "You're gonna kill somebody!"

"Yeah, do somebody a favor around here. Trouble is, I'm not that nice." She rounded a corner and jammed herself through a set of double doors into an empty recreation room. Rows of tables, chairs tucked neatly in. Stacks of bingo games arranged on shelving along one wall. Not a single molecule of fresh spring air invaded the fetid tang of nursing home "air."

The doors swooshed back and forth behind them, the oxygen tube knocking gently at the tank with a small "ting" as Big Jean labored to even her own breathing.

"Goddamn it all to hell." She shifted her tiny ass in her seat, clutching a hankie with a big K embroidered in the corner. She looked around the empty room. "Son of a goddamn bitch."

"Ma—"

"Don't 'Ma' me. While we were back there jawing about nothing I was missing my games. And I had a big pot last time. I'm on a streak."

Ginger came around to the front of the wheelchair, bent down to her mother and looked into her rheumy eyes. "Ma, we were just here."

"Whaddya talking about, we were just here?"

"We were just in here, an hour ago, and I watched you play and you did win—"

Big Jean snatched her daughter's hand with her arthritic one. A light came into her eyes. "Twenty-three dollars and eighty-one cents!"

"That's exactly right. But it was an hour ago, not yesterday."

Big Jean let her hand go and looked away. She scanned the room, turned behind her and squinted at the doors, then back at Ginger. In a soft voice she said, "That wasn't yesterday?"

"No. Today."

"So I didn't miss it."

"No."

"Well, all right then." She shifted again, still glancing around with narrowed eyes. "Cuz I look forward to this every day, you know. I swear it's what I drag my ass out of bed for in the morning. Otherwise I'd just lie there sucking on this thing" —she banged at her tank with a bony elbow— "all damned day and night, just staring at the TV like a vegetable. Like a damned beet."

"I don't know, Ma, you never miss Bingo or Elderobics."

"I don't?"

"That's what Sally tells me."

"Is that that Oriental girl? Sally? With the bad teeth?"

"...Yes."

"I do like cuttin' a rug."

"You were a great dancer. I have pictures."

"Well, bring 'em next time, for chrissakes." She rolled herself up tight to one of the tables, her flat birdlike chest meeting the edge of it. Her hands fiddled with nothing on the worn oak table top. "So tell me what else I don't remember. Christ, it sucks getting old, Gin. Let me tell ya, I wouldn't bother but here I am. And on your dime. Sorry about that, hon."

Ginger pulled up a chair and sat across from her at the narrow table. "Well, we were in your room, just catching up."

"Did you bring me anything?" she said with a wink.

"A box of taffy from Voorheesvrankinville Farms."

"That's it?" she said, flipping her empty hands up in the air.

"You can't have that—Mom, I can't get that for you any more."

"Connection dry up?"

Ginger nodded. Big Jean loved pot. Sprinkled it on her Cream of Wheat in the morning.

"Damn. Well, work on it."

"Problem is, it's also been kind of slow month," Ginger said softly.

"Haven't closed anything in a while?" Big Jean dug into her fanny pack, pulled out some cash and handed it to her. "Bingo's good for something."

"Thanks, Mom."

"Taffy, huh. We hid it, right?"

"All set."

"Where, though?"

"Between your—"

"—mattresses. It's comin' back. Was it the diet kind?"

"Mom, you don't need that—"

"I like to look good, you know. You've put on a few, haven't you?"

Ginger sucked in her gut. "I suppose—"

"Your dad tended to fat, so you got that, I think."

Ginger sighed. "So I was telling you about Dickie."

"He never comes to see me, the little prick."

"He hired someone new. From New York City."

"What?"

"Her name is Tandy."

"Sounds like a stripper."

"Wouldn't surprise me at all. But, Ma, the best is yet to come. Dickie's gonna start using computers. We're going into cyberspace."

Big Jean looked around frantically. "Why, that little...we said no computers! I said that twenty years ago when I retired and I'm sayin' it again now! They're a waste of time!"

"I know, but he won't listen!"

"What does Maxie think?"

"Oh, she's as mad as I am—"

"That woman was a legend in Coxsackie Neck, let me tell you, a *legend*! My sister knows her stuff."

"Maxie's the best."

Big Jean sighed and fluffed out her perfect silvery do with both hands. "That Dickie. I never liked him."

"Well, Ma, he is your son. And he does have some good qualities."

"No, he doesn't. You're my favorite, but you know that. Now take me back to my room. I need to have a little chat with that boy of mine."

⁂ ⁂ ⁂

Ginger's car chugged and pooted as she idled outside of Squamskootnocket Valley High. Finally, she caught sight of her daughter, head down and alone, in layers of ripped black clothing and chunky black shoes. She watched her navigate her way through throngs of pretty, chatting girls and gawky teen boys. Shoulders pulled forward, as if against a wind only she could feel, Harvest ran-walked across the parking lot and jumped in the car without a word, tossing her oversized knapsack in the back seat.

"How was your day, honey?"

Harvest stared straight ahead. "Perfect."

Ginger pulled out from the line of mothers-in-waiting to the school parking lot where she hovered at the entrance to the main street.

"Really? Did you do well on that science test?"

"Actually, I failed that. The reason I had such a great day was that I got harassed because my mother just listed an outhouse. Oh yeah—there's also picture of her looking like a psycho on the front page of the *Bugle*."

"A listing is a listing, honey. And besides, it's no longer a working outhouse. But, you know, the memories are there."

Harvest sighed, sank back in her seat and gazed out the window at fluffy clouds scudding across a ceramic blue sky.

"Such a beautiful day to go shopping," Ginger chirped. "So where should we start? Sears?"

"I don't want to go shopping any more. I want to go to Shelley's."

"I thought we were gonna at least check out that bra sale at SaveMart."

"Buying bras with your mother is weird."

"It is?" Ginger peered at Harvest through her curtain of black hair. "Well, I didn't know that. I thought you wanted to hang out together this afternoon."

"I never said that. I said I needed bras. Can't you just take me to Shelley's?"

Ginger pulled the car over to the side of the road. Her unused cell phone rattled around on the floor, dangerously close to a rusty hole big enough for it to drop through. She let her hands fall from the wheel into her lap. "Thanks for asking. I had a really hard day too." Harvest rolled her eyes. "Your Uncle Dick just hired a new hotshot know-it-all bitch from Manhattan—"

"Mom, your language—"

"—and then he announces Kanadoo's going online—"

"—well, hello and welcome to the twenty-first century—"

"—and I told him, forget it. I'm never doing that—"

"—great, Ma, that's just great—"

"—so I saw Big Jean and she's with me on this, all the way."

Harvest yawned. "Mom, this is all very fascinating but can we go to Shelley's now?"

"And then I pick up my daughter and she doesn't want to buy bras with me 'cause that's too 'weird', and it's just...it's just..." Ginger choked up.

"Mom, are you crying?"

She snuffled. "Yes, I'm crying. Mothers have feelings too."

Harvest sighed and yanked on her fish nets. "OK, OK, we'll go buy bras."

"But you don't want to buy bras. You're just saying that. You didn't used to be like this, Harvey. You used to like being with me, doing things together, having fun. Getting ice cream, going on the Ferris wheel, going to the circus, getting our hair cut together. We had a ball. You were a nice kid, don't you remember?"

"Yeah, I was like, seven."

Ginger wiped her eyes with her sleeve. "I guess that was a while ago, that circus thing."

"I'm a teenager, Mom. I'm supposed to hate you."

"Really?"

"Mm hmm."

Ginger started up the car again. "Well, I had no idea. You've been nice until now. Still, it does seem like you could kind of muffle things a bit."

Harvest was silent as Ginger pulled away from the curb.

"How's that boy you like? Trevor, was it?"

"Trevor is soooo last month."

"Oh. Any new boys on the horizon?"

Harvest gave her a searing look. "Nope, no new boys on the horizon. Anyway, that's none of your business, my love life."

"Sorry, didn't mean to pry."

They pulled in to Shelley's driveway and Harvest sprang out the door. Shelley, a heavy, moon-faced girl, also all in black, stood in the doorway, unsmiling.

"Hey, honey, what time should I pick you up?" Ginger called out.

"Don't worry about it. I'll get a ride." Harvest clomped down the walk, disappearing behind the screen door.

Chapter 6

Ginger drove home thinking about her daughter, how she barely seemed to recognize Harvest these days. She grasped the whole teen rebellion thing pretty well, but lately felt there was something else going on that she just couldn't put her finger on, as if a new wall had been put up completely blocking her out, as opposed to the usual picket fence which still kept her out but where she could at least peek through the slats and make sure the girl was OK.

It had been such a long day. Definitely high time for a cocktail, but just as Ginger turned onto her street, she remembered she was completely out of white zin. She did a three-pointer and headed back to town.

Ginger pulled in to Squamskootnocket Liquors, puzzling for a moment about the parking lot full of cars. Was some kind of sale on? She rarely missed those...and look, there was Maxie's ancient Beemer, a brand new Lexus, a Porsche...

She checked her hair in the rear view, puckered up and painted on a coat of Coral Madness, and got out. Laughter tinkled from within the squat brown building. She caught Maxie making her way along the handicapped ramp and scooted up behind her.

"Max, what's going on?"

"White zin tasting. You didn't know? Was in the *Bugle.*"

Ginger held the door for her. "I must have missed it. I woulda dressed up..."

"Ah, you look fine..."

Eddie, the proprietor, a small, nervous man with watery eyes, rushed to take Maxie's arm. "You made it! Come on in. I was just about to pop a Taylor Country!"

"My favorite!" Ginger gushed.

He handed her a plastic glass filled to the brim with something pink.

"What's this?"

"Just the last of the blush."

Maxie and Ginger gathered around a card table where several open bottles surrounded a plastic tray of Triscuits and cheddar.

"It must be realtor day," Eddie said, opening a fresh box of Ritz. "Your new partner just got here too. Gotta grab some supplies. Back in a flash." He disappeared into the walk-in cooler.

Tandy, standing near the Australian wines, did a finger wave at them. She wore a pencil skirt and heels and a fitted red silk shirt. A scrawny older man in rainbow suspenders gesticulated as he spoke to her.

"Oh my God, Old Man Higgins is here—" Ginger began, her mouth full of Triscuit.

"Keep it down," Maxie hissed, nabbing a healthy slab of Country Crock as she passed.

Eddie reappeared with a case of wine. "So, ladies, how's the market?"

"We're hoppin', Eddie. No rest for the weary," Maxie said.

Ginger gulped her wine while monitoring Tandy who laughed heartily at something Billie said. They clinked glasses as Tandy slipped her a look.

"Great story on you in the *Bugle* today, Ginger," Eddie said.

"That's Kanadoo's first listing of the year," Max said.

"Well, you must be very proud."

"We're always proud of our Ginger," she said, topping off her sparkling Chablis.

A customer gestured at Eddie and he ran off to the cash register.

Ginger took a step closer to Max. "This is bad, this is really bad—"

"Why, because she's everywhere? Like air? Like a cliché? Like a friggin' Squamskootnocket plague?"

Ginger watched as Billie broke free from Tandy and strolled over to her. By the time he reached her, his expression had changed from bliss to that of a man about to discipline his pet pot-bellied pig.

He grabbed a bit of her sleeve in a bony grip and led her around and behind a mountainous potato chip display.

"I been wondering why you haven't been answering your phone. I musta tried you six times at your office today."

"Well, I was out—"

"Also tried your cell phone."

Ginger reddened and finished her wine. She ached for more. She saw between bags of Tastee Fries that her best friend from high school, Regina Freenspeet, had joined the gathering.

"Been having a few problems with the cell phone. Damn technology! I remember when things were easier. You just made a call and if you weren't home, nobody cared—"

"So I just wanna know, what's going on with my out-house? Any offers?"

"We've had tons of interest, you know, inquiries, and I've been talking it up all over town—you saw the article, right?"

"Yeah, how could I miss? But no offers, huh."

"It's only been two weeks. Things are percolating, I can feel it. I wouldn't be surprised if we had a bidding war by the weekend."

"My ass. Well, the least you could do is have an open house there. I mean, what the crikey am I paying you two percent for? Ginger, this is a test, remember? Like they do on the radio. This is how you're gonna show me you can list my thirty-five acres and make me a lot of money. Make me a rich man! If you can't even sell a goddamned outhouse then what am I gonna do?"

"Billie, relax, I got everything under control. We're gonna have an open house there this weekend! I'll have a huge ad in the *Bugle*, balloons, cookies, games for the kids, door prizes, pony rides, magic shows, heck I might even get us on cable or CNN—"

"Yeah, well, you better not be blowin' smoke, cause I'm gonna take a cruise by there and check it out myself."

"Right, OK—"

"And let me tell you, my friend, you've got some real competition over there," he said, wagging a craggy paw toward Tandy. "That girl's gonna make a name for herself in this town. I can feel it. So you better mind your p's and q's. Now, how many balloons ya gonna use this Sunday?"

"Two, I figured."

"I want at least six. I want to see them from Highway 25, so if folks catch sight of them they'll be inspired to come on over.

"Six it is. Maybe more."

"That's what I'm talkin' about! Sky's the limit. You show me what you can do, Ginger, and the world will come to your doorstep. Mark my words." He tossed back his wine, placed his plastic cup down, pinkie outstretched, and turned to leave. "I'll see you on Sunday."

Ginger gave a lifeless wave and stared after him. She felt someone bump into her and turned around. Maxie stumbled backwards a few steps, eyes huge in her thick glasses, nearly crashing into the brandies and cordials before Ginger caught her arm.

"Whoah! Didn't see ya there, Gin. I was looking for the Slim Jims. Zin always gives me a craving."

Ginger snapped back to life. "He is such an old—"

"Wet fart. I know, some things never change."

"Hey, what's Regina doing with Tandy over there?"

Maxie found a Slim Jim, peeled off the plastic and started to gum it. "Talking about her house."

"Her what?"

"Her dom-i-cile, my friend. Hey, go try the Almaden blush. It's got some real zip."

"You bet I will, Max, you bet I will." Ginger brushed by her, almost sending her into the sale rack. Three glasses of wine and no dinner had suddenly kicked in, and she was really feeling, well, like herself.

She charged up to the table of wine and snacks, blustering, then told herself to count to ten, as she had been counseled to do at various times in her life. She got to one.

"So I see you've met my best friend," Ginger said, grabbing the blush by the neck and pouring.

"Yes," Tandy smiled. "Regina is lovely. She speaks very highly of you."

"She should. She's my best bud. Since grade school."

"Hey Ginger," Regina said, giving her a big hug. "What's new?"

"Oh, nothing much," she said, nearly cracking a molar on a chunk of carrot.

"Tandy here was telling me about her exciting life in Manhattan! It sounds just like a TV show or something."

"It was thrilling, but I needed a change of pace," Tandy said, sipping at something blood red. "And this place, this town, well—it's such a welcome change."

"What's that you're drinking?" Ginger asked. "That's no zin."

"I begged Eddie to open a Pinot Noir for me." She wrinkled her nose prettily. "And he obliged. Such a doll. Shhh, don't tell anyone."

"Well, anyway, she sure got the truth out of me." Regina giggled into her hand. "I'm in love!"

"With...who?" Ginger asked, mentally scanning every possible man in town and coming up with: zero. Null set.

"I met him online. He's wonderful. He's in jail. But he didn't do it. He's an angel."

Tandy's eyes narrowed. "I guess you two haven't spoken in a while."

"We're best friends, not joined at the spine," Ginger said, giving Regina the hairy eyeball. Which was utterly lost on her.

"Anyway, this all happened so fast. But love is like that, you know! He has a couple of kids, well, OK, five kids, which is why I'm going down to Virginia to live with him, which is why I have to sell my house!"

Tandy's eyes glittered with reptilian hunger. She reached for something small and efficient in her small, efficient bag.

"Here you go." She offered Regina her business card. Ginger and Regina stared at it. On it was a hologram of Tandy at a desk, smiling and holding a pen to an offer, then signing, then holding, then signing, depending on how Regina held the card.

"Now run your finger across the signed offer part," Tandy said.

As Regina did so, Tandy's recorded voice said, "Congratulations, you have a deal!" Regina gasped, and did it again. "Congratulations, you have a deal! Congratulations, you—"

Maxie slipped in behind Ginger and peered at the card. "Hell's bells, look at that."

"This is impressive," Regina said, playing the little recording in the card over and over. "This is amazing. Can I really have this?"

"Of course. And I know you're friends with Ginger here, but if you have any questions at all about real estate in the area just give me a call or"—sidelong sneer to Ginger—"email me."

"Oh, I will, thank you!" Regina heaved a great sigh of happiness, as if she just learned she'd won some grand sum of money. "Well, I gotta run," she said, picking up her purse. "Me and DeeShaun have an e-chat scheduled at nine, so I can't be late!" She made for the door, Tandy's business card in hand.

Ginger picked up the bottle of Pinot Noir and sniffed it, made a rank face, put it down, then freshened her own glass of white zin. She paced in front of Tandy, who held her ground between the snack spread and a Zima display.

"Is that the tradition in the city, stealing each other's customers?"

"Just remembered-got a casserole in the oven," Maxie said, turning to leave. She waved goodbye with her cane, knocking over several bags of fried pork rinds. Nobody moved to pick them up.

Ginger kept her eyes on Tandy. "Later, Max."

Tandy nibbled at the browned edge of a butter wafer. "As they say, nobody owns a client. You should know that by now, after—how many years in the business?"

"Thirty-nine. Longer than you've been alive. Much longer."

"Impressive. Experience is priceless. I commend you for your patience, years of hard work, and dedication to the business."

Ginger popped a chocolate-covered strawberry in her mouth and chewed athletically. "By the way, what are you doing here?"

"Excuse me?"

"Shouldn't you be in college getting some kinda nineteenth-century English lit degree?"

"Already have one. Balzac. Good way to starve."

"Well, let me tell you another good way to starve. Reaming people out of their paychecks. Stomping on your colleague's territory. Screwing the people you work with, day in and day out—"

"I get it, I get it. Don't worry. I won't call her."

"She has your card."

"Now, Ginger," she said, placing one hand on a slender shell of a hip, "what kind of best friend would she be to call me to list her house?"

Ginger was flummoxed for a moment but rose, Phoenix-like, from the ashes of flummoxation. "Mark my words, Tandy, this is going to come back and bite you on the ass."

"Are you...threatening me?" she asked with a kind of horrified curiosity.

"I sure am."

"My, things did seem primitive around here but I didn't think they'd be—"

"You stay off my turf, or else."

Tandy's perfectly glossed mouth twitched at the corner.

"You mess with me and I'll toss your skinny ass back to Rockefeller Center faster than you can say P&S."

Tandy glanced around, as if craving a witness.

"We're alone. This is between you and me."

"Well," Tandy said, gathering herself. "I'm glad we cleared all this up."

Ginger thought she detected the slightest tremor in Tandy's fingers as she put down her glass and walked away, blowing a kiss goodbye to Eddie as she headed for the door.

Chapter 7

Still congratulating herself on her performance, Ginger took the turn into her driveway wide and crashed head-on into her shed. A raccoon whose real estate she'd violated scurried out, stood on its haunches and stared at her with burning red eyes, then trundled away under the bushes.

Cursing, she pulled back and got out to survey the front end of the car by its headlights. Actually, the car didn't look too bad but the shed was starting to rack up the scars from a number of such enchanted evenings.

As she made her way around to the passenger side she noticed a lump in the back seat. Harvest had forgotten her school knapsack. She grabbed it, groaning a bit under the weight of that and her real estate bag as she squelched across the overgrown lawn to her mailbox.

There was only one letter sticking out of the old-fashioned metal box, but it gave her a chill. It was business-sized, thin, ominous. Its implications not softened by trashy circulars or fluffed out by the *Bugle*, it lay there alone and self contained, like something armed; an assassin. She took a deep breath and held it for a few moments as she listened to the spherical croak of bullfrogs from nearby Lake Squamskootnocket. Exhaled.

She knew the return address without having to look, but she did anyway. There was plenty of moonlight. The letter was from Squamskootnocket Valley Savings and Loan.

She slipped the letter in her coat pocket and let herself into the house.

⁕ ⁕ ⁕

On the kitchen table lay two items: Harvest's knapsack and the letter. Ginger sensed there would be no joy in realizing the contents of either item. However, she felt that as an adult who must accept her responsibilities, she ought to face reality every so often. Of course there was always the possibility of burning the letter in the fireplace or burying it in the backyard under a rock; with the knapsack, simply returning it to Harvest's room without a second thought was certainly an option. Then she could pile into bed and burrow down into it, ostrich-like, endlessly replaying her slam-dunk evening with Tandy (or at least the part until she crashed into the shed), and subsequently fall into a zin-fed slumber.

Speaking of zin, she wondered if there was anything left in the fridge. A quick check revealed a third of a bottle. Honestly, who could blame her if she was going to go the "adult" way: opting for a wee bit of fortification. She poured herself a healthy swallow or two, then wandered off to the bathroom to check her hair, floss her teeth, and examine a filling that looked as if it might pop out momentarily. She killed ten more minutes reading a *Ladies Home Journal* article—"Make Cheerful Summer Doilies for Your Garden Parties!"— before she realized she better quit screwing around, since Harvest could walk in the door at any moment.

She marched over to the table, picked up the letter and held it up to the yellowish light of the hallway. Yup, sure was a letter in there. A letter with words, news of some kind. Maybe it was a bank statement. A really thin one this month. Or maybe a—

She ripped it open, almost in half. With badly shaking hands she read:

> Dear Ms. Kanadoo:
>
> This letter is to inform you that foreclosure proceedings have begun on your property at 25 Weenicket Way, Squamskootnocket, New York. If you do not pay $5,987.11 in back mortgage payments, as well as all monies due going forward, your property will go up for sale with the bank 120 days from this date, August 20.
>
> Our foreclosure officer will be in touch soon.

Sincerely and with best wishes(!!) and thanking her for her business, and so on. Her heart thumped gangbusters in her chest. She imagined the oceans of zin it would take to make her feel better, the waves of it crashing over her wasted life, sucking her back into its bosom of blissful insensation. But she knew it still would never be enough.

Never enough zin to tell Harvest they were going to lose the house and they would live God only knew where. Never enough zin to forgive herself for not selling a house in nearly a year. Never enough zin to hold her dear husband Carl's photo, look him in the eye, and tell him that she'd let everyone down so completely, so utterly.

Although maybe a touch of vodka and OJ might do it—No! Stop it!! she thought. Halt! Alcohol was Not The Answer.

Time to stand up to things. Be accountable. Be positive.

Or at least time to move on to the next problem before Harvest got home.

After checking through the blinds first for any approaching vehicles, she circled the knapsack on the table like it was an unexploded bomb. Why did she feel it contained the explanation for the fact that her daughter had become almost unrecognizable to her? This black, ragged scrap of canvas, heavy with over a hundred key chains she collected—Smurf, Spongebob Squarepants and other strangely childish icons—went with her everywhere now, not just to school. She lugged it to the mall, to overnights with friends, she'd even taken it to the junior prom. The jangle of the key chains was the harbinger of her approach to the house. The bag was by her side even at night, and she always zipped it shut the minute Ginger appeared.

And now here it was, its teen, goth, backtalking, Mom-bashing secrets about to be laid bare. One last time Ginger asked herself: do I really want to know why my daughter hates me? The answer again was: yes.

She unzipped the main compartment, which was crammed with books. She pulled out, one after the other: *Geology Today*, *English Composition II*, and *Applied Calculus*. She rested a moment, enjoying the stunning normalcy of these textbooks. But there was more in this bottomless pit of a bag. She reached in deeper. A workbook called *Introduction to Chemistry*. A novel: *Catcher in the Rye*. Aw, Ginger thought, and I thought she just read *Megadeath Monthly*. Was that it? Piece of cake. But her hands closed around one last thing in the bottom of the bag...a thin paperback: *Bisexuality for Teens*.

Hmmm.

Was this the big secret? So it wasn't Trevor any more, it was Shelley? Or Trevor and Shelley?

She pulled up a chair and sat down with a heave. She stared at the nearly dead plants on the windowsill without seeing them or, for that matter, hearing their silent shrieks for water. Huh, she thought, she likes boys and girls. Ginger's intellect: clouded, disordered and tangled as it was, took that thought and tossed it back and forth across the frayed net of her mind. The volley went on peacefully for some time. To her surprise, nothing bad happened. All she came up with was: well, that's different. In the end, she'll be with a girl. Or with a boy. It was OK. Just be a good person and have a good life.

After a few moments of second guessing herself (should I be upset? is this wrong? am I missing something?) she began to concern herself with the endless remaining pockets and secret cavities of Harvest's bag.

Extracted from a side pocket: clove cigarettes, a lighter from the Pussycat Lounge with a retro-sexy winking woman with kitty whiskers perched on a lamppost, a condom that looked like it had been in her bag for decades, a deck of cards...tarot cards. She stared at those a moment. On the cover of the box a man hung upside down from what looked like a diving board, his hands tied behind his back. She fished out a blue chamois cloth bag with five smooth stones inside, each with some sort of engraved lettering from an unknown alphabet. A small clear plastic bag of— hah!—pot! She opened it, smelled it. Nope. From bringing Big Jean the good stuff over the years she certainly knew her weed, and this smelled more like Italian seasoning. A long black stick with a silvery grey tip.

And one more thing. It felt like just a piece of cardboard until she pulled it out and unfolded it. A Ouija board.

A Ouija board?

A car door slammed. Laughter.

Action trumping thought, Ginger jammed everything back in the knapsack in seconds, ran to Harvest's bedroom and tossed it on her bed, raced up to her own bedroom, shut the door and peered out her blinds just in time to see Shelley's car pull away and Harvest turn toward the house.

Chapter 8

French toast spit and crackled in the pan as Ginger, humming tunelessly in her fluffy pink robe and bunny slippers, busily set the table and poured out orange juice for two. Finally she heard what she was waiting for: the creak of Harvest's door. From the corner of her eye she saw her daughter's slim form slip into, then a few moments later, out of the bathroom. The form hesitated at the bedroom door.

"Ma?"

"Yes, honey?"

"What are you doing?"

"What does it look like I'm doing?"

The whisper of bare feet on wide pine boards. "Is someone coming over?"

"It's for you. Your favorite."

"What's wrong?"

Ginger got out two plates. "Nothing's—"

"Something's going on. You've never made me breakfast in my life."

Ginger glanced up from scraping dried egg off a fork. "I haven't?"

Harvest shook her head.

"Well, that's not good."

Harvest continued to study her. "Did you, like, sell a house or something? Is that why you're in such a good mood?"

"Can't I make you breakfast? For the...first time?"

Harvest sat at the table, curling one leg under her. "Yeah, well, whatever." She poured a generous amount of maple syrup on her stack of French toast and took a bite.

Ginger went to a basket by the fireplace and brought back a jumble of orange and brown yarn, sat across from Harvest and began to crochet.

"Aren't you going to eat?" Harvest asked.

"Just waiting for my appetite to find me this morning."

"Do you have a closing?"

"No."

"Then why are you making that?" She gestured with her fork.

"Well, I'll have a closing someday. Just want to be ready."

Harvest shook her head and continued eating. After a moment she said, "Come on, what's really going on?"

"Harvey—"

"You have at least five finished 'throws' or 'throw ups' or whatever you call them by the couch over there. What do you need another one for?"

It was true. There were eight hideous rust and dung-colored throws with scalloped edges neatly folded in her rattan crochet box.

"You know things happen all at once in real estate! What if I have a bunch of closings all at once? This way I'll be all set, with closing presents from the heart."

Harvest pushed her plate away and tamped a clove cigarette on the table. "When was the last time you sold a house, anyway?"

"Harvest, I've been meaning to ask you. I know you're busy with your friends and hobbies and everything, b—"

"Are we broke?"

"—but I was wondering if you might consider getting a job—just something part time, maybe down at the *Bugle*? I know you like to write and it might be good for you to have that kind of experience—"

"Was it six months? That disgusting ranch on Vandeleer with the lady with fifteen cats?"

"—just some pocket money, and maybe also...it was a year."

Avoiding Harvest's eye, she set the crochet project aside and began to gather the plates. "That was a year ago, Harvey."

"Are we gonna lose the house?"

"Well, no, but—"

"Jesus, Ma, if you would just learn how to use a computer—"

"Now don't go there, young lady. You know how I feel about that. I've sold real estate perfectly well for thirty-nine years and never needed—"

"We're going to starve to death."

Ginger crashed some dishes in the sink, ran some water. "Don't you say that—"

"You're just going to drink it all away, and we'll be homeless and starving—"

"Look, young missy, you just listen up here. I am a functioning alcoholic just like everyone else in this damned town, just like your dear old dad—"

"Don't talk about Dad like that!"

"Oh, you think he didn't like his Riuniti on the rocks? Well, you think again, young lady. He was with me one for one and then some, and if he hadn't fallen down that tank—"

"Oh my God, was he drunk then?"

"It was ten o'clock in the morning!"

"So was he drunk??"

"It's possible but that's not my point!" Ginger lost steam a moment, tightening her pink belt around her plump middle.

"I'm ready for your point whenever you are, Ma."

"My point is," —one more jerk on the belt— "that we are Kanadoos. From the proud Kanadoo tribe of the Squamskootnocket Valley Region—"

"Oh, God, not the proud Indian crap again—"

"—a proud and noble Native American tribe that survived to this day in the form of this renowned real estate family. We survived to list and sell another day."

"If we're Indian, then we shouldn't drink, right?"

"For Indians, we hold our liquor pretty good. Besides, Big Jean is a quarter Swedish."

Harvest got up and stomped off to her room. Ginger ran after her. "Hey, we were talking—"

"Shelley'll be here in a minute." She slammed the door behind her.

Ginger spoke through it, right into Marilyn Manson's bleeding cat-eye. "Honey, why are you like this? Is it because you can't get past your dad's death? Should I take you to a shrink?"

"With what, an IOU?" Harvest stepped out wearing a black leather jacket and jeans. A horn beeped outside.

"When will you be back?"

Harvest hesitated at the door. "I don't know. Dinnertime maybe."

"Don't worry, everything's going to be OK. We'll be fine. It's spring. Things'll be hopping soon."

Shelley beeped her car horn again.

"OK, Ma, whatever you say," and she was gone.

⁕ ⁕ ⁕

Ginger watched them drive off from her tiny front porch, her daughter and her perhaps-lover, perhaps-just-friend, neither even offering a wave goodbye.

The morning air was cool and delicious, the sky clear and blue over the freshly blooming flowers and green green grasses of spring. Just the kind of weather that made you want to fall on a sword, Ginger thought as she made her way to a clot of deep purple crocuses nosing up through her neglected crust of a yard. She picked a flower and smelled it. Smelled like nothing. Flowers! What was the big damned deal.

She was overcome by an urge to sit down in the front yard in her robe. Just to plop right down. She saw herself doing it before she did it, then did it, rolling onto her back in a kind of slow motion, her feet churning a bit in the air like a beetle until she found her balance and strained to sit back up, cross-legged.

She took a deep breath. It had been a while since she'd sat on the earth. There was something lovely about it—the rich smell of moist soil, the birds chirping in the trees above her, but also something wet about it; her ass slowly cooling and dampening through her robe and sensible waist-high panties.

Her eyes filled with tears.

I've taken a wrong turn somewhere, she thought, staring out across her lawn at the road.

A car with tinted glass drove by, slowed, then kept on going.

I've let things slip. It's even possible, she thought, wiping her fluffy sleeve across her eyes, that I've reached rock bottom.

My husband is gone, I'm about to lose my house, I'm forty pounds overweight, and my daughter has Italian seasoning and a Ouija board in her backpack. I don't understand her life at all. These days, I don't even understand my own.

The tears flowed heavily now. A part of her tried to get up and go inside but it was as if she was rooted there. It was a big old messy cry. A healthy, cleansing one. After several minutes she looked up and saw the neighbor's cat Bootsy sitting a few feet away, staring at her.

"Hi Boosthy," she said through her clogged nose. "Boosthy, you think I'm a good real estate agent, don't you?"

He flicked something away with his tail.

"Cuz y'know, I usta be number one."

He stared, as if interested.

"I was the go-to gal. I was a gal on the go. I was—"

Bootsy got up and crossed sideways in front of her, passed her, then sauntered toward her backyard.

Ginger yanked up a handful of grass and tossed it, like a little kid. Her ass was wetter and colder than it had ever been. It wasn't half bad, really, to have a numb ass. She thought, I'll just stay here. When they come to repossess the house they can just take a forklift and scoop me up and set me down in the homeless shelter in Vanderskleet. I'll quit selling real estate altogether (like anyone would notice!) Maybe I'll set up a booth in the center of town and sell my throws.

The thought inspired a fresh round of tears.

Not about selling her throws, she was sure that would go well, but ending her career as a realtor? That was too much!

She had a choice, and it was clear: either stay on the grass and wait 'til the bank man came, or get up.

Time passed.

The school bus came and went, wide-eyed school children ogling her as it roared past. Still she sat and thought.

An hour later, a prop plane putt-putted overhead. A father piloting as his son watched the world unfold beneath them. "Dad, what's that big pink blob down there? A cow?"

His father threw a glance down at Ginger. "I don't know, son. Do we have pink cows in New York?"

His little son giggled and they veered west, into the horizon.

Ginger shielded her eyes as she watched the plane swerve away. Sun was beating down on her now, and she began to sweat under her robe. Bees buzzed around her hair, loving the smell of her new perm. She barely bothered to swat them away. Her big pout was lasting longer than even she thought it would. The major problem being that if she did get up, there had to be, in her mind, no possibility of failure. So much easier to wait out the three months on the lawn for the man from the Squamskootnocket Valley Savings and Loan.

Dave, her profoundly deaf mailman, started to walk across her lawn, bent under the weight of his bag. It was obvious he hadn't seen her because he was headed right toward her, since she sat between him and her mailbox on the other side of the lawn. Dave was a burly sixty-year-old with wiry silver hair escaping from under his blue cap, from out his ears and his wide nose.

His strong thighs bulged under his striped post office shorts as he slogged across the lawn. He was six yards away, four, three...Ginger watched in amazement as he barreled toward her. She yelled, waving her arms, "Look out, Dave!!"

Two, one...

She tucked and rolled to her left, but Dave's foot caught in the belt of her robe and he went flying, a blizzard of mail bursting from his bag and scattering on the grass.

Tangled in her robe, Ginger struggled to her feet. She ran over to Dave and helped him up, apologizing over and over. He brushed himself off and looked dejectedly at the white sea of mail on the lawn.

"What were you doing sitting on the lawn like that?"

"IT'S A LONG STORY!" she shouted, slapping her ass now and then to get some feeling back.

"Are you OK?"

"I'M FINE!" she yelled. "JUST A LITTLE DEPRESSED!"

"Ginger, why are you shouting?"

"BECAUSE YOU'RE DEAF!" she shrieked, pointing to his ears. "YOU CAN'T HEAR!!" She did a double take at him. "AND HOW DID YOU KNOW THAT I WAS SHOUTING IF YOU CAN'T HEAR?"

"How many times do I have to tell you," he said, gathering the mail from the lawn. "I lip read. I read your lips."

"OH!" and then a softer "oh." After a moment, her shoulders shook, and she began to cry. When Dave finally looked up at her from tending to his mail, his face registered concern and he put a friendly arm around her shoulder. Given the inch, she took the mile and sobbed into his polyester jacket, leaving goobers there as he patted her on the head.

"Are you having a hard time, Ginger? What's the problem?"

Through vibrations in his chest, he understood she was talking to him, but of course couldn't hear her. He pulled her away from him. "What was that?"

"Dave, my life is falling apart. I haven't sold a house in a year, I got a foreclosure on this place, I can't even use a cell phone, my daughter has Ouija boards in her backpack—"

"She has wh—"

"She hates me, OK? She usta think I was a queen. Wanted to be like me, sell real estate just like Mommy, and now" —sob— "I'm losing everything. You don't understand—"

He took her by the shoulders. "Why wouldn't I understand? I've never told you what happened to me."

She wiped her eyes with her sleeve. Afternoon sun was starting to throw long shadows, and she had a flash of the nice ham in the sandwich drawer and the thick sourdough bread in the bin. "Whad habbened to you?"

"I was an attorney for a big law firm in New York. I had a beautiful wife, two kids, a great house in the 'burbs. One day I come home from work to a note from my wife saying she's leaving me for her aura consultant. Everything was gone—the kids, furniture, everything. Then, that night, my hearing began to flag, it went in and out, like bad reception. It was terrifying. Long story short, by morning I was completely deaf. Some bacteria from our Jacuzzi got lodged in there, they say, but they don't really know. So I lose my job, my family, my house—"

"Wow, that's terrible. You must feel like shit."

"The point is this: I'm alive, I'm basically healthy, I have enough to eat, a place to live—hell, who cares if I live over the Squamskootnocket Dollar Store—I love life! Life is good, full of possibilities. Now that I can lip read, I can get back into law again, get back on my feet. But it's going to take hard work and persistence. I mean, hell, I was so desperate for a while there, I almost got my real estate license. No offense."

"No offense taken!" Ginger began to stand a little straighter as he was telling his story, a fresh lump rising in her throat. "In fact, you got me feeling a little better!"

"I hope so."

"Where there's a will, there's a way! Nowhere to go but up! It's always darkest before the dawn!"

"When the going gets tough, the tough get going!"

They high-fived each other.

"Time to pull myself up by my bootstraps!" she said, adjusting and tucking her robe. "There's a reason you ran into me today, Dave. Say, are you up for a little ham on sourdough?"

⁂ ⁂ ⁂

A brisk spring wind wilding her cottony locks, Ginger hustled down Main Street, Squamskootnocket toward the Coffee Pit where she had a date for decaf with Maxie.

The place seemed empty at first, and for a moment she wondered if she'd gotten their meeting time wrong. Then she found her in a booth in the back, head down on the table, a ciggy immolating in an ashtray. For an awful moment she watched for the rise and fall of breath in Maxie's diminutive form, saw it, relaxed, and tapped her on the shoulder.

"Hey, Max, it's me. Rise and shine."

Maxie lifted her head. Her face was covered with stamps. Birds of America. She blinked at the yellow bright of the diner, her brow wrinkling as her brain gathered the information necessary to recognize her wake-ee. "Oh, hi. I was just working on my mailing..."

Ginger peeled a few stamps off her friend's face: a Great Blue Heron, a Tufted Egret. "Thanks for meeting me. I really needed to talk to a genuine pal."

Maxie scratched at a stamp on her glasses with the craggy nub of a nail. "Damn things. 'Spose I could start buying those peel-off kind but I just don't trust them. The kind you lick work just fine for me, so why'd they have to go'n change things?"

Ginger settled into her seat. "I hear you, Max! Change is the enemy!"

"Damned straight." Max craned her head toward the counter and stools where curling, badly misspelled menus covered the walls. "Now where's that little tart to heat up my bean?"

Ginger flagged the waitress, Sheena, who sat smoking in a far corner of the restaurant. A stripper on weekends in downtown Vanderskleet, Sheena made ends meet on weekdays at the Pit.

She sauntered over, eyebrows penciled, teased locks high.

"Hi, hon," Maxie said. "Got any a those coffee buns from this morning?"

"For you? Sure. Ginger? Turkey on white?"

"Coffee bun sounds good today, Sheena. And Sanka."

"Set ya right up," she said, heading back toward the kitchen.

"Nice girl. Body like that, I'd prolly shake it for a living too." Maxie handed Ginger one of the postcards she was mailing. "Hey, you ever send this one out, lemon bundt?"

"Nope, not that one. I did a thousand of the blueberry cobbler once, though. 1971, I think."

"That's a yummy one." She took a sip of cold coffee, grimaced, and pushed her cup aside. She slapped her hand down on the table. "Ginger, I'll be honest. You look blue."

"I'm broke."

Max looked at her a long moment. "Wish I could help you in that department—"

"Oh no, I'm not asking you—"

"I mean I've got my social security, a little money from the Guinness people—they're so nice, and the recognition is great but no real cash—"

Ginger held up her hand and cleared her throat as Sheena freshened their cups and laid out their coffee buns. She said under her breath, "I wasn't asking you, really I wasn't."

"What about Big Jean?"

"Can't keep going to that well. Besides, Dickie's holding those purse strings."

Maxie tore off a piece of her bun. "How'd that ever happen, anyway?"

"Hell if I know." But she did know. Even though she was the favorite, Big Jean trusted Dickie over her for cash flow.

"Things'll pick up. The season's just starting! You're blue now, which means you'll be happy soon. It's the cycle of life."

"Yah think so?"

"Absolutely. I didn't get to be this old and not learn a thing or two. Besides, you're the best realtor in town, always have been!"

Ginger puffed up a bit. "Ya think so?"

"Course you are. Nuff said."

Ginger leaned forward. "You have a point. Nobody knows Squamskootnocket like I do." She jabbed her finger at the squiggly pattern on the linoleum table. "I know every house, every store, every hill, every valley, every clod of soil, every damned soul in this town!"

Max chowed on her bun and slurped her coffee. "There ya go."

"Hell, Max, I've always sold things. Remember when I was in Brownies?"

"Sure I do. You were a pip."

"—and I sold the most cookies ever in Squamskootnocket? And I got all those badges and I sold every single one of them—"

"—for a tidy profit I'd say—"

"I tell you, selling's in my blood."

"Atta girl." Max wiped her mouth and reached for her pile of stamps and cards. "Ya wanna hand me that wet sponge?"

Ginger did so. "I need to kickstart my life! Spin into action! Just spinspinspin! Get back into my old tricks: door knocking, cold calling, pens with my name and number on them—"

"I gotta lot a those."

"Today was special. I ran into Dave—"

"Deaf Dave?"

"And he told me his story and it was so inspiring, how he lost his hearing and how he used to be a big lawyer in the city—"

"Dave's always been a mailman, far as I know. Deaf as a shoe. Can't hear himself fart. A sad thing." She slapped an

American Vulture in the corner of a card, tamping it down with a tiny fist.

"The point is, he has dreams! Big ones! And he's going for them! I don't know, Max, it's like today I took the time to take a long hard look at myself. I asked myself: who am I? WHO AM I LOOKING AT?"

"And who'dja see?" she asked, not looking up from her cards.

"I saw Ginger Kanadoo!! Your kana-doo realtor! I'm still me, Max, I still got it, I just gotta get it in gear again. But I'm not getting any younger, so this is it! This is now. Hell, not only am I gonna sellsellsell, I'm gonna win that goddamned trip to Hawaii if it's the last thing I do! I've just gotta get my groove back."

Maxie waved at Sheena for more coffee. "Get jiggie with it."

"Busta move, as Harvey would say! It's true, some self improvements are in order. Nobody can help me but me, I know that. I've gotta reach deep inside myself. Hell, maybe even get another perm."

"Perms are always a good pick-me-up."

"I may even join Shapes and shake off a few!"

"There's a thought."

"I swear to you, Max, I'm going to sell that damned outhouse this weekend if it kills me!"

"You go, girl."

"I'm not gonna let Tandy get to me, or Old Man Higgins—"

"Mmm hmm—"

"And I will not, I will NOT, I swear to you, EVER ask Dickie for money again."

"That's probably wise."

Ginger sat back in the cracked naugahyde booth. "Thanks, Max. You made me feel so much better."

"Oh, now, you did that all by yourself. You didn't need old Max." She waved for the check. "You got this, right?"

Chapter 9

Ginger sat in Dickie's office, her hands held together as if in prayer. "Please oh please oh please lend me some more money, Dickie. I promise I'll pay you back the second the crapper closes—"

He heaved himself to his feet, hiked up his pants and shut the office door. Tandy passed by, cell phone to her ear, laptop in tow. She waved at Dickie as she sauntered to her work station next to Maxie, who looked deeply absorbed in something at her desk.

"Did she just...wink at you?"

"Course not. I don't know. Maybe. A friendly wink. What's the harm?"

Ginger chose her battles. "You know I've had a run of bad luck lately."

Dickie sat on the edge of his desk. "Gin, you've never paid me back. Ever."

"I haven't?"

"No, not in—"

"Damn, Dickie, I thought we were square—"

"How can we be 'square' when I've never seen a dime?"

Ginger pouted. "Harvest, your very own and only niece, needs new ripped black stuff, and not only that—well, trust me, Dickie, the wolf is at the door!"

Dickie folded his arms and looked at her. "If I had it to give, I would, Gin. I'm tapped out. Look at the sales this year. Pitiful. That's why I hired Tandy. She's gonna help turn this place around. And there'll be more Tandys."

"More Tandys? How could you—"

"I gotta survive, Gin. You and Max, and Mom when she was here, you were at the top of your game. But now..."

"Now, what? You're putting us out to pasture? You can't fire me, Dickie! Mom loves me!"

Dickie rolled his eyes and walked around his desk back to his seat. "How is Mom, anyway? Still keeping her in hooch?" He pulled out a file and began to shuffle through it.

"I don't know what you're talking about."

"Like hell you don't—"

"She has glaucoma. Cut her some slack!"

Dickie shook his head. "Just get back into the swing of things, and start taking care of yourself. Tandy said she saw you sitting on your lawn this morning. She gave me a call. She was very concerned about you."

Ginger reddened. The thought that Tandy had seen her that morning during her little event tightened her windpipe to the size of vermicelli. "Can't a person sit on their own lawn? Is there some new law in Squamsquoo—"

"I'm just worried about you, is all."

Ginger snorted and got to her feet. "I'll show you, Dickie. I'll show you who's going to save this office."

Dickie nodded and gestured at the door. "I'm sure you can do it, Gin."

Ginger harrumphed. "And I'm going to Hawaii to boot." She stomped out of his office, giving his door a bit of a slam behind her.

Head held high, she strutted past Tandy's desk.

It was a study in simplicity, elegance and order: a laptop, BlackBerry, desk phone, standup files color-coded and off to one side, even a small bunch of freesia in a slip of a vase. Interior photos of what looked like new construction flashed and faded across her PC screen. Ginger froze a moment, staring, then broke away and meandered over to her own desk, which was next to Maxie's.

Countless files were stacked in yellowed piles, while several half-filled coffee cups teetered next to bits of old doughnuts. Hundreds of brightly colored Post-it notes with directives like "Pick up Harv today at 2:30, not 3, DON'T FORGET!!!" covered every available surface. Ginger picked up a folder for a slab ranch she'd sold years ago but never filed, flipped through it, then tossed it listlessly back on her desk. She stared at her silent black phone, its dark heart concerning itself with millions of other real estate transactions, none of which she had absolutely anything to do with. Out of the corner of her eye she watched Tandy exit the bathroom and walk toward Dickie's office. Smiling, he held the door open for her.

"Hey, Max," Ginger stage whispered at her, one eye still on Tandy. Max stayed focused on what looked like a coloring project. Ginger sat down and nudged her with her foot.

"Watch it, Gin. I'm busy."

Ginger got up and looked over Maxie's shoulder. She was gluing a yardstick to the back of a good-sized square of white cardboard. "So is he gonna help you out?" Maxie asked, not looking up from her work.

"I told you—I'm never asking him for a dime again," Ginger said, shifting her weight.

"So he said no, the prick. The thing is, he has it. He just won't cough it up."

Ginger sighed and tucked a wacky strand of hair behind her ear. "What are you doing?"

Maxie turned the sign over. In huge letters it said: "Hell, No, We Won't Go—Online!!" She held it up and smiled. "We're bucking this technology trend, my friend."

"We're technology-buckers!" Ginger clapped her hands. "I love it! Where's mine?"

Maxie pulled out an identical sign from under her desk and handed it to her. "Ya gotta remember, Gin, we are the backbone of this organization, and if he thinks he can push us around with this bloggie woggie website crap, he's got another thing comin'!" She pushed herself to her feet, grabbed her sign and held it high. "Come on, time to stand up for our rights!"

With tiny marching steps, Max made her way to Dickie's office, Ginger right behind with her own sign. For a few moments they stood in front of his windowed door holding their signs. They ogled Dickie and Tandy as they pored over some new construction plans spread out on his desk.

They shook their signs a bit, then started to march in a little circle. Max hummed tunelessly. Ginger started to chant, "Hell no, we won't go—online!" Time passed. Nothing happened.

"This is just like 'Nam," Ginger said.

"They're ignoring us," Maxie said. "The nerve."

"Just intimidated."

Maxie continued in their tiny circle. "Hell, I would be."

The phone rang and everyone jumped. Maxie dropped her sign, and Dickie and Tandy finally looked up and saw Ginger with hers. The phone hadn't rung for so long and the sound was so foreign that everyone was momentarily in shock as to what to do about it.

Breaking from his trance, Dickie lunged for the phone. He said a few words and laid it down on his desk, his face darkening as he read the signs bobbing outside his office.

"He looks kind of mad, Max," Ginger said.

"Oh, screw him." Max kept circling around her. "This is the writing on the wall. Let him read it."

Dickie wrenched the door open. "You two get rid of those goddamned signs this minute, you hear me?"

"Ever hear of freedom of speech, Mr. Smartie Pants?" Maxie said, circling around him with her sign. "Or is that something that went out with respecting your long-term employees?"

Dickie grabbed both signs from the women, knocking Maxie into Ginger, and stormed to the back room where they listened to him curse and thrash about. The snap of balsa wood, the furious rip of cardboard. He came out liver-colored, slammed the door behind him, and steamed past Ginger into his office.

"Phone's for you, Ginger," he said before disappearing inside.

Maxie blinked as Ginger helped her get her balance. She pushed her away. "Gin, ya gotta phone call. Look smart!"

Ginger straightened. "Probably just Harvey."

She went to her desk and picked up. "Regina! ... Great, you? ... Three o'clock? ... Sure, I'll be there! With bells on!" She hung up.

Ginger jumped up and down and clapped her hands.

"What? You win the lottery?"

"I got a listing!"

They high-fived.

"I told you it would happen!" Maxie sat down and picked up her knitting. "Ya just gotta be patient."

"This is it! My luck is changing!" Flushed with excitement, Ginger grabbed her jacket and purse. "Max, I'll see you later." She careened into Dickie's office. Dickie looked up, still red-faced. Tandy gave Ginger a constipated little smile.

"Just wanted to let you know that I'll be unavailable the rest of the day."

Dickie rubbed his forehead. "Why's that, Ginger?"

"Because this afternoon I'm going to list my best friend Regina Freenspeet's house."

Chapter 10

Ginger bounced along in her junker, ignoring the cold rain that pelted her windshield and spewed up from the street through the holes in the floor of her car and onto her Easy Spirits. She sang along loudly and tunelessly to the golden oldies, belting out along with Elvis: "I'll have a boooooo Christmas without you, I'll be so blooooo just thinking about you..."

The entire time she was driving, and singing, and slapping the steering wheel in time with the music, she was also fighting a niggling, naggling little wretch of a thought that tapped and rapped at the back door of her tangled and obfuscated frontal lobe like a Jehovah's Witness. She thought if she sang loud enough, and long enough, and forcefully enough, she could banish the wisp of memory, the pesky backbeat, the sinewy thread of raw reality that simply would not take its bible and go away.

The thought was this: Regina Freenspeet's house smelled.

And not just any smell. Not some memory of old dog, or mildewy books in a damp basement, not staleness or kitty pee or strange cooking smells or exotic spice, not plastic new-house smells or smoke from an old fire, or cigar or tobacco or pot, not the sickly sweet smell of a baby's room or the acrid reek of a teenage son nor the pukey powder of teenage girl, not the smell of the aged just removed to their ultimate home...

No, no, no, no, no...and finally...no.

Regina Freenspeet's house smelled

like

shit.

"You'll be doooin' all right, with your Christmas of white..." she yodeled, "But I'll have a blue, blueblueblue Christmas..."

Oh please please please, God in heaven above, make it not smell like that any more, she prayed as Love Me Tender kicked in and she hooked a hard right onto Regina's street. Maybe Regina had finally smelled it herself and taken care of it, or maybe someone had told her and she had gotten rid of it somehow. Maybe, after thirty years of visiting Regina at 25 Applebee Way, Ginger wouldn't leave her house gasping for air. Today, anything was possible!

Regina, pear-shaped with a halo of dyed-cinnamon hair, waved gaily at her friend from her screen door as Ginger gathered herself and her paperwork from the car.

"Look at this crazy rain!" Regina yelled out good naturedly. "This wasn't supposta happen!"

"Well, you know how things are around here," Ginger said, running across the wet lawn with her bag of files. "If you don't like the weather, wait a minute!"

"Get yourself inside, Gin." Regina ushered Ginger across the threshold. "I got brownies coming out of the oven, your favorite. Frosted with nuts."

They hugged briefly, then stood apart. Ginger couldn't help but see, whenever she looked at Regina, the popular, slim, pretty girl with the big knockers who first dated the football team, then made her way through the basketball team, the hockey team, and so on. Though renowned as the school slut, she was so well meaning about her encounters with boy after boy, so chronically re-enthused about love each and every time, that she never thought of herself in a negative way. She had an irreducible sweetness to her, and Ginger knew that when she did move away, she would miss her a great deal.

Ginger took a deep lungful of air and let it out. Pure, unmitigated, unexpurgated, undiluted, odeur de shit. That is, mixed with the dark sweet smell of brownie. Made things almost worse.

"You look wonderful," Regina said, leading Ginger into the kitchen. "How's work? How's that new girl, you know, the one with the crazy business cards?"

"She's nice enough," Ginger said, pulling up a chair and accepting a cup of coffee, "but between you and I, she doesn't know squat about real estate, never mind Squamskootnocket."

Regina scooted out a hot brownie from a tray, then poured herself some weak coffee from an ancient pot. "Oh, give her some slack. She'll catch on."

Ginger harrumphed and took a bite of brownie. "You can't 'catch on' to experience, Geena. You can't" —finger quotes— "'learn' real estate. You have to eat it, breathe it, sleep it, live it for decades in order to have something truly valuable to offer people."

Regina clapped her hands. "And that's why I'm hiring you, the best, to sell my house!"

Ginger buried her nose in her coffee for a moment to give herself a break from a fresh wave of stink issuing from Satan knew where. "Geena, here's the plan. I want you to give me a tour of your home, before we sign all this paperwork."

"But Gin, you've seen it a thousand times!"

"I need to see it like a realtor, and take some notes."

"What a great idea! That sounds like fun!"

So she got the tour. A solid 1955 cape with original kitchen and baths but a lot of character under the frilly curtains, religious trinkets and drawings, endless family photos and tchochkes stashed in every corner. And in every corner of every room Ginger inhaled deeply, yet casually, trying to determine the source of The Smell. Oddly, it was less pungent in the bathrooms than the rest of the house. Its presence seemed to have nothing to do with where those smells normally emanate. It was also inconsistent, which gave Ginger hope that perhaps she was imagining it.

But she wasn't. Imagining it.

It would disappear for a moment, then usher itself back in, waft down a hallway in a gushy wave, stink up the laundry sink, belch up from the linen closet; dissipate again, then balloon out all around them, almost through them, as if making up for lost time. It was, in fact, like an entity unto itself. A great, flatulent, crapping ghost.

Ginger decided to feign innocence. She stopped short halfway down the second floor hallway. "Geena, did you smell that? Just now?"

Regina paused at the door of her office. She had been about to show Ginger a picture of her new boyfriend, DeeShaun, and his five children, who each had a different "mom." A bilious haze hung in the air all around them. Geena sniffed at it, right in the thick of it, Ginger noted, observing the twitch of Geena's tiny upturned nose. "What?" Geena said. "I don't smell anything. Why? What do you smell?"

"I don't know ... it's a sort of ... kind of ... an earthy smell..."

Geena sniffed again. "Brownies? They did burn a little—"

"No, earthier than that—"

"Oh, no, not gas! Did I shut it off?!" She started toward the stairs but Ginger cut her off.

"No, I checked that. Maybe it's just me, but I smell something a little...odd. In fact I've smelled it for a long time."

"Well...what are you trying to say? That my house smells? I clean it every week. In fact, I just had the place professionally cleaned, even the windows. I think it looks great—"

"It does! It does look great! I love your house, I always have, but you know how you go into a house sometimes and you smell something and you just can't put your finger on what it is—"

"Oh, like Karen's house on the lake? That place stinks like wet towels! My God, does my house smell like that?"

Ginger recalled Karen's house fondly, the rather comforting smell of damp towels compared to...

"No. Not like that. More subtle, more like...more like..."

"More like what? Spit it out! We're friends. You're my realtor. You have to tell me!" She was reddening, arms crossed hard, photos of DeeShaun and his smiling, cornrowed kids clutched in one hand.

"S-something brown—brown things—"

"Brown things?"

"Like old brownies" —that have passed through an intestinal system— "or maybe just burned ones." Ginger gave it up and collapsed in a tattered loveseat. Her life felt loathsome to her. She wanted to drop thirty-five years, thirty-five pounds and one bisexual child, and head off into the shrill and frightful but ultimately gorgeous hills of youth knowing what she knew now.

"Well, I can get rid of that," Regina said, thrusting the photos into Ginger's hands. "Just some potpourri or something. Boil cloves on the stove. Whatever. You must know some tricks."

"I do," said Ginger, looking at the photographs without seeing them. "Don't worry. I know all the tricks."

Chapter 11

As Ginger drove home it occurred to her that she had absolutely no idea what to do about Regina's house, or about her outhouse, or about her own house, or any house in the world. Her mind was a tabula rasa where puffy white clouds and the occasional glass of Sutter Home floated past. Some plug had been pulled on her energy as she left the poopy house, and all of it had drained out of her and through the holes in her car and out onto the road. She was housed-out; in fact the only thing she could hear was the sweet centurion call of zin. A call she heeded as soon as she got in the door.

After she changed into her fluffy robe and slippers and poured herself a tall, cool glass, she padded over to Harvest's room where she heard the tinny sound of the TV behind the door.

"Hey, Harvey, honey."

Nothing. She rapped at the door. More nothing. Knocked a little louder. A few seconds later Harvest's little face appeared, framed tightly by the door and the wall.

"I have company."

"Oh! Who's your little friend?"

Harvest rolled her eyes. "Shelley, who else?"

"Well...how was your day?"

"It was fine. Can I go now?"

"I got a new listing today."

Resigned, Harvest stayed in the doorway, though Ginger's view of her grew narrower and narrower. "Anybody I know?"

"Just your Auntie Regina's place!"

"You're kidding! That place smells like shit!" She sighed exasperatedly, giving in a bit with the door. "Are you even gonna tell her?"

Ginger exhaled as she shifted her weight in her slippers. The floor creaked. She felt a hundred years old. She cleared her throat. "Of course not."

Harvest closed her eyes and dumped her forehead on the edge of the door. "We are going to starve to death. It's as simple as that. We're going to be homeless and naked and go begging through the streets of this godforsaken bunghole of a town—"

"Now you stop that right now, young lady!" Ginger whispered hoarsely. "A listing is a listing. It's a great house, lots of curb appeal, beautiful land, lots of room for a young family, great neighborhood—"

"Except it smells like—"

"I know what it smells like! I'm working on it. I have a plan in place that's going to take care of that problem, going to get rid of it completely, so don't you worry. And don't you get smart with me!" she added without conviction.

Harvest disappeared for a second, then bobbed back into view. "We're hungry."

"Well," Ginger said, softening at the normal turn of conversation. "Find out what your friend would li—"

"Chinese or pizza?" Harvest asked from behind the door. Ginger looked at the slim hands that held the door in place, nails painted black and bitten to the quick. She remembered Harvey at five, begging her to paint her nails pink, "just like Mommy."

"Pizza, OK? Mushroom and olive." Harvest shut the door, half an inch from Ginger's nose.

Ginger stared at it a moment, shook her head, and went to the kitchen to make the call. Instead of ordering the pizza first, she dialed Maxie's number.

"Hey, Max..." She heard the phone drop, a clattering. "You there?"

"Yup, just resting my eyes."

"You up for a drink?"

"Everything OK?"

"Just wondering why I gave birth. Thought you might want to come over and share the pain."

"Oh, she's not so bad. I remember when she was the cutest, sweetest, happiest little girl—"

"Well, that's not the case any more."

Maxie sighed. "Gotcha. I'll be right over."

* * *

Ginger pressed her ear to her daughter's door. Maybe the girls were saying something that would explain the contents of Harvest's knapsack, or just why Harvest hated her so much these days, or maybe there was something bisexual going on that she as a mother should—DING DONG!!! Ginger jumped, flustered, tossing wine in her eye as she dropped her glass which shattered on the floor. Cursing, she stepped over the mess and made her way to the door, wiping her eyes on her sleeve.

Maxie and the pizza boy had arrived at the same time. They stood under the front porch light, the oddest of couples: the scrawny whip of a boy holding the pizza in one hand and playing with a zit with the other, next to Maxie who stood dwarfed in a heavy Irish sweater, though it was a warm night, eyes blinking huge behind pink tortoise-shell glasses. A full moon hung behind them as if lighting the scene.

"Hey, Max, you hungry?" Ginger scrambled in her pockets for bills.

"Always and never." Maxie took small birdy steps past the boy and into the house. The boy took the money wordlessly and with a quick nod, disappeared into the night.

Max looked around. "Hey, I like what you've done with the place."

Ginger headed to the kitchen counter with the steaming pizza box. "I haven't touched this house since the day I moved in, Max."

"Maybe it's my cataracts. Everything looks...softer."

Ginger grabbed a broom and dustpan and started to clean up the broken glass outside Harvest's room.

"Little accident?"

"I tell you, Max," Ginger whispered, "I just don't feel like I'm living in my own house these days. I feel like a stranger here."

Max shook her head as she watched Ginger sweep. "I remember when my little Joey hit puberty. Little bastard was hell on wheels. Worst ten years of my life."

Ginger looked up at her. "Ten years?"

"Started at twelve, ended at twenty-two when I kicked his grand-theft-auto ass outta my house—"

"Shhh, keep it down." Ginger took the dustpan full of glass and started back toward the kitchen, Max shuffling along behind her.

"Little no-good punk was just like his father, screwing everything in town, stealing money from the till at the station, then blowin' it on the horses on the weekends up at Saskawee-gee-on-Lake, comin' home tanked and ornery, all pissed that he lost and beating on his little dog Spoot—"

"Not that Chihuahua—"

"Can you imagine hitting a Chihuahua?" She tossed up her toothpick arms in her enormous sweater. "There's nothin' to hit!"

Ginger shook her head as she gathered plates, napkins and placemats. Max pulled out a bottle of Riunite and poured out two generous glasses.

"Whatever happened to Joey, anyway?"

"Oh, he's fine now. On the Spackenkill city council. Two kids. Works at the plant. Talks about running for president someday."

Ginger sighed. "So, there is hope, I guess—"

"Well, I didn't say that—"

"I just want to be able to talk to her. I want to understand her. I want her to like me again."

Max climbed up on a stool at the kitchen counter. "And I want Dolly Parton's tits."

Ginger popped an olive in her mouth. "Don't be so negative. I really think that with love, all things are possible."

At that moment Harvest burst from her room, disappeared in the bathroom and slammed the door.

"Ya got any red pepper?" Max asked, helping herself to the pizza.

Ginger handed her a small glass spice jar, then went to the bathroom door and hesitated there.

"Hey, this is paprika—"

"Harvest?"

A pause. "Can't this wait till I'm out of the can?"

"Harvey, we have a guest here, and I would really like it if you and your friend joined us for dinner."

Sound of the toilet flushing, the squeak of faucets. She emerged, glancing over at Max who winked at her as she chewed.

"Oh, hey, Aunt Max."

"So why don't you go get Shelley and join us for dinner with your Auntie Max—"

"OK, Mom, chill. I'll go get her." She disappeared into her room.

Ginger threw her hands in the air. "Chill. I hate that word. 'Chill.' I'm fifty-nine and I don't chill, OK? It's just nasty. Why can't she say: sure, Mom, we'll be right out. Thank God she likes you, or the answer would have been a flat out no anyway."

"It's always easier to like your auntie more than your Mom when you're a teen, honey."

The door opened and the girls emerged, lit blue from the back by the glow of the TV. Both wore all black but had opposite body types. Harvest was rangy and high-strung, her wavy black hair falling heavily in her face from her center part, while Shelley had a generous figure, flaxen blond hair cut short and punky, and didn't seem the type to move unless absolutely necessary. Each had painted thick black kohl circles around their eyes and wore deep red, almost purple lipstick. Both reeked of clove cigarettes.

Shelley held out her hand to Maxie, her numerous silver bracelets clanking. "Hi, I'm Shelley."

"Nice to meet you. I'm Maxie."

"Oh, sorry," Harvest said dully, tossing a piece of pizza on a plate. "I should have introduced you."

"You girls want some Coke?" Ginger chirped.

"I don't drink that garbage," Harvest said, getting herself a glass of tap water.

"I'd love some, Mrs. Kanadoo." Shelley settled onto a stool and politely accepted the piece of pizza Harvest handed to her.

"Oh, dear, call me Ginger. Mrs. Kanadoo—so formal!"

"Hey, Mom," Harvest said, polishing off her first piece of pizza in record time and reaching for another. "Why in the world did you name me Harvest? It's such a lame name."

"I don't know, honey. Hmmm." Ginger put a hand on a jaunty hip. "As far as I remember, one afternoon your Dad and I got the munchies after a couple of toots and started chowing down on pb&j's. We were staring at the label on the bread and it said: 'Harvest Nut'! Boom! You, my girl, had a name!"

"You named me after sandwich bread?"

"Not any old sandwich bread—damned good sandwich bread!!"

Harvest and Shelley stared at each other, chewing.

"Mom, we have to go out in a few minutes."

"Where are you going?" Ginger said in an unnaturally cheerful voice.

"Just going for a ride."

"A ride where?"

Harvest threw her pizza crust down. "Who cares where? A ride!"

Maxie pointed a tiny, sharp finger at her grand niece. "You tell your mother where you're going, or you're not leaving this house."

Harvest dropped her eyes and sipped her water. "We were thinking of going back to Shelley's. She has cable."

Ginger folded her arms. "What about your homework? It's a school night, you—"

"I know what night it is, Ma."

"I want you home by ten."

"But it's already seven—"

"I know what time it is," Ginger said as she wiped down counters and stacked dishes, "and I want you home by ten. If you can't do that, then you can't go out."

Harvest slapped a half-eaten slice of pizza down on her plate and got up. "Come on, Shelley, let's get out of here." She stomped into her room and slammed the door.

Shelley sighed and calmly finished her slice of pizza. "She's such a hothead." A sip of Coke. "But I love her anyway."

Ginger gulped as Maxie narrowed her eyes. "You two in the same grade?"

"Well, I'm with the 'special' kids. You know, the short bus."

"Oh," Maxie said.

"Learning disabilities. Also known as: I'm dumb."

"Don't say that." Ginger wiped her hands on a dishcloth. "Everybody learns differently."

Shelley got up and brought her dish to the sink. "That's OK. I don't really care. School's a ridiculously small part of my life. I pass, I fail, no big whoop."

Harvest burst out of her room, backpack slung over one shoulder. "Ready, Shell?"

"Lead the way," she said, tucking a blond strand behind one ear. Her nose ring glinted in the light.

"Bye, Max," Harvest said. She brushed past her mother in her quest for the front door.

"Good night, dear. It was nice to see you," Max called after her, sipping her wine. "Don't forget to say goodbye to your mother."

Shelley turned and held out her hand. "It was nice to meet you, Maxie."

"Same here, dear. I'm sure I'll see you again soon."

In the foyer, mother and daughter stood enmeshed in a heated discussion.

"I didn't say anything—"

"It's not what you said, it's your attitude—"

Shelley pushed open the screen door and stepped out into the beautiful spring night. "See you in the car, Harv." Harvest waved her away. Shelley added, "I mean, we better get going. Thanks for the pizza Mrs...Ginger."

"I'll be right there—"

"'Better get going?' Get going where? I thought you were just going to watch TV—"

"Mom, you're so paranoid these days. She means we're going to be late for our show!"

Ginger folded her arms. "What show?"

"Some...piece of reality crap she likes. I don't know the name of it. Something about plastic surgery on pets. What difference does it make?"

"Harvest, what's going on?" Ginger asked in a softer tone.

She shifted her heavy bag to her other shoulder. "What's going on?? What's going on is that my mother is going insane and doesn't trust me any more and needs to get a life!"

"I have a life! My life is here, with you!"

"Mom, you need a boyfriend or something. All you do is...not sell houses. And knit those...things you knit."

"You just be back here by ten o'clock. And I'll thank you to keep your advice to yourself."

Harvest shook her head and walked into the fragrant night, breaking into a run across the lawn to Shelley's waiting Volkswagen.

⁕ ⁕ ⁕

As soon as Ginger shut the door behind her daughter she sprinted back to the kitchen and snatched up her car keys.

"Grab the wine and let's go!"

Maxie was reading "How to be a Top Producer in Ten Seconds!" in one of Ginger's old real estate magazines. "Says here if we go door to door with a box of home-made cookies we can dominate the listings in our neigh—"

"Put that away!" Ginger ripped the magazine out of her hands and threw it in the trash. "I have a daughter to track!"

"We're gonna follow them?"

Ginger pulled Maxie gently but firmly off the stool and gave her a little shove toward the door. "Now! They're getting away!"

"Oooh, sounds exciting," Maxie tittered, turning back to cork the wine and stash it in her purse. "I always have so much fun with you, Ginny."

But Ginger had already raced across the lawn and started up her ride, revving the motor and blowing blue-gray clouds into the starry sky. "Move it! Just pull the front door shut behind you!"

Maxie did as she was told, taking petite yet brisk steps across the lawn, the bottle of wine in her bag bump bumping against her munchkin hip. "Hold your horses. I can't go any faster! Sheesh! I'm the oldest realtor in America, remember?"

"Living realtor! Show me some life, for crying out loud!"

Maxie paused to catch her breath at the car door, handed Ginger her bag, then turned her small backside around and carefully, slowly, planted it in the seat next to Ginger. Her Irish sweater poofed out as she descended, almost engulfing her completely.

Ginger lunged across her and pulled the passenger door shut, at the same time charging backwards out of the gravel drive and into the street.

"Whoah, sister!" Maxie said, falling forward into the dash. "Ya trying ta kill me or something?"

Ginger's eyes were wide as she flew down her street. "Buckle up, Max. We got some fancy driving to do."

* * *

They raced out of the Flats, passing rows and rows of neat bungalows with one car in the drive and washing on lines waving like ghosts out in the back. Magnolias drooped with the weight of their waxy blossoms while delicate plum petals fluttered like snow in the night air. A full, bone-white moon seemed to follow them as they drove, lighting their way as if it were daytime. They roared past Dickie's place, a bungalow identical to Ginger's, past the darkened high school with its dilapidated, gothic columns and deserted lot, careened around the old gummy bear factory and out onto Main Street.

Ginger gunned it. Squamskootnocket was asleep already at eight on a Thursday night. The road was hers.

"Hey, Ginger!" Maxie yelled over the engine.

"Yeah!"

"What are we doing?"

"Just look for a white Volkswagen, plate NY 529."

Maxie saluted and peered out her window. "They break the law or something?"

They raced through downtown Squamskootnocket, past Shapes, the town hall, the fire station, Kanadoo Realty, the Coffee Pit, Squamskootnocket Liquors, Bargain Gas, and finally the *Bugle*, where Jim Steele labored late, a black silhouette in his tiny office on the third floor. He glanced up from his desk as they hurtled past, then just as quickly bent back to his work.

"That's just it, Max, I don't know what's going on. But I'm going to find out!"

Ginger drove even faster once they were out of town, shooting past her outhouse listing and the lurking Squamskootnocket Lake on her left, past the acres of open land owned by Old Man Higgins, and past Regina's house on the right. Finally, she hooked a hard left into Shelley's hoity toity subdivision, Vanvronkenskasket Arms.

Maxie cleaned her glasses on a hunk of sweater. "That Shelley seems like a nice girl. A little heavy, but a real pretty face—"

"Shhhh!" Ginger said, as a white VW pulled out of one of the many cul de sac arms of the development and took a left several hundred yards in front of them. "That's them!" she whispered hoarsely, jamming the brakes so they came to a crawl. They watched as the taillights of the car flickered and disappeared over a hill. "I wonder where they're going," Ginger added, downshifting further.

Maxie popped open the wine and took a long swig. "Maybe they're going to Shelley's house to watch cable." She handed the bottle to Ginger. "Here, have a hit."

Ginger took a meditative swallow, never taking her eyes off the hills of the subdivision. "The only way out of here is on this road, so if they leave, we'll know about it."

"Did we bring any snacks?"

Ginger's concentration broke. "Damn, Maxie, you eat more than I do and you weigh ninety-five pounds."

"Ninety. What can I say? I got a good metabolism. Probably explains why I'm the world's longest living rea—"

"Shit! Here they come!" Ginger pulled into a ditch and turned off the car just as the little white VW came hurtling back toward them, then past them, flying down the access road of the subdivision toward the main road. They watched in the rear view as the car's right-hand blinkers flashed and the car turned and disappeared.

Ginger turned the key in the ignition. Every cylinder and gear ground and wheezed and chafed. Nothing. They sat listening to their own ragged breathing, the soft chirp of insects outside, a plane passing far overhead. Ginger tried again, cursing softly.

"How long have you had this car, Ginny?"

"Shut up, Max."

She tried again. This time: life! The engine caught and sputtered like something that had flat-lined only to be shocked back to reluctant duty. Revving the engine a few times, Ginger put it in gear and put her foot to the floor. The tires spun in the cool spring mud, shooting reams of it behind them into the dark nests of trees. They hadn't moved an inch.

"Son of a goddamned bitch!" Ginger slammed her hands down on the steering wheel.

Maxie sat blinking. Hummed a tuneless tune. Slapped a mosquito on her wrist.

Ginger tried again. The engine squealed as the spinning tires dug them deeper into the shoulder. They could actually feel themselves sinking.

"Want me to get out and push?" Maxie asked. "I'm stronger than I look."

"Yes," Ginger said, then slapped the wheel again. "I mean, no—are you nuts?" She got out and slammed the door. A rusted piece of the handle broke off in her hand. She threw it high up into the manicured woods.

She slogged to the back of the car and leaned on the trunk, waiting as Max scooched over to the driver's side. Again and again Max gunned it as Ginger pushed with everything she had, sheets of mud flying back to coat her. Finally the car lurched forward, soaring out of the ditch and onto the road.

Ginger scrambled around to the driver's side. Maxie looked up at her through the open window. "You look like a Milk Dud. With eyes."

Chapter 12

They raced up and down Main Street, then back to the subdivision, and were about to give up when Maxie saw something just as they were passing Old Man Higgins's land for the third time.

"Hey, Ginny, is that a road?"

"Good eye, Max." Ginger lurched to the right and onto a dirt road just barely as wide as their car. They climbed up and up, until the road ended at a flat grassy field, across from which an even narrower road disappeared into the forested hilltop. The white VW sat parked at the mouth of it.

Ginger killed the ignition.

"You think they saw us?" Max said, peering out.

"Keep your voice down, will you?"

They watched as the silhouettes of two heads joined for a long moment, then came apart.

"They're kissing!" Maxie yelped. "I think they're gay!"

Ginger rolled her eyes in her muddy face. "Well, I know that. What I want to know is why she carries oregano around in her backpack."

"Italian cooking class?"

They watched the heads join again, separate, then lean against each other. Cigarette smoke snaked out of the car windows, a peal of laughter reverberated in the woods. The air was fresh with the smell of pine.

Ginger picked a piece of dried mud out of the corner of her mouth. "And a Ouija board. She carries that around too."

"Show and tell?"

"Just be quiet and let's see what they do."

"Maybe they just want to be alone, Gin."

"Yeah, well, too bad."

A light sparked in the woods above them, a bright white flash that grew into orange and yellow flames that danced higher and higher in the moonlit sky. Ginger and Max watched as Harvest and Shelley, wearing white robes with wide sleeves and hoods, got out of the car. Arm in arm, they started up the wide path toward the fire at the top of the hill.

"Holy shit! They're in the Klan!" Maxie gasped.

Ginger turned toward her. "Just put a sock in it, get out of the car, and follow me. If you're going to make noise, you can stay here. Got it?"

Max held a finger to her lips.

They got out, Ginger in full crouch by the door. She scuttled to the front of the car, cringing as twigs and branches snapped beneath her feet, and motioned to Maxie to follow her.

"Can you make this hill?" Ginger whispered.

"Piece of cake."

The sound of chanting stopped them cold. Several male and female voices joined in a deep-throated round of sound that floated up out of the woods and toward the sky along with the cinders and ash of the growing fire.

"Ooohhmmmmmm, ooooooohhhhmmm, oooohhhhm..." The voices folded over and entwined with each other.

"It's a cult!" Maxie hissed, stumbling along behind Ginger.

Ginger ignored her and pressed on. They left the trail and started through dense woods, pulling aside brambles and climbing over logs.

As the chanting grew louder, Ginger worried less about how much noise they were making in their ascent. Finally they were just yards from the break in the woods. Ginger got down on her hands and knees and crawled behind a fallen tree. Speechless, she watched what took place before her.

Five white-robed figures circled a raging bonfire, chanting and holding hands as they moved slowly around it. Ginger felt the low notes of the ohhmmm in the pit of her stomach as the procession stopped, turned, circled the other way, and stopped again.

The enrobed figures held each others' arms high as they took a step toward the fire, their voices rising as if riding the crackling flames up to the sky, then released each other and stepped back. In unison, they pulled off their hoods. Four women: Harvest and Shelley; Francis, the Seniorobics teacher from Shapes; Sheena, the waitress from the Coffee Pit; and one man.

They took off their robes and stood naked in the moonlight.

Maxie began to whimper but Ginger clapped a hand over her mouth. Her eyes bugged out of her face.

Francis stepped forward and raised her arms. "I conjure thee, O Circle of Power, that thou beest a boundary between the World of Humanity and the realms of the Mighty Ones, a guardian and protection, to preserve and contain the power we shall raise within; wherefore do I bless and consecrate thee."

Shelley stepped forward and lifted her heavy arms. As she spoke the group continued to chant, but softly this time. "I call the power of Earth, the power of the body, foundations, the material plane."

Harvest stepped forward, raising her arms, her long dark hair flowing backward. "I call the power of Air, of the mind, of intellect and imagination."

Francis took a step forward, her frizzy blond hair like a halo in the moonlight. "I call the power of Fire, of vitality, will, and purpose."

The man stepped forward. "I call the power of Water, of emotion, of intuition."

Sheena reached down and opened a box. From it she took five candles, lit one and gave it to Shelley, who gave it to Francis, and so on to all in the circle as she spoke these words: "We welcome this night the Hare Moon, the great moon of May, a night for the celebration of sensuality, of love, and the power of life." She turned and gestured first at Harvest, then Shelley. "We are here to celebrate the new love between these two women, to call upon the powers of the North, of the South, of the East and of the West, to fortify their relationship and make it strong, and have their relationship be accepted and cherished by family and friends alike."

Harvest and Shelley embraced, then parted, facing the fire.

Harvest spoke up. "We are also here to work magick for Francis, who will soon undergo hip replacement surgery, and who needs our light and our blessings so that she may fly through this surgery and return to teaching aerobics and not lose her class on Tuesday nights at seven, which we all enjoy so much, to the new girl at the desk." Francis nodded, held her hands in prayer, and looked skyward.

"And we welcome Brian, who is new to our circle. We pray to the four quarters that he be healed of his tendency for premature ejaculation, that he might bring forth all the pleasure in his mate before he finds his own..."

"Ohhmmmm...."

"...and lastly, let us celebrate Sheena. We call upon the gods and goddesses that bring inner strength, fortitude, and will power, that we might empower Sheena to shed her addiction to exotic dancing and apply herself to cosmetology school with the same dedication she has shown for shimmying up a pole—hear us!"

"Ohhhmmmmmm!!"

"Thank you, oh spirits of the quarters! Mighty Ones of the East, West, North and South, we thank thee for attending...and if go ye must, we say Hail and farewell!"

"Hail and farewell!" intoned the group.

There was silence as all held their lit candles high, then a gush of wind blew up from the earth as if from the heart of the mountain they stood upon. Several candles went out. Those whose candles weren't extinguished by the wind blew theirs out, and all reached for their robes. The spell was broken.

Ginger grabbed Max by the shoulders and physically turned her around, gesturing frantically that they had to scram. They made their way down the hill, the sound of talk and laughter filling the night behind them.

⁂ ⁂ ⁂

They burst out of the woods just as the first white robe began to descend the hill.

"Max, you have got to MOVE!"

"This is as fast as I go!" she said, her arms flapping with her tiny steps.

Ginger got to her knees, her back to Maxie. "Climb on."

"What??" Maxie bumped up behind her.

"Get on my damned back! Now!"

She clambered onto Ginger, who hoisted her up, then ran, piggybacking her all the way to the car. She tossed her in and they spun out and back down the dirt road to the street.

"I think my teeth are back there somewhere," Maxie said, holding onto her jaw.

"Who cares about your teeth! My daughter's a witch!"

"A gay witch."

"She's bi."

"What's that?"

"She likes boys and girls."

Maxie shook her head and watched the dark trees shooting past. "Young people have so many more choices than I did growing up."

"I mean, crikey, why can't she just be a vegetarian or something? I can handle that. Just cool it on the cold cuts! Ixnay the olive loaf! Not a problem. None of this 'Mighty Ones from the East' crap!"

"Relax, it's probably just a phase."

"Max, they were naked, in the woods! Naked in the woods is not a phase! It's some serious shit!"

Max took a hit of wine and sat back. "That was pretty weird about Sheena and Francis, huh? Who knew they were witches? Learn something every day."

"And who is that guy Brian?"

"Mr. Quick Dick?"

"Max, stop making fun!" Ginger turned into the Flats, slowing down in front of Maxie's bright yellow bungalow. She turned off the car and dropped her head in her hands. "Do you mind if I stay at your place tonight? I'm scared to death of my own daughter."

"Sure you can. My zin is your zin. But this way you won't know if she's home by ten. She may be a witch but she still needs discipline."

"I don't know, Max. Why do I have the feeling she can take care of herself?"

Maxie shrugged. "Stay here if you like. I got cable, jammies with feet, and a case of Gallo spritzers. You're golden!."

"Thanks, Max," Ginger said, dragging her mud-caked self out of the car. "You're the best."

Chapter 13

The next day arrived as cranky and occluded as Ginger's tangled and knotted brain. Phlegmy clouds scuttled like nasty thoughts in church across a mustardy spring sky. Blots of rain would fall here and there, hang on for a while in a pudendous cloud sac, then let loose again, randomly and viciously. The girls slept in.

Ginger lay in polka dot flannel pajamas in a knot of sheets and blankets on Maxie's foldout. Though it was a day for cocoa and knitting orange things, a matinee and early to bed, Ginger remembered, as one bleary eye opened and focused on Maxie's smiley face clock, that today was the day she'd promised Old Man Higgins an open house at the outhouse, replete with balloons, cookies, pony rides, bungee jumping, Geraldo Rivera, satellite coverage, a lunar launch... She groaned and rolled over.

At one-fifty p.m. she hauled ass out of Maxie's with a tray of burnt-black brownies and a bag of ancient balloons Max had scared up from a mildewy box in her basement. Ginger raced to the outhouse; to its black cragginess, its leaning teeniness, its dour decrepitude. It was all waiting, just for her.

Two o'clock seemed awfully early to have an open house, she mental-noted as she unloaded her signs, listing sheets and assorted crap from her car. She placed four signs strategically around the structure, one facing either direction on the street, and in case anyone missed those, two directly in front of the place. Each sign carried a different photo of her. One featured her with a big smile and a thumbs-up gesture; one had a determined gonna-sell-that-house-and-right-now face; one was somewhat wistful as in: I don't do this for the money, I do it because, hey, I care; and the last had her holding a fistful of cash. Underneath all of them was the same text: "Ginger Kanadoo—Your Kana-doo Realtor!" with a phone number sans area code. She felt that each sign expressed different sides of herself and that each was a crucial selling tool.

After staking the signs, she clambered up to the outhouse and unlocked the door. Nuggets of corroded metal fell off in her hands. Considering what the building had been used for for a century, things smelled all right inside, more like old pine boards with a touch of mold than anything else. This was, of course, thanks to the fact that the business "ends" of the place had been sealed long ago. Compared to Regina's house, it was aromatherapy heaven in there.

Ginger kicked aside a few dead bees that remained, whisked away the worst of the cobwebs with an old *Bugle*, then ruminated over which potty to sit on: the right or the left. It was a tough call. On the right she had a view of Lake Squamskootnocket through some holes in the rotting slats, but on the left she could get a bead on the traffic flow and know right away when an interested party pulled up. She decided to mix it up and spend the first hour on the right enjoying the lake, and the second on the left.

For an hour she nearly burst a lung trying to blow up Maxie's nasty old balloons. They tasted like condoms of yore, and brought back some funky memories of high school and certain virginity-shattering moments not so very far from the very potty she was sitting on. By the end of the hour she had only one sad yellow balloon blown up, its pooty old end flopping around like a hundred-year-old nipple. It simply wouldn't inflate any more than that. She tied it to a tree near one of her signs as she scanned the street for traffic, though not one car had passed in the last hour and fifteen minutes.

The tray of sooty brownies was looking better and better all the time. It was nearly three-thirty, she hadn't eaten since the day before, and her hangover was one hungry beast. She was making some headway on the tray when she heard a car pull up onto the gravel shoulder of the road just outside.

She froze, halfway through a chocolaty mouthful.

Customers. It seemed too bizarre! And she was kind of enjoying her time alone in an outhouse eating incinerated brownies...oh, well.

She wiped off her mouth, straightened her clothes, and opened the door with great ceremony, as if she were opening the door of the Taj Mahal for the leader of the free world. "Welcome!" she said with sweeping gesture.

A dark-haired woman in a close-fitting jacket and a tall blond man gasped loudly and jumped backward. "Good lord!" the woman said. "I had no idea someone was actually in there!"

In a flash, Ginger took it all in: the recent model Lexus, the man's self-adoring spikey haircut and precious retro glasses, his buttery leather jacket, keys to everywhere in the universe hanging loosely in tanned hands; her hair that shone like money, her body toned to a ruthless perfection she would never appreciate, her flawlessly manicured hands clutching the shoulders of a young boy she held in front of her who was dressed to Gap frothiness in coordinates he would loathe in a few short years.

They stood O-ing their mouths at her for a ridiculous length of time.

She hated them.

She needed to sell them something.

"Welcome to my open house!" she tried again, attempting to make her way gracefully down the muddy hill to the gravel shoulder. "I've just had a rush of folks but I still have some brownies left—"

"Mommy I want to go—" the boy said, plastering himself against his mother's low-slung jeans.

"Hush, Alexander, we just got here."

The second car in two hours appeared at the top of the hill. Old Man Higgins rumbled toward them in his Dodge Dart and slowed, staring. His face screwed up and reddened as he pointed at the lonely yellow balloon and shook his fist at her. Ginger painted on a smile and waved gaily at him, head-gesturing at the Lexus and its passengers standing in front of her. He snarled at her some more for good measure, then waved her away and peeled out.

"Friend of yours?" the man asked in an unreadable tone.

"Actually, that was a buyer just burning up for this place. This would have been his third time through but I think he wanted to experience it alone. He'll be back."

They looked completely confused.

Ginger held out her hand and smiled big. "I'm Ginger Kanadoo, your kana-doo realtor."

"I can see that," the woman said, stroking her son's blond locks and glancing around at the signs.

"Nobody knows Squamskootnocket like I do. I'm a native. Been selling homes here for thirty-nine years, nearly forty."

"That's quite an accomplishment," the man said, still inscrutable.

The woman pointed a candy-apple red fingernail at Ginger's face. "You've got a smear of something brown...right along your nose..."

"Oh, dear me," Ginger said, yanking a Kleenex out of her pocket. "Always was a messy eater—some things never change! You sure you folks don't want a brownie? Alex?"

The boy just stared at her, recoiling further into his mother.

"I'm sorry," the woman said. "His name is Alexander. He doesn't respond to Alex." She petted him some more. "Good boy, honey."

The man took a step forward, sinking into muddy ground. "I'm Raphael, and this is my wife, Angelique."

They all shook hands. Ginger even shook Alexander's sweaty, limp paw.

"So," Ginger said, perkiness personified, "care to take a look at the place?"

"Mommy, I don't wanna go in there!"

"You don't have to, honey. It's OK," Angelique murmured, tucking a flaxen curl behind his wee shell of an ear.

"Well," Raphael continued, "we had the weekend free and thought we'd take a spin out here and check out the town. Alexander has a lot of allergies and he does a lot better in the country—"

"Except I'm allergic to grass—" Angelique hissed.

"Anyhow, since we can't please everyone" —a glare at the wife— "we've been mulling a compromise of sorts."

"Well, if Squamskootnocket isn't a compromise, I don't know what is!" Ginger spouted as she turned to lead them up the hill. "We've got more charm here than you can shake a stick at! Plenty of downhome Squamskootnocket hospitality—wide-open spaces, a few roads, a gas station, you name it! It's all here."

They reached the outhouse but the family made no move to go inside.

"And let me just toss in, on the QT," Ginger went on, a bit winded, "the seller is mulling a price change on this place, so don't feel too confined by the asking price."

They just stared at her.

"It's really a lot roomier than you'd expect in there," Ginger said, gesturing at the open door. "The view from the south side is a stunner."

"Isn't it...an outhouse?" Angelique asked.

"Where you go poo!" Alexander shrieked. "And peeeeeee!" he added gleefully, collapsing in giggles. Angelique shushed him.

"It used to be, dear," Ginger explained sweetly, "but now it's an historic landmark. A proud piece of Squamskootnocket history."

An awkward pause had its time on the dance floor.

"But aren't you...selling it for the land?" Raphael asked.

"Well, it's just a tenth of an acre—"

"But what's a buildable lot in this town?"

"An acre. Hey, I admit, it's a bit of a roadblock."

"A bit. Is there anything else in town that we could build on?"

"You know, I have lots of irons in the fire in that department. I'm done here in a few minutes. When can you come to my office? We can cover things better there."

⁂ ⁂ ⁂

Angelique's tiny nose wrinkled prettily as she passed on Ginger's offer of decaf and donut holes. Alexander reached out to grab one but she slapped his hand. "We don't...eat those things, Alexander."

"Oh, Angel, loosen up, will you?" Raphael said, popping a powdered sugar hole in his mouth.

"OK, well then you deal with his sugar highs because I'm not going to—"

"So, where are you folks from?" Ginger asked, closing the conference door behind her and settling herself across from them. A hard rain had finally broken loose and pelted the windows that looked out onto Main Street. Alexander sat on his mother's lap, shrinking back after his reprimand and poutily playing with her hair.

"Upper East Side. We love it but we've had it. Need to give the country life a shot," Raphael said, knocking back a glazed hole, then a cinnamon one.

"He's just sick of working for a living," Angelique said.

"Who isn't? I'm an architect. I specialize in wine cellars and media rooms on yachts. I'm at my office at five in the morning, I leave at nine at night. Why? So I can have a heart attack by the time I'm forty-five? So I can keep paying a four-thousand-dollar-a-month mortgage for fifteen hundred square feet? So I can keep her in Manalo Blobicks and him in, well, whatever the hell he's got on?"

"Blahnicks! You never get that right. And yes, I want my son dressed properly. Besides, you act like I don't work for a living."

"You call that work? Now that's the kind of work I'd love—"

"I design very high end products," she said to Ginger conspiratorially.

"And what are they?"

"Every other month she draws a pair of sunglasses on a board—"

"I don't design the sunglasses, actually, just the temples." She scrambled in her purse and pulled out a pair of sunglasses with "AngeliqueWear" inscribed in gold on each temple.

"They're beautiful," Ginger said, examining them.

"Eight hundred dollars a pair. Can't keep them in the store."

"I can understand why. Very snappy." She handed them back. "So tell me, are you just looking in Squamskootnocket?"

"I'd like to, but Angie here—"

"Actually, the idea of moving here makes my skin crawl," Angelique said, shuddering as she glanced around the paneled office as if she were entombed, "but I am sick to death of having no space for my stuff. And I suppose fresh air is nice now and then."

"Would you mind sharing your price range with me?" Ginger asked as she took notes in a beat-up notebook.

Raphael gazed at the rain and crossed his legs, leaning back in his chair. "Oh, I'd say one point seven, one point eight."

Ginger looked up. "One point eight...what?"

Raphael and Angelique looked at each other with knitted brows, then back at Ginger. "Million," they both said. Raphael took a sip of coffee, studying her.

"Oh-oh! Of course." Ginger wiped a sweaty palm on her skirt under the table. "Certainly the high end of what's available here."

"I would think so. New construction of course. None of these haunted, rotting old mansions for us."

"Of course. So you're talking about all the bells and whistles here, granite kitchen, Subzero—"

"God, no," Angelique said, rolling her eyes. "Granite is *so* 2006. We've been looking at the new 'Dungbell' for counters. Have you heard of it?"

"No."

"It's gorgeous," she said, cresting with joy. "It's this composite of dung, plastic and recycled cell phones. Very green. It's just dreamy, though it can get slimy, but it doesn't crack like those cement composites. It's in all the showrooms in the city."

Ginger scribbled furiously in her little book.

"And we must have a twelve-top stove on one of those kitchen islands suspended from the ceiling by invisible trip wires—have you seen those?"

"No, I—"

"Angelique, honey, remember where we are," Raphael tossed in. "Middle of Nowhere, USA."

"Oh, right. Anyway, it's got sensors over it—the kitchen island—so if a child puts his hands anywhere near the cooktop, it turns off."

"And of course we'll do a media room with IHOD," Raphael added, flicking a piece of coconut off his sleeve.

"Absolutely," Angelique cooed. Ginger gave her a questioning look. "Interactive Holograms-On-Demand. You know, so you can have a chit chat with Brad or Angelina, or whoever. Whenever."

"It's great stuff—" Raphael started.

"Except we're turning off the adult option. No more porn stars interacting with you in the family room, dear—"

"That was once! One time!" He held up a rigid finger. "And I'm still paying for it," he added, his grin erasing any glimmer of remorse.

"And, oh yes!" Angelique said, already over it and tunneling for something in her purse. "We have to have this, too."

She handed Ginger a pamphlet which read:

HouseAlive!

A Necessity for Today's Sophisticated Living

Today's new HouseAlive! goes beyond the ho-hum of the ordinary wired home. We've got everything the competition has, including ShopNow: email notifications to let you know you're almost out of milk, the WeSpy feature that tracks your teenagers wherever they go, in or out of the house (or your mate for that matter!) and the perennial favorite: the Time4Love Tickler, where your house reminds you that it's been a wee bit too long between special encounters with your spouse.

But now there's so much more to enjoy. Today's new HouseAlive! is an even better friend than ever before. It simply knows when you're down, and comes right to the rescue! Our new HappyTime option senses when your synapses need a boost and lets loose with special dopamine spritzers before even YOU know you're blue.

A general malaise you can't place? A certain je ne sais quoi? Perhaps associated with the incalculable amount of money you've not only spent on that cavernous box but on

> the sums soon to be spent to actually heat it, cool it, and landscape it, never mind clean it in the coming months? The reasons don't matter. Stop worrying! HouseAlive!'s new HappyTime feature not only spritzes you happy but plays music at a frequency only your tortured subconscious can hear, soothing you into a submissive and dreamy peace.

"Wasn't there another feature that came out after this pamphlet was printed—what was that again, Raff?"

"Oh yeah, the AutoExam thing. This special room with a gizmo that does prostate exams and pap smears—"

"That's right. I want that. One less shlepp into the city."

Ginger cleared her throat. "How many bedrooms and baths did you have in mind?"

"Well, there's us, then there's Lucette."

"Is she your nanny?"

"Oh, no, that's Betty. Lucette is...French."

"So she's a tutor for Alexander?"

"No...no," Angelique said, as if that had never occurred to her. "She's just French. We thought it was important for Alexander to have some sort of European person living in the house, right, hon?"

"Mmm, yes, honey," Raphael said, engrossed in the pamphlet. He finished it, turned to Ginger, folded his arms and considered her. Ginger inhaled the poof of fine leather and aftershave. "So, Ginger, what have you got for us? Five bedrooms, nanny suite, four full baths at least, couple of acres, all of the above?"

I've got a three bedroom, wallpapered, tsotskhe-crammed 1955 cape that smells like shit, she thought, busying herself with a few papers. "I don't have anything right at the moment, but let me make a few calls—"

The door blew open and Tandy stepped in with a grand smile, arms spread wide. "Raffy! Angel! Alexander! Oh my God! What are you doing here?"

Much merriment, hugging and cooing while Ginger sat and stared, papers in hand.

"I'm sorry to interrupt your meeting, Ginger, but when I saw these people I had to say hello! They were my neighbors! In New York!"

"Small world."

"It is, isn't it?" Tandy tweaked Alexander's cheeks. He blushed and turned away. "He's so big! I remember when you were just a little thing in your Mommy's snugglie! And now look at you, all grown up!"

Angelique laughed. "I think he still has a big crush on you."

"Tandy sold our place a couple of years ago when we were in the Village," Raphael added, not able to loosen his gaze from Tandy for an instant. "I mean, what are the chances...?"

"How nice," Ginger said.

"And, oh my God, we were looking for you when it came time to sell," Angelique gushed, "but we called your office and nobody knew where you were! We never dreamed you would come to a place like this!"

"Tandy gave us the best closing present possible, don't you think, Angelique?"

"Oh my god, that's right! Frozen stallion sperm for when Alexander starts his own stud farm. What could have been more thoughtful! He LOVES the sperm. He says he wants to go 'visit' it all the time. It's the cutest thing."

"It's all about planning for the future," Tandy said with winning self-effacement.

"So, what are you doing here, Tandy? Are you looking to move out to the sticks too?"

"I already live here! I'm a broker here at Kanadoo!"

"No kidding," Angelique said with a sidelong glance at Ginger who now stood awkwardly behind the conference table. "That's so interesting!"

"Listen..." Raphael got to his feet and brushed the doughnut crumbs off his faux well-worn jeans. "We were just wrapping up here with Ginger," he said with a head-nod in her direction, "but what are you doing for dinner? Do you have plans? We're all set, aren't we, Ginger? We have your card—"

"Well, I thought I'd—"

"Thanks a lot. We'll call you." He tailed his wife and child out of the conference room. "Anyway, Tandy—God you look great—Angie and I know a great place in Vanderskleet Neck—"

"Oh, please say yes," Angelique said, taking Tandy's arm. "We haven't seen you in forever!"

⁂ ⁂ ⁂

Ginger slouched at the front desk staring at the phone, arms folded, going over the past hour again and again in her mind. What she needed to do was write the copy for the outhouse as well as for Regina's place, but all she could do was sit with her pen and paper laid out neatly in front of her. She was in a mild state of shock. Just outside her window, a malevolent grey rain beat down on the lone car in the parking lot, which was hers. Dickie was away for the weekend, Tandy and her old friends had taken off an hour ago, and Maxie was probably still sleeping off the night before. All Ginger could see as she stared out at the rain were her hands wrapped around Tandy's skinny neck, Tandy's eyes wide as she begged for mercy.

She shook away the thought, pleasurable though it was, and forced herself to take a shot at writing the coverage for Regina's place.

"'Inviting cape in prime town location filled with the sights and smells of home—'"

No.

"'Talk about opportunity! Delightful surprises await you in this roomy cape filled with character—'"

The phone rang; she jumped.

"Kanadoo Real Estate, Ginger Kanadoo here. How may I help—"

"Where have you been?" came Big Jean's booming voice.

"Oh, hi, Mom. I've been busy with work...I've got two listings!"

"Yeah, Dickie told me about 'em. Coupla tough sells if you ask me!"

"A listing is a listing. You taught me that—"

"Why haven't you been out to see me?"

"Well, that's what I was saying. There's work, and Harvest has been keeping me busy—"

"Jesus Christ, she's not pregnant, is she?"

"Um, no—"

"Well, listen, I'm fresh out of you know what and I'm getting pretty goddamned cranky over here! Do you know what it's like living here with absolute clarity?"

"I can imagine—"

Line two rang. "Mom, I'm gonna put you on hold, OK?" She pressed the hold button. "Kanadoo Realty, Ginger Kanadoo. May—"

"Mom?"

"Harvey?"

"Where were you last night?" Her voice sounded small and younger than her years.

"Oh, I'm—I'm sorry, honey, I went over to your Aunt Maxie's and we had a few and you know how that goes—"

"Mom, she lives across the street—"

"I know, but you know how we are when we get going—"

"But you could have called and let me know where you were! How was I supposed to know you were over at Maxie's?"

"...So you were worried about me?"

A pause.

"Can you hold on, honey? I've got Big Jean on the other—"

Line three rang. "Hello, Kanadoo Realty. May I help you?"

"Ginger? This is Regina!"

"Oh, hi, Geena. I was just thinking about you, writing up some notes—"

"What notes? I thought you were gonna take pictures of my house today and you never called me. What's going on?"

"God, you know, I'm sorry. It completely slipped my mind. Say, Regina, can you hold?"

She jabbed at the hold button. The three lines blinked angrily at her.

Line four rang.

"Kanadoo Realty. May I help you?"

"Hi, my name is Mary, and I was just noticing your signs around town. I think my Mom may have listed her house with you years ago. Do you remember Katharine Datherack?"

"Katie? Sure! Oh, you're Mary? I remember when you were just knee high to a grasshopper. Mary, can I put you on hold a sec?"

"Sure—"

She hit line one. "Mom?"

"You can't be that goddamned busy over there! What the hell are you doing? Haven't you learned how to use the phones yet? You were never too bright with things like that—"

Ginger jabbed at line two. "Harvey? Harvey, honey are you there?"

She heard the muffled sound of crying. "We're not even a family" —sniffle, sound of phone dropping, recovery of phone— "real families communicate with each other—"

"I'm sorry, honey. I had a rough night last night—"

"I was home by ten and you weren't even here! You're so full of it, Ma—"

"I'm so sorry, honey, but I have to put you on hold." She punched line three. "Geena? Hi, Geena? Are you there?" Dial tone.

Cursing, she jabbed at line four. "Mom, listen, I've got a bead on some great shit. I just need to get in touch with the usual suspects—"

"This is Mary."

Sweat gushed like tiny geysers from Ginger's every pore. "Oh dear! That's funny! That was just a private joke I have with my Mom. She's such a cutup—"

"That's...all right. The point is, we really need to list right away. My husband got transferred and I'd like to get this going by tomorrow if—"

"How's nine o'clock?"

"Great! We're at 45 Schuyler Place."

"Looking forward!" She hit line two. "Harvest? Honey? Are you there?" Nothing.

Big Jean throbbed on the remaining line. Ginger watched it a few moments, wrestling with herself. Guilt won, as usual. "Mom?"

"No, the Queen of fucking Sheba. Now, when am I gonna see some hooch? And if you put me on hold again I'll disinherit your sorry ass."

Chapter 14

It was seven o'clock by the time Ginger had finished calming down Big Jean, writing copy for her listings, filing things away and getting ready for her listing appointment the next morning. A soul-deep exhaustion weighed on her as she went around turning off the lights and copy machine, closing up the same way she had for going on forty years.

She was just shutting off the main switch when she saw the silhouette of a burly figure at the door. Startled, she hid behind a filing cabinet, then slowly lifted her head and peeked above it. The figure tucked into itself against the beating rain, then turned toward a street lamp.

It was Jim Steele! She rushed to the door and opened it. Rain beaded on the outside of his aviator glasses; fog steamed the inside. His coat was soaked through and his sparse hair matted flat on his head. He held a velvety-wet paper bag.

"Jim! What are you doing here?"

"Is it OK to come in for a minute?"

"Of course!" She ushered him into the conference room and helped him out of his heavy coat. "Is everything OK? Do you need me for a fast-breaking news story? A quote or something?"

"No, no," he said, combing his hair back with his fingers, his big blue eyes blinking nakedly at her as she dried his glasses with the hem of her skirt. "I was just finishing up at the *Bugle*, and I know how crazy Sundays are for you and you probably needed a boost and I was over at the Pit having dinner by myself anyway so I thought I'd bring you a little something." A bit winded from his speech, he handed her the bag. "It shouldn't be wet. I had Sheena triple wrap it. She says 'hi,' by the way."

Ginger did a double take at Jim when she heard Sheena's name as a flash of the previous evening's revelry flitted by unbidden on the clotted screen of her brain. She pulled out a heavy lump of something and a cup of coffee, then began to open the package which was wrapped in paper, foil and Saran Wrap for good measure.

"Holy cow, is this what I think it is?"

Jim laughed, watching her face.

Ginger unveiled a deep-fried peanut butter and banana sandwich. "You got me an Elvis! Thank you!" She hugged him briefly.

"Is it still your favorite?"

She took a big bite. "Mm hmm, absolutely! Here, have a seat and split it with me." He sat but passed on the half a sandwich. "Sheena always did make a mean Elvis. Do you realize all I've had today are burnt brownies?" She took another healthy bite and a slurp of coffee as he watched adoringly. "How are your bee bites, anyway?"

"They're all pretty much healed—just some scarring, that's all. But listen, I came here for another reason. Do you remember Danny Ezerstadt?"

"Little Danny? The youngest of the Ezerstadt kids, right?"

Jim took a sip of her decaf. "Well, he isn't so little any more. In fact he's all grown up. Went to trade school for a while for construction and just got his builder's license."

"So he's all straightened out, huh?"

"He's all squeaky clean now, as far as I can see. Anyway, he came to my office last week and wanted me to write an article about him and all the new construction going on in Squamskootnocket."

She choked a little on her sandwich. "What new construction in Squamskootnocket?"

"Well, it seems that Old Man Higgins—you know, we really shouldn't call him that any more. We are out of high school—"

"OK, Billie, go on—"

"Billie and Danny have an agreement for Danny to develop his land."

Ginger swallowed hard. "All of it?"

"All thirty-five acres. He's thinking a twenty-five lot subdivision. Million-plus homes. Five-thousand-plus square feet, three-car garages, the whole nine yards. It's really going to change the face of Squamskootnocket."

"This'll never get by the planning board."

"It already has."

"I guess I've missed a few meetings." She put her head in her hands. It throbbed as if something wanted to get out and run away.

Jim shook his head. "I don't know where all these people are going to come from who have this kind of money."

"Oh, they're around," Ginger said from behind the curtain of her fingers.

"You OK, Ginny?"

She took her hands away from her face and sighed, sinking back in her chair. "I'm not gonna lie to you, Jim. It's been real tough for me lately."

"But I noticed you've got another listing—Regina's place! That and the outhouse..."

"I gotta say, Jim, nothing's moving. And, well, just some stuff with Harvest."

"What, your typical teen stuff? Boys? Breaking her curfew?"

"Yeah, just things like that. Guess I shouldn't let it bother me."

She burst into tears. She told him about everything: the foreclosure notice, her empty bank account, the fact that Regina's house smelled like shit (which he already knew and had wondered about for years), Tandy walking off with her big-bucks buyers, Harvest being part of some naked cult, the Ouija board, the oregano...it was like the gates were open and she couldn't get them closed.

He patted her hand. "Well, I have an idea. What about doing something for the Fourth of July? Maybe you could set up a booth or something?"

She put down her sandwich. "I like that idea, Jim. Now you're thinking! In fact, what about replacing all that Fourth of July birthday-of-our-nation hoopla and just calling it 'Realtor Appreciation Day'?"

"Well—"

Ginger sat up straight and began to gesture wildly. "We could put ads in the *Bugle* to announce it! It'll be all about realtors and what we do. Different kinds of houses I have on the market, maybe a sandwich board with the history of Kanadoo Realty. We could have balloons and streamers and rides and scratch tickets and raffles—"

"We might have to keep some Fourth of July stuff around—"

"Oh sure, I'll have a little flag on my booth or something, but the focus will be on appreciating your local realtor."

"Well," Jim said, his face reddening, "I sure do appreciate you, Ginny."

"Oh, well, that's nice, Jim," she said obliviously. "Anyway, we can give away little water testing kit key chains and—oh, I know—I'll sell my throws!" She clapped her hands. "What a great idea, Jim!"

He got up and struggled back into his wet coat. "I always like to help you out, Ginny, any way I can."

She walked him to the door. "You're a peach, Jim. Thanks again," she said, escorting him out into the rainy night.

She couldn't stop thinking about it all the way home: Realtor Appreciation Day—'RAD'— replacing traditional Fourth of July festivities! She fantasized about all the people she'd known over the years and sold houses to coming up and telling her what a great job she'd done, how she'd changed their lives forever, the speech she'd make, the confetti, the champagne...then she pulled into her driveway and saw Harvest's little light on in her room, and came back down to earth.

Chapter 15

Harvest hung back a few steps behind her mother in the mall, hair hanging in her face, chest concave, hands jammed deep in the pockets of baggy black jeans which dry-mopped the floor as she walked. After much discussion, Ginger and Harvest had decided to head for the mall at Vanderskleet, since the only other choice for dinner was the Pit, and neither had wanted to go there.

Music dead for decades treacled through from somewhere far above their heads while badly dressed, overweight American families strolled with lifeless eyes past half-clothed manikins in shop windows. It was like whoever was supposed to dress them said, 'Oh, screw it, this is just too boring.' Mother and daughter passed Orange Julius, Spencer Gifts, the Jeans Shed, Dress Barn, Hot Topics and Sears, as well as other sad relics of early-eighties malls. Ginger paused outside the Hair Shack.

"Hey, Harvey," Ginger said, waiting for her to catch up. "What about a nice haircut? One of these cute new bobs?" She pointed at some yellowing photos of hellishly coiffed women in the window. They all looked like coked-out realtors, seconds from a signed offer.

"Are you nuts?"

"Well, how about just a trim, then? When was the last time you had a haircut—"

Harvest protectively stroked her hair, twisting a mass of it together on one side and flipping it to the other. "Who cares when the last time was? I don't want to cut my hair. Ever."

"Okee dokee."

A Christmas Tree Shop, a Friendly's.

"How about some new clothes? You've been wearing the same—"

Harvest stopped walking. "Mom, we don't have any money, so don't—"

Ginger turned to her, hands on hips. "It's called credit. We have credit. We're OK."

"Let's just go home."

Ginger took her by the shoulders. Harvest looked around through her hair to see if anyone was watching. They weren't.

"You said you wanted to go to the food court, young lady. We're going to the food court. I'm buying you a nice dinner."

"All right. Let's go. Jeez."

They wandered toward the ass end of the mall and a halfhearted scattering of tables and chairs flanked by Antonio's Pizza, Taco Bell, Wendy's and Star of Thailand. They settled on pad thai, watching wordlessly as the tiny woman behind the plate glass stir fried noodles into a peanuty mound and piled two plates high.

Harvest pushed her dinner around on her plastic dish, occasionally taking a sip of diet Coke.

"I just wanted to say how sorry I am about last night," Ginger said, tucking into her plate of noodles.

"I'm over it."

"Well, I'm really glad you said yes to coming out tonight. It gives us a chance to catch up. A chance to talk. Maybe you can tell me a little about what you've been up to—you know, in school, or whatever."

"There's nothing to tell."

"You haven't been doing anything...new?"

Harvest squirmed in her seat. "What does that mean?"

"Honey, we're just talking. Don't get upset."

Harvest examined the ends of her hair. "My life is very exciting. I go to school, hang out with my friends, and go to bed. Snore city."

Ginger cleared her throat. "You haven't joined any new clubs lately? Like maybe an after-school sort of thing? Chess club? Glee Club? French? Drama...?"

"You know I hate all that stuff."

"You do, don't you. Hmmm. Let's see...how about...religions? Join any religions lately?"

Harvest's eyes grew wide. Ginger took her hand but she shook it off. "What are you talking about, Mom?"

Ginger tried again, unsuccessfully, to take her hand. "Honey, promise me you'll be calm, and understand that I did what I did out of love—"

"What did you do?!"

"Well, honey, Max and I—it was her idea, really—well, we sort of tagged along behind you last night—"

Harvest stiffened. The blood drained from her face. "You followed us?" She covered her mouth, eyes huge and unblinking.

"Again, Max's crazy idea—you know how she is—"

"And what did you...how did you...oh my God..." Tears fell rapidly; Harvest didn't bother to wipe them away.

"Is it a cult, honey? Are you brainwashed?"

"Holy shit—"

"Because I don't care how much it takes. We'll get one of those cult people out here right away. I hope they take Diner's Club, but—"

"I can't believe you followed me! You have no right to follow me! It's none of your business what I do! I'm eighteen!"

"You're my daughter. Of course it's my business! If you're involved in some sort of satanic cult then I want to know about it!"

Harvest dropped her head in her hands; her hair fell forward in a tumble of black ringlets. "It's not a satanic cult," she said very slowly and wearily. "I'm Wiccan."

"You're what? Honey, I can't hear you behind all that hair—I still say it's too bad that bob didn't grab you—"

"I'm Wiccan. I'm part of a coven. You saw who was there, people from town—"

"Oh my God, you are a witch. You're all witches!" she said, scooting back in her chair.

"You weren't meant to see what you saw. It was none of your business. I'm not doing anything wrong."

Ginger began to tear up. "I don't know what to do. I...we tried to raise you right, your dad and I. We took you to church on Sundays—"

"No, you didn't! You didn't raise me as anything! You and Dad just smoked pot on Sundays!"

"We did?"

"Yes, you did!"

"Well, OK, I guess we skipped the church thing, but honey, the dark arts? I knew I shouldn't have rented The Craft." She blubbered into her napkin, then blew her nose hard. "Do you think they have wine here?"

"Mom, it's a food court."

"I'm just glad I finally know what's going on with you. I don't mind about Shelley—"

"Also none of your business—"

"Boys, girls, whatever, as long as you're happy—though I gotta say: no more sleepovers, and the door stays six inches open, same as the rules with boys. But the witch stuff, well, I can't say I support your traipsing around the woods naked, praying for some strange guy's peter to stay up—"

"That's Brian! He's in my class! He's a warlock and a great guy!"

"Honey, you were naked in the woods with strangers!"

"Mom, you're shrieking."

"You would be too if you were your mother and learned your daughter was a witch!"

The woman who had made their food, as tall as Ginger and Harvest were seated, came by and took their plates off the table. "Five minute, we close," she said, and shambled off.

"I'll say it again: I am not a witch. I'm Wiccan."

"What the hell is the difference?"

"Wiccans live by rules. Witches don't."

"What kind of rules?"

"The first one is the Wiccan Rede: 'an it harm none, do as ye will.' In other words, don't hurt anyone, whatever you do. The second rule is the Threefold Law, and that is: whatever you do will come back to you threefold, or with three times the energy."

"OK, well, maybe I'm missing something but what does this have to do with you chanting naked in the woods?"

She rolled her eyes. "We were skyclad, Mom. Clad by the sky. It makes the spells stronger."

"Does Friendly's serve liquor, ya think?"

"Is that all you think about, booze?"

"Honey, I'm just having trouble with the witch—"

"Wiccan—"

"Wicked—"

"Wiccan—"

"Wiccan thing. How long has this been going on?"

"I don't know, a while."

"What's a while?"

"Like, a year."

"A year of prancing around naked in the forest?"

"God, Mom, we only did that like twice. Don't be such a prude."

"Can I ask you something else?"

Harvest just raised her eyebrows.

"Is Sheena really going to cosmetology school?"

"I guess."

"Look, honey, can't you just tell me why you're doing this? I mean, what have I done wrong?"

"Mom, it's not always about you, believe it or not. Maybe this is who I am. Maybe this is what I want to do, what I believe in. Maybe it makes me happy. Did you ever think of that?"

"But you're miserable! Honey, I can't have you doing this stuff any more. It's got to stop, and right now."

Harvest glared at her.

"Look, I never told you this, but there's this contest going on at work. Whoever makes the most sales by the end of the summer wins a weeklong vacation to Hawaii! Honey, it's a slam dunk for me! I've already got the two listings, another one coming on tomorrow, and it's not even June yet. So get yourself a coconut bra and Shelley a straw skirt and we are outta here in October! It'll take your mind off all this witch stuff once and for all..."

Harvest folded her arms tight across her narrow chest. "There is so much wrong with what you just said, I don't even know where to begin."

Ginger leaned forward and narrowed her eyes. "The fact remains that I am the mother and you are the daughter. No more wikky wikky stuff in the buff. That's it. Done. You will concentrate on your school work—"

"But Mom, you don't understand. It's not evil, it's spiritual! And I get straight A's!"

"To think that you've been meeting up with these weirdos for a year behind my back gives me the willies!" Ginger began to wipe invisible crumbs off their table with a napkin. "I've got enough to worry about and now my daughter is in some kind of wacky cult."

Harvest started to cry again.

"Now, honey, I'm sorry you're upset, but this is for your own good. And no Shelley for a month. She's the one who got you tangled up in all this, right?"

Harvest wouldn't look at her.

"You know, sometimes a mother's job isn't easy. We have to put our foot down, lay down some ground rules, be tough."

"Why?" she sniffled. "You never have before."

"All the more reason to start now. And one more thing: why do you carry oregano in your backpack?"

"Don't tell me you went through—" A fresh round of violated tears.

"Oh, honey, I had to! I had to find out what was going on. And I still don't understand...why oregano? Why? Why??"

"I'm taking an Italian cooking elective in school, all right? Is that OK with you? And we all had to bring in some spices—"

Ginger hugged her and said, "Oh, honey, I'm so relieved! Anyway, enough for one night. Let's just go home."

Harvest freed herself from her mother's grip, got up and walked toward the exit as Ginger ran to catch up with her.

Chapter 16

Ginger drove away from 45 Schuyler Place feeling all was right with the world. The paperwork was wrapped up, the listing signed for three months, the price was reasonable, and the house was in great shape. Mary and Jeff had a small but comfortable colonial painted in Pottery Barn colors, with a gourmet kitchen and a wrap-around farmer's porch, all on a storybook acre of land with its own precious little creek and miniature bridge. It was a ridiculously yummy listing that Dickie would love her for, and that would make Tandy snarl and rage inside as she congratulated her.

As Ginger drove through the Flats in the general direction of Regina's to photograph her house, she thought back dreamily to her warm meeting with the Jones's in their newly painted family room: the fresh coffee and homemade cinnamon buns Mary had made for her, their quick acquiescence to all the suggestions Ginger had made to spiff things up a bit before the house was listed, Jeff's strong yet gentle handshake, the sunlight streaming through freshly laundered lace curtains. Their two tow-headed children, Joey and Sarah, were brought out to meet this real estate legend. They greeted her shyly, then were ushered back to their playroom. Then, as if on cue, two adorable twin dachshunds ran out to greet her, licking her hands as if she'd known them all their lives. It was then that Mary had waxed nostalgic about Big Jean; how she'd grown up knowing her as her family's realtor, how she'd practically been part of the family. Mary and Jeff both oohed and aahed at Ginger's thirty-nine years in real estate, stating without reservation that they wouldn't have considered anyone else in a million years to list their home. Their only request was that she get the house on the market the next day if she could (of course she could! she was Ginger Kanadoo!) and that the twin dachshunds, Mopey and Dopey, be kept inside at all times.

Piece of cake! she thought. Just sign here!

She promised she would be at the house the very next morning to take pictures and write up a glowing blurb. Mary and Jeff beamed, handing her the key to the house as they insisted she take the rest of the cinnamon buns home with her. After demurring at first, referencing her attempts to cut back on such indulgences, she relented and accepted the whole tray. She did have a daughter to feed!

Now, as she drove, their sweet, buttery odor filled her car, their gooiness akin to her state of mind as she turned these recent memories over and over, fantasizing about how much these young people liked her, nay, idolized her. It was in this state that she drove right past two figures standing in silhouette at the top of Old Man Higgins's land.

It was an entire mile later that this image registered as something actually quite alarming. In fact—sinister. She slammed on the brakes, skidded into the shoulder, and did a screechy three-pointer back the other way.

She was, as the expression goes, loaded for bear.

As she approached the hill she slowed, then idled behind a stand of elms where she believed she could see and not be seen. Eyes never leaving the two figures on the hill—one slim, female and all in black, the other a man in jeans and a workshirt—she grabbed a handful of cinnamon bun and chewed hard. She opened her car door, crept out, and gently closed it behind her, then tiptoed into the low hanging branches of the trees and peered through them.

It was her.

Tandy.

Miss Snippy Snooty, Miss Complex Uptown Haircut, Miss I'll Steal Your Hot Buyers in My Spare Time, Miss My Website Kicks Ass, Miss All That.

And it was him.

Mr. Danny Ezerstadt, Mr. I Used to Torch Ladybugs in Old Soup Cans, Mr. I Sold Ecstasy to My Little Sister Only Five Years Ago, Mr. Squamskootnocket Bad Boy, Mr. Kiss Me I'm All Cleaned Up Now, Mr. Developer Big Shot I'll Turn This One Horse Town Around.

She knew them both, better than they ever imagined.

For whatever good that did her.

Because she was the one hiding behind the trees, jamming yet another sticky bun in her mouth, fuming as she watched them laugh and talk. She watched them as they strolled a few yards across the gently sloping hillside, pointing here and there and nodding vigorously, then stiffened as Tandy pulled her laptop out of a shoulder bag and opened it, right there on the hillside, its silver case catching the light and blinding her as she nearly stumbled backward into a ditch.

She gathered herself, shielding her eyes against the brilliant reflection, and just watched, finishing the bag of buns without tasting a thing. Finally, Tandy closed up her laptop and pulled out some papers. She held the laptop out as a sort of desk for Danny to sign them on, which he did, one after the other after the other. Afterwards they shook hands warmly, patted each other on the back, chucked each other under the chin (for crap sakes, Ginger thought, just get a room, will ya?) until Tandy broke away and walked off toward her Beemer which waited a few hundred feet away in a verdant spot of shade.

Ginger squinted her eyes, plotting, chewing.

OK, she had to admit. It looked bad. It looked real bad. But there was still a chance for her to get out there and blow Tandy out of the water. She crumpled up the pastry bag, tossed it behind her and started up the hill.

* * *

The soil was wetter than expected as she trudged up the slope in her Naturalizers, at each step sinking, then pulling her foot free with a ploop. Tandy had already driven away, but Danny was making his way across the ridge of the hill to places unknown. He was outpacing her. She wanted to shout but he wasn't in shouting distance, so she started to run, something she hadn't even considered doing in years. And it was damned hard, harder than she remembered in fact, this running thing. She pumped her arms as she had seen runners do, working her thighs hard in the sucking mud and regretting the bag of buns she had just consumed that bounced along with her in her voluminous insides.

But he was getting away! He had taken a turn and crossed over the ridge and was descending on the other side! First his boots disappeared, then his bluejeaned legs up to his knees, then his slim hips...she ran and ran, imagining herself and Harvest homeless and living on the streets of Squamskootnocket, her daughter's starving saucer eyes, countable ribs poking out above her distended belly under her torn black T, standing for hours in a food queue and finally getting to where they were doling out the slop and the toothless old charwoman saying, "Sorry, there ain't no more gruel. Come back tomorrow!" Harvest's accusing eyes turning back to her...

"DANNY!!" she hollered, stumbling forward onto her hands into the grassy muck of the hill.

He kept going, only his shoulders and head visible now...

"DANNY EZERSTADT!!"

He stopped, looked around. Kept going.

"DANNY! IT'S GINGER!"

This time he turned around, saw her, cocked his head, and started back up toward the ridge.

Ginger gasped with relief, pulled herself up and brushed herself off as much as she could, though the odd stick and leaf clung to her poly blend suit.

He made his way toward her, a small smile playing across his face.

She straightened her shoulders and approached him, holding out her hand for him to shake.

"It's Ginger Kanadoo, your kana-doo realtor!" she said, a little louder than she had intended.

He shook her hand slowly, looking into her face. "Yeah, I know who you are." Then he pulled his hand away and looked at it, brushing it on his pants.

"Oh! Sorry about that, just had a cinnamon bun in my car and no place to wash my hands—I'm just a gal on the go!"

"Okay...what can I do for you, Ginger?"

She laughed in a barky way. "Why so formal, Danny? How's everything? How's the family? Your brothers?"

He folded his arms, the papers he'd just signed tucked under one of them. He had turned out to be a good-looking man: broad shoulders, thick black hair and a strong chin, but that slight curl of his top lip remained. Even as a kid he looked like he was constantly sneering, which he probably was.

"Everything's good. The brothers are fine. Everybody's married off, you know—"

"Even you?"

"Even me," he smiled. "Just a couple of months ago."

She felt herself sinking in the sumpy grass. She rocked side to side as she freed one foot, then the other. "Who's the lucky lady?"

"Remember Helen Danaskew, from—"

"You married your high school sweetheart!"

"That I did, that I did. And we're expecting a child in December—"

"Wow, you didn't waste any time now, did you?"

He laughed again, stretching but never obliterating the sneer. "No we did not. We're very excited. Just bought a place up in Vanderskleet. We're closing on it next week. For sale by owner, sorry."

Ginger held up a hand and waved away the thought. "Hey, don't worry about it."

An awkward pause nosed in as Ginger listed to the left.

"So, what can I do for you, Ginger?"

"Well, Danny, I just got word that you got your builder's license. Congratulations." He nodded, smile gone. "And that you were talking with Billie Higgins about getting something going with this land."

"We're past the point of talking, actually. It's a done deal. A twenty-five lot subdivision is going in here. We're breaking ground in a few weeks, delivery in early spring. This is going to put Squamskootnocket on the face of the map. It's pretty exciting."

"It certainly is! It's thrilling! So—have you thought of how you'll market all these beautiful homes? You know I'm Squamskootnocket's finest realtor. No one's been selling real estate in this town longer than I have—except Maxie, of course, but she can't do stairs any more—"

He held up his hand to stop her. "Hate to say it, Ginger, but you're a little too late on this one."

Ginger blinked. The cruel spring wind did unflattering things to her hair, and she'd long since stopped trying to right herself in the muddy ground. She'd already sunk a good few inches. "Excuse me?"

"I just signed with your compatriot there, Tandy...Brick something."

"The whole thing? All twenty-five houses?"

"Whole kit 'n kaboodle."

"Do you really think that was wise?"

"Well, sure. She really seemed like she knew what she was talking about."

Ginger's hair blew straight up as if she had been electrocuted. "Danny, Danny, Danny, I think you're making a terrible mistake here! She just got to Squamskootnocket a couple of weeks ago! She doesn't know the old gummy bear factory from the Coffee Pit!"

Danny shifted uncomfortably. "Well, I don't know, Ginger, she showed me her website—which was pretty awesome—she's got a virtual reality tour streaming—"

"Hell, I'll give you virtual reality! The reality is she's never had a listing in this town, never sold anything in this town, hardly knows a soul in this town, and to be honest with you, Danny, she's just not Squamskootnocket material! She's wrong, all wrong!"

"To be honest with you, Ginger, I think it's good she's not from here. I need buyers, and they're going to come from the city. In fact she told me she already has some very well qualified buyers—"

"We all say that!" Ginger said, spitting a bit. She loathed herself beyond all reckoning as she sank ever deeper into the hillside. The cinnamon buns in her stomach had expanded into a demonic ball commanding liberty from her too tight waistband.

"You do?"

"Yes, we do, just to get the listing! It's a tactic!"

He shrugged. "Tactic or not, we're meeting with them next week."

She held up a conciliatory hand. "Danny, I understand. You're embarrassed at this point to tell Tandy you've changed your mind, that you've decided to go with the finest realtor in Squamskootnocket. You've seen my signs all over town. You know what I can do."

His face darkened.

"Don't worry, Danny, I know you're sensitive, a man of your word. Look, I'll break it to her. We're close that way.

She'll understand. We're a family at Kanadoo, you know that. But you're not stuck with her. You can tear up that contract right now. You're not obligated to it."

"But, Ginger, with all due respect, I don't want to tear it up."

She folded her arms hard across her chest. A stray cloud dribbled out a few drops of rain, wetting her forehead. She blinked them away like tears.

"You don't want to tear it up?"

"No, I don't."

She looked away, across the green valleys and gently rolling hills bursting with cash. "So let me get this straight: you want to entrust your entire investment, everything you've worked for, perhaps your very future and that of your wife and child, with an unknown quantity in a short skirt?"

"It's not the—"

"And the person who can make you a rich man, the one who can secure your assets, no—double, triple them—is standing right in front of you and you do nothing?"

"Ginger, I—"

"Look, Danny, I care about you and your family. You are a vital part of Squamskootnocket, its very soul, its identity! I will not, I cannot stand by and see you and your family bankrupted, doomed by this terrible choice!" She let her voice grow foggy with emotion. "I just can't watch it happen. It rips me apart. It's...it's too much."

His face grew hard, the sneer tightened and held. "No, Ginger. No." He took a few steps back.

She tried to take a step forward, forgetting how embedded she was, and nearly lost her balance. "Danny, don't leave! How can you do this?!"

"Ginger, what's done is done. You can always bring a buyer."

"Danny, this is Ginger Kanadoo talking here! My God, I babysat you! Don't you remember? I peeled you off the jungle gym when you climbed up too high and were too scared to come down! I kissed your boo boos! I filled your sippy cups! I changed your diapers, for crying out loud, and I can't even list the crap you build?"

He turned back toward her. "The 'crap' I build?" He shook his head and walked away.

Ginger took a few suctiony steps toward him. "Danny, I didn't mean it! I was angry! Danny, please come back!" He kept going, disappearing over the hill. "Well, don't look to me to bring you a buyer! It ain't gonna happen!" she yelled at the hill. "Don't come crawling to me when nothing sells!"

Chapter 17

The door swung open easily at 45 Schuyler Place, ushering out the smell of freshly laundered clothes and high quality leather furniture. Ginger stepped into the two-story foyer, set her purse and paperwork down on the stairs, and pulled out her throwaway camera. She traveled from room to room taking photographs from every conceivable angle: she stood on chairs, she squatted low for a fishbowl effect, she backed into closets to make rooms look bigger. Late-afternoon sun filtered through lace curtains onto the honey-colored oak cabinets in the country kitchen, striped through blinds onto the fluffy white comforter on the master bed, and glinted off the spotless, brushed-nickel appliances in the master bath. The house glowed with its own ineffable sweetness, like the smile of a coddled child gazing out from the arms of his parents.

When Ginger finally reached the finished basement, she heard the sharp yelps of the twin dachshunds in the garage. She ignored them, trying to get a shot of the water heater in its best light, until an idea hit her.

Why not get the little sweethearts in one of the shots? What's homier than the cute mug of a little dog peeking up from his own bed in the corner of the living room next to a blazing fire? It would sell the house in a second!

She could almost hear the accolades from Jeff and Mary about her brilliant idea as she tossed her camera on a pile of freshly folded towels and crossed the room to open the door to the garage. Behind the door the dogs yelped and scratched excitedly. Ginger fumbled through all the keys she'd been given, but not one of them opened the door.

She leaned against it, thinking. The only other way to get to them was through the garage door itself. She'd been given the garage door code but had no idea where she'd written it down.

She tramped upstairs and sorted through reams of paperwork, then found it, scribbled on the back of her checkbook. "Aha!" she cried, then ran outside and around to the back where she pressed the numbers on the little mechanical box on the garage door.

It opened.

They ran out.

Yipping and yapping with joy, their little hot-dog tails wagging their backends, Mopey and Dopey ran right past Ginger into the yard, then in

completely

opposite

directions.

There was an awful silence for a few moments, the singular silence of dogs that were no longer there. But soon the hush was filled with a loud roar inside Ginger's head, the sound of panic and terror, bearing down on her like an oncoming train.

She shook her head hard in a vain attempt to dislodge the noise, then whipped around, gasping. She lunged a few steps in one direction, then the other. "Mopey! Get back here! Dopey! Come on, boy!" She clapped her hands and called again.

Nothing. Chirping birds. Buzzing bees. Laughter of children playing nearby.

Ginger ran in the direction of one of the dogs. As she chugged along she realized this was her second sprinting session of the weekend, an absolute record in her lifetime, and wondered if being in shape might be a good idea for what she did for a living. But then she thought: naaah.

Still, it was nasty work, this "running." Jeff and Mary's yard was well kept but she had to bushwack her way through the neighbor's land, then their neighbor's, and so on, through piles of brush and logs, and thorny bushes that ripped at her sensible jacket. She even forded a narrow stream, balancing on a fallen log.

All the time shrieking, "MOPEY!!! DOPEY!!! GET YOUR ASSES BACK HERE!!"

Panting, she stumbled through yet another yard where children were playing catch. They paused in their game, staring at her as she climbed over their picket fence. After she regained her footing on the other side, she got up some pretty good speed, then skidded on wet grass right to the edge of a swimming pool that was flush with the ground, her arms windmilling. As she tipped forward, then back, then forward again, she saw her wildly distorted face in the water haloed by her crazy mane of fluff-hair and thought: I'm gonna have a freakin' heart attack, right here, right now.

Instead, she fell back onto the dewy grass. Hot tears pricked at the backs of her eyes, but she wouldn't let them out.

Crying would do nothing for her now. She forced herself to calm down, get her breathing under control, and listen...

She heard barking. Distant, but there. She scrambled to her feet and ran around the pool to where the lawn abutted conservation land. Jaw set, she stomped through the forest, following the high-pitched yelps. Over a hill and down again, through a grove of saplings, until she came to a clearing and the object of her desire.

Mopey stood on his hind legs, his front legs resting on the base of a pine tree. Far up in the branches, a white and orange tabby crouched, snarling and backing up into a nest of needles.

"Mopey!" she stage whispered, approaching him, her head in the center of a cloud of gnats. "Or Dopey!"

But all Mopey—or Dopey—cared about was the feline up the tree, not the realtor on his tail. He ignored her, clawing at the tree and growling at the cat, who hissed and yowled with gusto back at him.

"I'm comin' ta getcha, little doggie," Ginger said. She lunged at him and grabbed him around his sausagey middle.

He squealed as she pulled him away from the tree, still yapping at the cat, his little forelegs scrambling uselessly in the air. She turned and ran back into the woods with him.

After a short while running with a squirming dachshund in her arms she missed the time she'd spent running that day without one. No matter which way she held him, most of him drooped down and banged against her thighs, so that every step she took bounced his lower half against her. She tried every possible position until finally she held him like a baby; his four legs skyward, his cold nose in her face and his big, soulful brown eyes staring up into hers as if to ask: why, why, why?

She looked into his eyes as if to say: I have no clue why, Mopey, or Dopey. Life has simply given me no answers whatsoever.

After what felt like some sort of dachshund triathlon (wrestling underbrush, hopscotching over vegetable gardens, squelching through wetlands), she made her way up the flagstone path at 45 Schuyler Place. One of her heels had fallen off, part of her suit jacket was torn at the shoulder, and her face was streaked with mud. But she had her dachshund!

She locked him in the garage and turned right around in the direction the other one had disappeared. Gamely she trudged through yard after yard, calling "Mopey! Dopey!" until her voice was hoarse, then nearly gone entirely. Finally, when she reached the abandoned gummy bear factory, its strangely sweet orange smell still lingering in the air after all these years, she had to take a load off and rest on an old sugar barrel before starting back. Crickets had begun to chirp, nearby barbecues to smoke and the fresh earth smell of a cool summer night to lift up from the ground.

The last tangerine rays of the setting sun limned her defeated form as she trudged up the drive and let herself back in the house. She stood in the middle of the living room, her mind numb with panic. Another force led her into the kitchen where she opened the refrigerator, hoping against hope for just a taste from a bottle of cold white zin.

Only low-fat yogurt, carrot sticks, soy milk, gourmet mustards, blah blah yuppie blah. Not even a lousy Coors.

She raced through all the cabinets, closets, pantry, all the various high-end nooks, until she finally discovered a cunning little door in the kitchen island where she hit the alcoholic jackpot. Vodka, gin, whiskey and all the mixers, plus a cache of wines. All reds, but she gamely uncorked one, since desperate times certainly called for desperate measures.

The first glass went down on the tannic side but by the third she was feeling a bit better, and had really started to get into the porn collection she'd stumbled upon at the back of the master bedroom closet. She was having fun imagining Mary and Jeff in all those wacky pretzel positions, and was even starting to feel a bit, well, something she hadn't felt in what seemed like decades, when she promptly fell asleep.

She woke up hours later with a start. Someone in the middle of a particularly shrill, pseudo big-O had bitch-slapped her into a consciousness she wasn't sure she wanted. But there she was: sloppy drunk in her seller's house, watching Two-Timing Asian Sluts, and down one dachshund. Quickly she gathered herself and put everything away where she had found it, wiped the counters, fluffed the pillows and locked up. Hiccupping softly, she stashed the empty bottle securely in her purse and headed home.

Chapter 18

Ginger made a ridiculously wide arc into her driveway and rammed into her shed, this time sheering the left side clean off. Swearing like a longshoreman, she backed up and idled. The shed was supernatural, for crying out loud, it was like the thing kept moving closer and closer up the drive every time she'd had a few drinks!

Not stopping to even glance at whatever damage she might have done to the front of her car, Ginger got out, beelined to her front door and jammed the key in the lock.

It wouldn't open.

Cursing in several different dead languages, she tried again and again, but the key would not turn. What could this be, she thought...maybe...is this really my house? She took a step back, looked around. Yup, 25 Weenickett Way, peeling pea-green bungalow, droopy porch, shutters hanging on by a song. Is this the right key? Had to be—it was the only key she had other than her office key.

She stared at the key, as if the answer were written there somewhere. My God, she thought, has my child changed the locks? It was the only conclusion left. The thought made her more sad than angry, and she felt tears nagging behind her eyes. Her own daughter, changing the locks! There was a message in there somewhere!

She peered a couple of yards to her left at Harvest's open window, from which heavy metal music blasted forth. Through her grapey eyes she could almost see the music jangle out the window and swirl up into the starry night. She blinked hard, climbed off the porch and squeezed herself between creaky clapboards and the horrible shrubs she'd planted years ago in a fit of home improvement, bushes she'd never been able to kill since, no matter how viciously she poisoned or hacked at them.

Now they wreaked their vengeance on her as she inched along toward the window. Her head arrived a few inches below it, so she had to reach up and bang on the screen with the palm of her hand. No response. The music blared on. She did it again, then screamed, "HARVEST!"

The music stopped. "Who's there?" Scared little voice.

"It's your MOTHER! I'M LOCKED OUT!"

Harvest's heart-shaped face framed in hair appeared at the window. "Mom, you look awful! What happened to you?"

"Just let me in!"

"OK, OK!"

The face disappeared. In one heroic heave, Ginger launched herself backward through the demonic clot of bushes out onto the grass where she landed in a pile of career wear and ripped support hose.

Harvest ran out onto the lawn in her nightshirt. "Mom, are you drunk?"

"No," Ginger said with besotted exasperation. "Jeez!" She rolled over and started to jockey herself to her feet. "You always just assume—"

Harvest shook her head with disgust and headed back toward the house.

"You stop right there, young lady. I have a question for you."

Harvest hesitated at the base of the porch, put her hands on her scrawny hips and turned. "What?"

Ginger climbed the porch stairs in her wrecked suit, a tuft of grass sticking out crazily from her hair. "Why did you change the locks on this house, missy?"

"I have no idea what you're talking about."

"My key," Ginger said with exaggerated formality, "no longer fits the lock of this domicile." She held her key high. It glinted in the porch light. "Observe." She put it in the lock and made a great show of how it wouldn't turn.

"Mom, that's the deadbolt."

She turned to her daughter, blinking big. "Excuse me?"

"Since when have we ever had a key for the deadbolt?"

Ginger held fast to her confusion. Harvest put her hand over her mother's and guided it down to the lock just under the doorknob. Together they inserted the key and turned the lock.

"You've only lived here thirty-five years, Ma. Why would you remember a silly thing like which lock we use?"

"Don't get smart—"

"You're drunk, and I don't talk to you when you're drunk." She headed inside, Ginger on her heels.

"Since when? What are you, Amish or something? Sometimes I feel like you're somebody else's daughter. Immaculate or something."

Chin uplifted and slightly pigeon-toed in her bare feet, Harvest brushed by her mother as she headed toward her room.

"Or is it some kind of wicky thing...you can't talk to me when I've had an adult beverage."

Harvest whipped around and shrieked, "I'm Wiccan! Wiccan! Not wicky!"

"OK, OK, I heardja! You're Wiccan. Now come on in the kitchen and talk to me a second. Don't be so damned high and mighty on your broomstick or whatever."

With a pouty mug, Harvest turned on her heel, marched into the kitchen and plunked herself into a chair.

"Now," Ginger said, pulling delicately at the viciously torn fabric on her sleeve. "How was your day?"

"How was my day? How was my *day*? How do you think it was? I can't see Shelley, I can't be Wiccan, I can't go to meetings, I have nothing. My life is over!"

"How about..." Ginger opened the refrigerator and looked around. A half bottle of white zin winked back at her. "...employment? I never said you couldn't get a job. A job might cheer you up, honey. Adds character, that's for sure. Why, I started working when I was—"

"What does getting a job have to do with anything? I want to be Wiccan, practice magick, have a life! You just don't care about who I am! You have no idea who I am!"

Ginger uncorked the bottle and poured herself a juice glass full. "You know, that's possible, that I don't know who you are. I'll give you that. But do you know what would be really nice, honey? Something nice you could do for your dear old mom?"

Harvest paused, sensing a trick question. "What?"

"If you could, maybe just once in a while, if you weren't too busy, ask me how my day was?"

Harvest folded her arms. "How was your day, Mom?" she asked with syrupy sweetness.

Ginger took a healthy gulp of zin. "It sucked ass, if you really want to know."

Harvest let out a burst of air. "I can't believe how you talk. You talk worse than the kids at school."

Ginger swirled the wine around in her glass, staring at it. "So you're not gonna ask why? Why my day was so bad?"

"I don't know, you still can't sell the house that smells like shit?"

Ginger pointed at Harvest with her juice glass. "*You* said shit."

Harvest rolled her eyes and hid under her hair.

"As a matter of fact, young lady, there's been a lot of interest in that house, if you really want to know."

"But you still haven't had any closings all year and we're going to starve to death."

"Hey, watch it! Don't act so spoiled. I got you your broadband, whatever that is." She got out a box of crackers and a jar of peanut butter. "OK, my day. I know you're dying to get the 411 on that. First, in the morning, I learned that the new broker in my office—"

"Tandy? The 'bile spewing bitch from hell loosed from Satan's gate'?"

"That's the one. Good memory!" she said, a peanutty finger jabbing the air for emphasis. "Anyway, she stole an entire subdivision out from under me. Love that! I'll have to send her a congrats card. And in the afternoon, I lost one of my seller's dogs. An accident. He took off. Couldn't find the little fucker to save my life." Ginger hiccupped and spread a thick layer of peanut butter on a cracker.

"So what are you going to do about the dog?"

"Haven't figured that one out yet. That's a tricky one. Especially since they're coming home tomorrow night."

"Well, you're going to tell the seller, aren't you? That their dog ran away?"

"Of course not! Are you nuts?"

"I'm not the one who's nuts around here, that's for sure."

Ginger threw the crackers down on her plate. "You want magic? You know what would be magic? If you would be nice to your mother. Now that would be magic."

Harvest pushed herself to her feet. "Why should I be nice to you? I haven't done anything wrong, and you make me stay here in the house all day like a prisoner! I hate you!" She stalked into her room and slammed the door.

Ginger stood for several moments, the echo of the slammed door sounding in her head. Lifelessly she chewed the stale crackers, staring at them on the plate but not seeing them. She washed it all down with the last of the zin, and started to cry. She pictured the rest of her life being unable to communicate with her daughter, an eternity of doors slamming and phones clicking off, and it made her sadder than she had ever been.

She carried the plate of crackers over to Harvest's door, lifted her hand to knock, then let it drop, remembering all the times she had talked to Harvest through this very door. The thought exhausted her. She turned, leaned on the door, and slid down to the carpet where she sat eating her snack, listening to the music Harvest had turned back on. She couldn't comprehend one word the singer was screaming and she wondered, does Harvest understand what this guy is saying? If so, then there was no hope. All these songs full of a rage she could scarcely remember; the energetic fury, the furious energy of youth. I'm angry at everything all the time! I hate my parents! Life sucks! I don't have the right jeans/sneakers/hair/whatever.

Ginger drifted back to her own youth. She had been a bit of a goody-two-shoes, though on the slutty side. Typical rebellions included staying out an hour past curfew or changing from knee socks into fishnets once she got to school, but secretly she really liked her parents and cared a great deal about what they thought of her. Hey, Ginger posited, maybe Harvest was hiding her admiration for her own mom under a cloak of teenage angst.

She decided to give it another try. She got up and banged on Harvest's door. The music grew louder. She did it again. Louder still. She jiggled the handle of the door. Locked. She pounded on the door, calling out her name.

The music cut off suddenly. Ginger was mid-pound and mid-shriek. "Harvest!!" Silence. "I don't care if you're a bisexual Wiccan! I don't care who you are! You're my daughter and I love you!" More silence. "Harvey? I just want to get along!"

A click. The creak of bed springs. Ginger gently opened the door and let herself in. Harvest lay on her purple velvet quilt, facing away from the door. Her new pop art screen saver, a lava lamp imploding on itself in neon colors again and again, was the only movement in the room. They both stared at it while Ginger took a seat on the edge of the bed.

"I'm worried about the dog," Harvest said.

"Oh, don't worry about that."

"I am worried."

"I told you, I have a plan. Anyway, who cares about the dog? Why do we need to talk about that? We need to talk about us."

"Because what you do affects us, Mom. Did you ever think of that?"

"I guess...you're right. You're so smart, honey. You got that from your dad, I think."

Harvest rolled over and pushed herself to a sitting position against the head of the bed. "So what are you gonna—"

"I'll take care of everything, honey, don't you worry."

Harvest lifted a small bell from her bedside table and rang it, closing her eyes for a moment as if holding onto the sound, then cradled it in her lap.

"Nice bell," Ginger said.

"It's blessed. It's for cleansing toxicity."

"Is it toxic here?"

"It's toxic almost everywhere."

Harvest handed Ginger the bell and she rang it. "There, that's better."

Harvest shook her head and looked away.

"So, honey, I had an idea. What if I just kind of tagged along with you on your next Wiccan meeting, how would that be? Showed up once in a while at these things, nothing scheduled. Just to sort of see what you're up to so I don't worry so much?"

"I'd rather you stabbed me through the heart."

"I'm just trying to find a way to—"

"Mom, you have to be Wiccan to go to these meetings. There are no box seats available."

"So I'll be Wiccan," she said with a shrug, ringing the bell again. Harvest snatched it from her.

"You can't just be Wiccan. You don't even know what it is."

"So tell me—"

"It's a spiritual thing. You're not spiritual. I—I don't know what you are."

"I am too. I love Halloween. I love vodka."

Harvest put her head in her hands. "I hate my life."

"Oh, don't say that. First you sound like you're fifty years old, then you're back to...what are you—"

"I'm eighteen!! Don't you know how old I am?"

"Of course I do, honey," she said, yanking at her waistband and wishing she'd gotten into her robe and bunny slippers before she'd embarked on this discussion. "OK, where were we? Why don't you start by telling me what goes on at these orgies...I mean meetings."

"Promise you'll listen and not ask stupid questions?"

Two fingers up. "Scout's honor."

"OK. It's pretty simple. We meet once a month during the full moon, which is the time when spells tend to hold together better. We do spells to help each other out, nothing bad. And then sometimes we meet at other times, if someone really needs the strength of the coven for some reason."

"OK, coven, spells, I gotcha. Do these spells work?"

"Yes."

"All the time?"

"Yes. So anyway, we have our ceremony, which you saw," she added sarcastically. "Then we break for cakes and wine."

"That sounds fun."

"Well, not literally. That's just what the Wiccan tradition is. Can be sandwiches and coffee. Anyway, you know I don't drink."

"I think I'd like to talk to the other members of this... coven."

"Go ahead! You know everybody in town except for Brian. He's captain of the computer club at school. He's very cool."

"Mmmm. And once he gets that problem of his worked out, he'll be even cooler—"

Harvest's face cracked into the tiniest of smiles. "Don't make fun. This is serious."

"All right. No more jokes. But listen, I think I can do it. I think I can be Wiccan."

"Mom, this is my thing—"

"Then I've got to come to one of your meetings and just observe. That's the deal, Harv. I can't just let you run around doing this without sitting through one of these things."

Harvest jumped out of bed and started to pace. "It's not my choice, Mom. I'm part of a group. Everyone has to agree."

"Then ask."

"All right, all right. I'll email everybody tonight."

"Now, have you talked to Shelley?"

"She broke up with me. Because of you."

"Oh please. Not everything is my fault."

"This is."

"No it's not. I told you you couldn't see her for a while."

"A whole month!"

"Well, that's over, isn't it?"

"It's only been a week!"

"So Shelley can't wait a month for you? What kind of girlfriend is that? A lousy one, I'd say!"

Harvest burst into tears and plopped back on the bed. A bit at a loss, Ginger just sat a few moments, watching her daughter's small rib cage expand and contract under her thin T-shirt. "I th-th-thought she loved me and she c-c-couldn't even wait a week" —unintelligible— "before she nod only dumps me b-but she joins another coven!"

Ginger patted her daughter gently on her back. "Not another coven!"

"Yeah! Just like that! She joined a coven in Vanderskleet."

"Ah, honey, these things happen. People break up with each other. Wiccans...change covens...I guess. Plenty of Wiccans in the sea, I'll bet."

"I already joined an online coven, but it's just not the same." The waterworks slowed and Harvest wiped her eyes, then got up and sat in front of her computer.

"What are you doing?"

"I'm gonna email everybody right now." She tapped the machine, zapping the screen into business mode. Ginger picked up the little bell again and rang it. Harvest turned around, still sniffling.

"You like that bell, huh."

"I do."

"Then why don't you borrow it for a while."

"I won't lose it."

"It'd be great if you didn't, Ma."

Ginger picked it up and palmed it. "Thanks. Now don't stay up too late on that thing. You have to get up for school tomorrow."

"Mom, it's summer. I also graduated last week."

Ginger just rang the bell, smiled, and left the room, pulling the door softly closed behind her.

Chapter 19

Ginger hung in Dickie's door like a big moth.

"I really don't care that you don't like her, Gin, that's not my problem."

"It's not that I don't like her, she seems like a very nice person, it's that she went to Danny Ezerstadt behind my back! *My* builder!"

"Your builder?"

"Well, you know I practically raised that boy, and this is the thanks he gives me? I think you should get rid of that Tandy and do it now! She is a scourge on the family spirit of Kanadoo Realty!"

Dickie shifted a pile of folders from one arm to the other. Florescent light shone off his balding pate. "Ginger, do the words 'just listed a subdivision' mean anything to you? Do you have any idea when the last time was that anything like this has happened at Kanadoo?"

"Yeah, well, how about that day I convinced the Vanderskleet Drive-In to project a picture of me with my sign right before the feature? How about that?"

"That was very creative, Ginger."

"I thought out of the box."

"Yes, you did. But you did not, repeat: did not, bring me a subdivision this week. Now, if you'll excuse me, it's time for our meeting. I'll see you in the conference room."

⁂ ⁂ ⁂

Ginger didn't hear a word Dickie was saying. All she could do was stare at the open pastry box with a kind of rageful wonderment. She raised her hand. "Excuse me, Dickie?"

He glared at her. "Yes, Ginger?"

"Um, what's in the box here?"

He slapped the palm of one hand with a pen. Maxie glanced up at the pastry box from her knitting, smirked, and returned to her work. Tandy, her black hair freshly streaked in roan red, visibly shut down a smile that was working itself free, never taking her eyes off Dickie.

"Looks like pastry to me, Gin."

She folded her arms. "Where are the donut holes?"

Dickie glanced at Tandy, who had succeeded in controlling her face, then at Maxie. "It's a nice change of pace, don't you think, Max?"

She didn't look up from her ball of yarn. "I think it sucks. I miss my holes."

"Is this why you didn't want me to pick them up this morning, like I have every Tuesday for thirty-nine years?" Ginger said. "So you could buy this..this..."

"Rugelach, petit fours and—"

"—just to get my goat?"

Dickie cleared his throat and began to speak.

"Have you tried the new coffee?" Maxie said. "It'll blow your head clean off."

Ginger poured herself half a cup of syrupy brew and gasped. "This can't be from the Pit!"

"It's not," Tandy said, turning and smiling sweetly. "There's a new Starbucks in Bangerlangersville. I figured it was worth the drive."

"Excuse me, ladies, but can we get back to talking about the business at hand?"

Ginger scowled as Tandy tilted her head, an exaggeration of listening.

"First up: an announcement. As of August first, I will no longer be receiving the weekly books from Squamskootnocket Valley's real estate service company. All of our business from that day forward will be conducted online. You will be—"

"But that's not fair!" Ginger said. "Why can't we have both?"

"Because, Ginger, after August first the books will no longer even be printed. I couldn't get them if I wanted to. Besides, it seems to be the push we need here at Kanadoo to come out of the Stone Age." Dickie and Tandy shared a private smile. "We should all be looking at this as a welcome change."

"Like global warming," Maxie said, mid-crochet.

"Excuse me?"

"Well, I don't see how we're supposed to go online if we have no computers."

"I have three on order. They'll be here Monday. Or you can get your own laptop and be mobile, like Tandy here."

Ginger and Maxie sputtered and harrumphed.

"Let's move on. The market. I have my views on it but you're the ones I'd like to hear from. You're the ones out there on the front lines, day in and day out. Why don't you tell me what your impressions are."

Ginger glazed over while Maxie knitted. Tandy raised her hand. "We are entering a changing market, with real signs of a slowdown in appreciation on the coasts. But I think with the five pillars of the economy still going strong: financial markets, technology, education, medical and defense, this will be more a correction of the bubble, more a slow release of air, than a bursting bubble."

"What is this bubble thing you're talking about?" Ginger said, effectively shutting down the room for several seconds.

Maxie's needles clacked. "You know, the eighties, when everything went to shit." Ginger gave her a confused look. "I'll tell you later."

Dickie looked like he was passing a ham. "Continue, Tandy."

She smiled winningly. "Well, I was just going to say that since the interest rates are still at historic lows, and with the economy still strong, I don't see the bubble bursting. Also, with all this new construction in Squamskootnocket, I can see a real boom coming."

"The challenge will of course be finding the buyer who can accommodate these kinds of prices," Dickie added.

"Of course," Tandy said, warming to her subject, "but they're out there. In fact, I've already had a few calls via the new website I'm building, and it's not even really..."

But that's all Ginger heard. She stared at the rugelach and cannoli and chocolate lace cookies and all she saw was a dachshund's weinery ass disappearing over a grassy knoll. It was finally hitting her that in only three hours her sellers at 45

Schuyler Place would come home to just one dachshund. Perhaps it wasn't premature to spring into action at this juncture, she mused.

She nudged Maxie and whispered, "Hey, I need a dachshund."

"You need a refund?"

"No, a dachshund. I need a dachshund," she whispered. "Stat."

"...but these are very sophisticated buyers with certain lifestyles—"

Dickie held up his hand. "Excuse me, Tandy. Ladies, is there something you wanted to share with the group?"

"I, uh, have a meeting I have to go to," Ginger said, getting to her feet.

"Me too," Maxie said, gathering her knitting.

Dickie gave them a dismissive wave and turned back to his star pupil.

Chapter 20

Ginger held the door of the Vanderskleet Valley Humane Society for Maxie who stepped inside, tripping slightly over the threshold. A wave of doggie smells washed over them as they signed in at the pee-stinky foyer. A woman in her sixties with thick glasses looked up from a sea of papers at her desk. She'd been attractive at one time in a delicate blond way but the sun had baked the pretty right out of her. Dogs barked, yelped and howled behind a thick glass partition. A small, piggy looking dog was caught behind the woman's chair, legs churning as if he were trying to burrow his head into it.

"What is wrong with that dog?" Maxie said, peering down at him.

"He's blind." The woman picked up the dog and nuzzled him. Ginger and Maxie stared at the clouded eyes of the pug. She set him down and he snuffled in circles on the linoleum. "I'm Ellen Franks, the supervisor here. How can I help you ladies today?"

"I have an emergency," Ginger said, stepping forward. "I need a dachshund, right away—"

Maxie kicked her in the ankle and piped up. "Today's my granddaughter's birthday. She's going to be eight, and oh what a cutie she is! Little dickens! Anyway, she's got her heart set on a dachshund. Do you happen to have any?"

Ellen squinted at Maxie, then at Ginger. The blind pug had come to an impasse in the form of filing cabinet this time, his head butting up against it. She snatched him up again. "Has she ever had pets before?"

"Oh, yes! Goldfish, birds, snakes, everything," Maxie said.

"But never a dog?"

"Well, this will be her second...dog."

"What happened to the first one?"

"Died." Ginger interjected. "It was...an old dog, and it died. Terrible thing. Also a dachshund, so you can see why she wants another one."

"And where's your granddaughter today?" asked the woman, still coddling the pug.

"She's at home getting prettied up for her birthday party," Ginger said. "So, do you have any dachshunds?"

"And you are...?"

"I'm her aunt. Her Auntie Ginger."

"And the girl's name?"

"Lucy—"

"Nancy—"

"Lucy Nancy." Maxie glared at Ginger. "And I'm her Grandma Maxie. So do you have any dachshunds? We're in just a bit of a hurry because—"

"All right, then, hold your horses." She reached behind the desk and collected a metal circle of keys hanging on the wall. "Can't let my dogs go to any old family." She unlocked a heavy door that led into a wide corridor.

They passed by all manner of dogs, many lunging at their cages, most dying to be petted, some resigned to their fate of lousy temporary housing, asleep in tight balls on skimpy blankets. Basset hounds, beagles, terriers, huskies, nippy little schnauzers, collies, retrievers, all manner of mutts, until the final cage, where a doe-eyed dachshund gazed up at them. A handwritten sign said, "Oscar, M, 5 years."

Maxie stooped down and poked her finger through the dachshund's cage. He sniffed at it, then looked away, not in the least impressed. "What a sweet doggie," she said.

"Hi, Oscar," Ginger cooed. "This looks just like little Lucy Nancy's old dog, doesn't it Max?"

"You got that right. Spittin' image."

"We'll take him," Ginger said.

Ellen Franks crossed her arms and cocked her head. "Don't you want to spend a little time with him? Take him for a walk outside?"

"That's all right. We know just what we're looking for. Nancy Lucy will be thrilled."

Ellen scratched the little pug behind his ears. Pleasure registered on his squinched up features. "Well, I can't let him go just like that. There's paperwork to be filled out, and there's also my policy that everyone who's going to live with the animal come and at least meet him."

"Oh, we can't do that!" Maxie said. "This is a surprise! It would ruin everything for little Nancy...Lucy!"

"She'd be scarred for life!" Ginger said. "No, we really need to take Oscar this afternoon."

Ellen gave her a tight smile. "I believe I just said that was impossible. Lucy's going to have to wait, at least until tomorrow. Or she can come later today. I'm open till seven—"

Ginger planted her hands on her hips. "Look, how much do you want for him?"

"That's not the point."

"Ellen, dear, why don't you just tell us what you charge for the little guy, and then we can at least make plans," Maxie said.

"Well," Ellen said, looking down at Oscar. "He's a purebred dog. A show dog with a stud history. His owner died and we took him in. He's beloved by all the staff here—"

"How much?" Ginger said, digging in her purse.

Ellen gave them a surreptitious once over. "Five hundred dollars."

Ginger stopped mid-search and gaped at Ellen. Maxie ogled the dog. "Five hundred dollars? Ginger, we're in the wrong business."

"Like I said, I've got his papers. He's pure. He's a fabulous animal. He won second prize at Westminster two years ago. He's practically royalty."

"Do you have any other dachshunds? Plain ones?"

"Nope. He's it."

Sighing deeply, Ginger pulled out her checkbook.

"But like I said, you can't take him today. I have to meet this...Lucy Nancy."

Maxie tapped Ginger on the shoulder and head-gestured behind her. "Will you excuse us a moment, Ellen? We have something to discuss."

Ellen shrugged. "Of course." She wandered over to a rambunctious beagle.

They huddled near the bulk kibble. "Ginger, we're getting reamed here."

"I know but I gotta have that dog! Max, I don't have the money."

"I don't either."

"Please, Maxie, you have no idea—"

"Ginger, there's gotta be another way out of this—"

"But there isn't! They'll be home in an hour! I guess I could tell them the truth but—"

"Don't be crazy, you can't do that..."

"Look, Max, I know I owe you, but please, just this one last time...I promise, when this thing closes, I'll pay you back with interest. I'll take you out for ribeye at the Meat Barn in Vanderskleet-on-Hudson."

"All right, all right." She sighed. "You drive a hard bargain, my friend." Maxie turned, leading the way back toward Oscar's cage, where Ellen joined them.

"Ellen?" Maxie said sweetly. "How many dogs have you sold today?"

"Well, none."

"This week?"

"None yet."

"And it's Friday. So don't you think a sale this week would be nice for you, you know, for the books?"

"I don't compromise my animals, so if that's where you're going with this—"

"We have a little girl whose heart will break clean in half if we don't bring her home a dachshund in an hour."

"The answer is no."

Maxie turned to her friend. "Now, Ginger, where was that other pound?"

"There is no other pound—nearby, anyway," Ellen said breathlessly. "You'd have to drive clear to Voorheesvrankinville to find something open now."

"I guess you'll have to sell us Oscar, then."

"I will not compromise my principles."

"How does five-fifty sound?"

"Fine," she said, reaching down to unlock Oscar's cage. "Cash only."

Chapter 21

Regina stood at a podium behind a long table festooned with flowers and candles. On her left sat Ginger, all gussied up in a sparkling gold gown, her hair in a French twist, a glass of champagne in hand. After a rousing round of applause, Regina took the mic and gazed adoringly back at her friend.

"And if Ginger hadn't gone the extra mile to sell my house for full price in one day," she said, welling up, "well, I don't think DeeShaun would have waited for me. I think my life would not be what it is today—happy and fulfilled!" The crowd—realtors, Dickie, Maxie, Big Jean and a variety of sellers and buyers Ginger had worked with over the years—clapped and smiled, tears evident in the corners of many eyes.

Old Man Higgins stood, hiked his suspenders, and took the mic from Regina. "Just one more voice in the chorus here, but I've gotta say my piece. This woman you see beside me...well, it's simple: she changed my life" —he choked up— "not only did she list my subdivision and turn the whole thing around in a week—we hadn't even poured the foundations yet—but she has shown me what it's like to be a stellar human being." Danny Ezerstadt, dashing in a tux and tails, jumped to his feet in a burst of impassioned applause. Ginger lowered her head in humility as Old Man Higgins turned to her. "I. Love. This. Woman."

"Mom!!!!!"

Ginger turned her head toward the sound of a distant voice, pouring herself another glass of champagne in the dream as she did so. "Go on with what you were saying, Billie."

"MOM!!!"

A hush fell on the crowd.

"MOM WAKE UP THE PHONE IS FOR YOU!!!!"

Ginger lifted her head from the pillow. For several seconds she had absolutely no idea where, who, or especially why she was. However, she was shocked to look down and see, not a sparkly gold gown, but her jammies, the ones with little yellow chicks on them, all gathered in a bunch around her waist. She wrenched herself into a sitting position.

"Tell whoever it is I'm not here!" Yikes, hadn't Harvest learned the most basic tenets of the Kanadoo household?

"IT'S DICKIE! HE SAYS TO GET YOUR FAT ASS OUT OF BED OR HE'LL COME HERE HIMSELF AND DO IT FOR YOU!"

OK, now that gave Ginger a bad feeling all around—did not sound like a congrats call about her new listing, a how ya doin' call, even a "your check's here if you want to pick it up" kind of thing. At all.

She opened the door and took the phone from Harvest.

"GET IN THIS OFFICE IN TEN MINUTES OR I SWEAR TO GOD I DON'T CARE ABOUT BIG JEAN YOU ARE FIRED!!"

"But Dick—"

Slam.

Ginger pulled off her jammies and threw on a pants suit in thirty seconds flat. She stumbled down the stairs and rustled around in the kitchen. Her hair stuck up every which way.

Harvest sat sprawled in an easy chair watching cartoons.

"Is there any coffee, honey?"

"It's one o'clock in the afternoon."

"I don't believe that was my question, dear."

Harvest chewed on the end of a pencil, eyes never leaving Spongebob. "Mom, did you buy a dachshund yesterday?"

Ginger slammed the refrigerator shut. "What in the world are you talking about?" She grabbed a can of coffee and scrambled in the drawer for an opener, found one and went to work on it. As she wrestled with the rusted thing she noticed the receipt from the Vanderskleet Valley Humane Society on the kitchen table: "One purebred dachshund, rec'd: $550."

"Don't worry, it's deductible."

"From what?"

Ginger slammed the drawer on her finger and yelped. "From all the damned money I'm going to make this year, dear! It's a business expense!"

Harvest channel surfed.

"If you're so nervous about money, Harv, feel free to get a job! No one is stopping you!"

She didn't answer. Ginger grabbed a jelly doughnut, put it in her mouth, and left the house.

⁕ ⁕ ⁕

Ginger screeched to a stop outside of Kanadoo Realty. She took a deep breath and let it out, then finished her donut, wiping the powdered sugar off her clothes as best she could. It was a gorgeous June day, flowers in bloom, sweet breezes blowing, but there was only terror in her heart. He couldn't fire her. He couldn't. He was her brother.

She thought of taking off. Just keep on driving, out of Squamskootnocket, past Vanderskleet and never stop. Try her luck in Hollywood, become a big movie star, wire money home to Harvest until she could send for her in grand style to join her in the seaside palace she lived in. Then she realized she had never been west of Vanderskleet and reconsidered. She took Harvest's bell from the dash, squeezed her eyes shut and rang it a few times, gathered herself, and went in.

Head down, she walked past Tandy and Maxie and went into Dickie's office without knocking, shutting the door gently behind her. He didn't lift his head from his paperwork.

"In all the years of buffoonery, in all the cockamamie BULLSHIT situations you have landed yourself in in all your years at this company, I would never in my wildest dreams have ever, ever imagined your doing such a stupid, boneheaded thing."

Ginger cleared her throat and examined her nails. "Well, maybe, Dick, you should tell me what the problem is before I—"

"What the problem is???"

Ginger shrank back in her chair as if blown there by a mighty wind, Dickie's voice clanging in her skull. She tried to imagine cool ocean breezes, a freshly opened bottle of chilled Sutter Home; to recall that peerless feeling of joy that moment in 1972 when she learned she'd been named Realtor of the Year for the first time, her smiling face all over the *Bugle*...

"Are you listening to me?" Dickie raged, his face a bright red balloon inches from hers.

"Of course I am, Dickie, along with everyone else in the office, I would imagine. But you still haven't told me the problem."

Dickie got up, hiked his slacks, crossed to the front of his desk and parked a lobe on the east corner. The buttons strained across the belly of his shirt. "Oh!" he said, shooting a finger skyward. "The problem! How could I forget? OK, play along with me. Are you with me?"

"Yes," Ginger said, eyes rug-ward, hands folded in her lap.

"It's a lovely summer evening. Our clients, Mary and Jeffrey Jones, return from a long weekend away after having listed their house that Friday with a well known Kanadoo realtor. When they arrive home, they go to check on their twin dachshunds who they've left in the garage over the weekend. Are you with me?"

"Mm hmm."

"Everything looks hunkey dorey until later in the evening when their young children, Joey and Sarah, start frolicking with the dogs on the living room rug. Suddenly, out of the blue, one of the dogs begins humping Sarah and tries to have sex with the little tyke—"

"Those pesky male dogs, you have to watch them—"

"Don't interrupt my story," Dickie said darkly. He resumed his sickly sweet tone. "Pulling the dog off her child, Mary calls her husband over. Evidently, something extremely unusual has happened to this dog over the weekend. Can you guess what that thing is, Ginger?"

She blinked. "I—"

"Over the course of the weekend, their dachshund has grown a penis! He's had a little weinie sex change! It was really quite startling!"

"I didn't do it! I swear I—"

"Two twin female dachshunds had morphed into a male/female pair over the weekend—just like that!"

"That's not—"

He got up and shook a fat finger in her face. "You can't get out of this one, Ginger! Your accomplice" —Ginger shot a look out at Maxie who was fast asleep at her desk— "came clean. For chrissakes, if I had any brains I'd fire the both of you!" he said, slamming his fist down on his desk.

"But, Dickie, what choice did I have? The dog ran away! I had to think fast, I had to think out of the box! It would have been better if it was a girl dog, but I couldn't think of everything!"

Dickie sat back behind his desk and folded his arms, leaning his chair back to its tipping point.

"So...are they mad?" Ginger asked in a tiny voice.

"Oh, no, they're just fine. Everything's fine. They love you. They think you're doing a fabulous job."

"Really?"

"NO!" he barked. "EVERYTHING'S NOT FINE! They fired you and they said they will never deal with a Kanadoo realtor again! They said they considered suing you and Kanadoo Realty, especially since little Sarah is so traumatized, but they said they would settle for having this strange dog removed immediately, and for you to tell them just what happened with Moopsy, or whatever the hell the missing dog's name was—"

"I'll call them right now—"

"They don't want to talk to you, believe me. Just tell me what happened and I'll have Maxie go pick up the dog. They don't know she was wrapped up in all this."

* * *

Head hanging low, Ginger left Dickie's office, pulling the heavy door shut behind her. She shuffled to her desk and put her purse down. Maxie snored in her cubicle.

Ginger took a rubberband and snapped it at Maxie's shoulder.

"Hey," Maxie lifted her head, her hair flat on one side. "Watch it."

"Thanks for ratting me out, Max."

Max rubbed her eyes and checked her watch. "He would have found out anyway. And don't be such a baby. This way I'm taking some of the heat."

"I guess. So, do you want a dachshund?"

"Umm, no." She resettled her head on her desk and went back to sleep.

Dickie's head emerged from his office. "Ginger! Call on two!"

Ginger picked up. "Yes?"

"Is this Ginger Kanadoo?"

"Speaking."

"This is Darlene Vandersloot of the Vandersloot Historical Society. We have a historical home that we'd like to list with you—"

"That sounds great—"

"Well, let me tell you a bit about the home first. It's an estate sale. It's my own family's home. It's been in the Vandersloot family for generations, so this will be a very emotional thing, but all of us have thought long and hard about it and in the end have decided we could all use the cash."

"I see. When would you like me to come take a look at it?"

"Oh, you could go anytime. It's vacant and the locks haven't worked for years."

"I'll have a look this afternoon."

"Good. I'd like to get it on the market as soon as possible."

"Ms. Vanderslot—"

"Sloot."

"Sloot—you have nothing to worry about. You've hired the most competent realtor in the area. I'll do some research on the price, then call you right away and we can do the paperwork."

"Sounds wonderful. The home is at 666 Phantom Lane, in the heart of Vandersloot. I'll leave my card in the house. I look forward to doing business with you, Ms. Kanadoo."

Ginger tenderly replaced the phone in its cradle, clasped her hands and looked skyward, thankthankthanking the random gods of real estate.

Chapter 22

Maxie sat in the passenger seat, hair blown straight back by the hot summer breeze through the open window.

"Stupid dachshunds. Why can't they be like birds or something, where you need their DNA to know what sex they are."

Ginger turned off Main Street, Squamskootnocket, onto Highway 48, the quickest way to Vandersloot. "Hey, a dog is a dog, in my book. They should have been satisfied with what they had when they got back: two dachshunds, count 'em: one, two, just like when they left."

"Amen, sister. People are just spoiled."

"They don't appreciate what they have."

"Ain't it the truth."

They drove in satisfied silence until Ginger took the exit for downtown Vandersloot. The road jagged off to the right, then took a steep dive down a hill into a horrifically decayed part of town. The hollow eyes of abandoned industrial buildings watched them as they drove deeper into a tangled clot of one-way streets until they finally entered the dead heart of the city. Ginger followed Maxie's directions to Beezelbub Court, a short street which ended at the banks of a long-dead river polluted by Vandersloot Tire, a mile upstream. Noxious clouds funneled into the sky from the factory, filling the entire north side of town with a green smog. There wasn't a soul around except the occasional drunk who stumbled by on his way to someplace better, which was anywhere.

Ginger clutched the wheel. "Where is this damned place?"

"Look for Incubus Road, then park," Maxie said.

Ginger took a left and stumbled onto the street. She parked and they got out. The river smelled like rubber as it slunk over slimy stones. A rotting, three-legged mailbox balanced on a broken concrete walk.

They looked up at the mouth of Incubus Road. Barely legible signs advertising Coca-Cola for five cents were painted on the brick sides of buildings. Summer blew its hot breath up at them.

"Why can't I get a normal listing, Max? Just a normal, boring listing where normal, boring people want to sell their house to normal, boring people and move to another normal, boring house?"

"You just had that and you blew it."

"With your help."

"Don't blame me," Max said. "I'll never get the dough back for that dog."

The sign for Incubus Road hung by a charm, swaying back and forth in the belching breeze. Ginger stared up at it.

"I don't even want to go down this street, much less go in the house and list it."

"Suck it up. You owe me five hundred and fifty clams." Max forged ahead down the warty sidewalk which heaved as if something evil was trying break its way through. "We take this till it ends, a left at Succubus, and we're there."

Ginger glanced back at the stream. Some kind of frog/fish/mammal thing was emerging from it, dragging primitive forelegs. "What the fuck is that?" Ginger said.

"Who knows. Just keep moving. Eyes on the prize, Gin."

They passed rows of triple deckers, their porches sagging with age. Overweight, tragic-looking people sat in ruptured wicker, smoking and drinking Kool-Aid, staring at them as their daughters pimped themselves on the random corner.

As they approached Phantom Lane, a hollow wind picked up. It toyed with Ginger's sensible knee-length skirt and rustled trash thither and yon in the yards of abandoned Victorians. Max and Ginger stood listening to the wind and to the almost imperceptible sound of moaning intertwined with it.

"Hold my hand," Ginger said, taking her first step onto Phantom Lane.

"Don't be a baby," Max said, grabbing it after a few yards.

660, 662, 664—every house put a deeper chill into them, until they reached...666.

The house of death.

Though it was midday, bats darted in and out of shadowy garrets that loomed like bad teeth over the decaying gums of the second floor. Ripped, filthy curtains waved and jerked to unfelt breezes far above their heads. A smell of something rotten wafted by. The front door hung on one hinge over a porch that was missing every third slat.

"I'm not going in there."

"Five hundred and fifty bucks. Plus dog food and vet bills for life if I can't unload the horny little sucker."

Ginger shook her hand free of Max's in a spasm of frustration. "Didn't you say you listed this house once? Like, a few years ago?"

"Try forty. Didn't sell then, won't sell now."

"Don't be so negative. Why didn't it sell before?"

"Because it's haunted, my friend. Haunted as the day is long. Haunted as I am short. Haunted as—"

"I'm not going in there."

"You're going in there."

"Can't you just go in and grab the woman's card and I can say I saw it? Just describe it to me."

Maxie shook her head. "No can do. You list it, you have to step foot in it."

Ginger stamped her foot in frustration. A giant black crow burst out of a first floor window, shrieking past their heads. Ginger nearly jumped in Maxie's lap.

"Please come in with me, please oh please, Max."

"Nope."

"Come on, I said I'd help you stage that overpriced slab if you helped me with this."

"Can't do the stairs, Gin, you know that."

"I'll give you a leg up." Ginger held out her hands, fingers woven in a basket.

Maxie folded her arms across her tiny chest. "I said I'd help you sell it, not go in it again. I'll never forget what happened to me forty years ago."

"Oh my god, what happened? What happened to you forty years ago?"

"I...I can't...it was too horrible..."

"Tell me!"

Maxie shrugged. "Wouldn't sell. Piece of crap. I mean, look at it. Pushed it for nearly a year."

"That is a nightmare." Ginger exhaled and squared her shoulders. "All right, I'm going in, with you or without you."

"Atta girl."

Ginger started down the weed-sprung walk and up the stairs to the porch. When she reached the last step, the front door creaked open as if to welcome her. She froze, one foot midair.

"Max, if you want a ride home from this godforsaken hellhole you get over here right now."

Grumbling, Max complied. Ginger helped her up the few steps to the porch. Together, they crossed the threshold. What must have once been a stunning foyer was now a creep show. Matching loveseats, covered in inches of dust, faced them as they walked in. High above their heads loomed an equally filthy chandelier, its great arms dipping down, then swooping up into the blackness above them. A magnificent staircase, its mahogany risers low and wide, swung in an elegant arc up to the mysterious reaches of the second floor.

Clutching each other's hands, Ginger and Maxie made their way down a dim hallway to a cavernous dining room, complete with a table still set for an elaborate dinner party for fourteen. A cookie-sized spider scuttled across a cracked china plate and disappeared. Sunlight filtered through jade and crimson stained glass windows, casting jeweled light on the antique wine glasses.

"Good sized dining room," Ginger said.

"Never goes out of style."

They passed through an echoing butler's pantry on their way to the kitchen. Iron pots hung in a row from a hammered tin ceiling. The counters were slabs of soapstone, nicked and hollowed from a century of use. Knives of every size jutted from a rough block of wood, while a butcher knife lay on its side next to it, as if it had just been used.

"Kitchen could use some updating, but we'll work that into the price," Ginger choked out.

They passed through swinging doors to a room so massive they couldn't make out the other end of it. Built-in bookshelves still filled with dusty tomes covered every wall. A yawning fireplace taller than Maxie emerged from the darkness as they walked across the room.

"Great family room," Ginger said. "Could even break it up a bit. Au pair possibilities."

But Max was gone.

Ginger twirled around, a cold sweat gathering on her brow. "Max? Max! Where are you?" She ran through the great room, tripping over footstools and antique dolls, their dead eyes lolling back in their heads.

"Relax, I'm over here," came Max's voice. Ginger followed it back to the foot of the staircase. "Time to check out the second floor."

"How did you do that?"

"Do what?"

Confounded, Ginger glanced all around her. "Max, I've had it. I've seen it. Let's go."

"You have to see the second floor, you know that. How else are you gonna describe it? Now get on up there."

"You know, Max, this might be a good time to tell me why this place is haunted."

"Naah."

Ginger put a foot on the first stair. "I won't be killed, will I?"

"You'll be fine."

"Maimed?"

"Doubtful."

"You love me, right, Max?"

"Like a daughter. Now go."

"Tell Harvey I love her, will you?"

"Shut up and climb. And keep your eyes open."

Whimpering, Ginger made her way up the stairs, sending up puffs of dust with every step. She peered down at Max when she reached the landing. She looked tiny, like glasses with hair.

"Can I come back down now?" Her voice echoed in the great hall.

"Stop being a wimp. Have a look around first."

Ginger turned away from the stairs and looked down the hall. The space was unsettling, the ceilings so high she couldn't make them out. Cold, strangely damp drafts of air wafted by as she walked. She peered in bedroom after bedroom, each with its own fireplace and each larger than the last. Ripped curtains fluttered at broken windows.

At the end of the hall she reached a room with a locked door. She tried it a few times with no luck. Shivering, she turned back toward the stairs.

After a few steps, she heard a click.

Feet melded to the floor, she turned to look behind her. The door of the locked room had opened a few inches. Perversely, and just like in the movies, she turned back toward the partially open door and tiptoed toward it.

It was a bathroom with an old fashioned metal sink and an impossibly ancient toilet. She had just convinced herself that nothing was going on when both faucets jerked to the right as if gripped by unseen hands.

Water dripped, then gushed into the sink. A few sponges lying at the bottom rose to the top. Soap bubbles began to form.

"Everything OK up there?" came Max's distant voice.

Ginger didn't answer. She stared at the sink as it filled to the point of spilling over. With shaking hands, she reached over and turned the faucets off. For a few moments she watched the taps drip into the foamy bubbles. She turned to leave, then heard two wrenching creaks, one after the other.

She whipped around. Both taps had been yanked back on. Water quickly overflowed the sink sending the sponges surfing over the lip and onto the floor.

Ginger screamed and ran helter-skelter down the hallway. She grasped at the banisters and flew down the stairs shrieking, "Maxie! Run! There's a ghost!" She grabbed Max and turned her toward the door, practically lifting her off her feet.

Max looked unimpressed. "Put me down, will you?"

Ginger replaced her. They listened to the pipes of the old house clang and bang, the sound of water coursing through them.

"What did you see, exactly?" Max said, leaning against a balustrade.

"Who cares?" Ginger's face was flushed, her hair wild. "There's something evil here, something that wants to tear us apart limb from limb, feed on our still-beating hearts, doom us to everlasting hell and damnation!"

Max put one finger to her chin. "Mmm, I don't think so."

"Then, what, Maxie, what?" Ginger sent a terrified glance up the staircase. "I'm telling you, you didn't see what I saw!"

"Which was...?"

"That thing! That—that horrible, horrible thing! You must have seen it. This was your listing!"

Max raised an eyebrow. In that instant the water pipes shrieked and banged as the water turned off.

Ginger's eyes grew wide. Maxie looked bored and even a bit sleepy. "That's it," Ginger said, grabbing her aunt by one spindly arm. "If you don't want to live, I do. We're leaving. Now."

Maxie shrugged as Ginger practically carried her out of the house and down to the sidewalk.

Ginger swiveled her around by the shoulders. "Max, I want you to run."

"You know I can't run."

"Then I'm going to have to leave you here to die, if that's OK."

"Go ahead," she gestured with her cane. "Save yourself. I'll meet you at the car."

Ginger turned and blasted off, Bass Weejuns churning over the broken walk. Fueled by fear, she reached the car in minutes and leaned on it as she caught her breath. Her hair was plastered to her forehead; semicircles of sweat stained the armpits of her white blouse. As she rested, staring up at the bruise-colored sky, she reflected that once again her profession had sent her on an unintended track and field event. She considered even more practical shoes.

She looked behind her down Incubus Way, where Max was only now turning the corner from Succubus Court, making her slow, steady way to the car. With a heavy sigh, Ginger wiped the sweat off her brow, started her car and headed down the road to pick her up.

⁕ ⁕ ⁕

Ginger and Max burst through the door of Ginger's bungalow, their arms overflowing with groceries. While Ginger put the food away, Max uncorked a bottle of Gallo, poured a couple of glasses, and wandered around the living room.

"Now, where's my favorite niece?"

"I'm in here, Auntie Max," came Harvest's voice from behind her door.

Max found her curled up in bed with her laptop, a greenish glow lighting her face.

"You on that thing again?" Maxie tsked. "What do you do with it all day, anyway?"

"Well, right now I'm doing a live chat on love spells. It's pretty cool."

"Love spells, huh? You kids. Why don't you wrap it up and join us. We're making your favorite."

"Sure, just give me a couple of minutes."

"OK, sweetie," Max said, shutting the door behind her.

"She is so nice to you, Max. Why is that?" Ginger asked, picking up the phone.

"Cuz I'm not you."

"I'll have two mushroom pizzas, large, extra cheese."

"But it's not healthy—her being in that room all day."

Ginger hung up the phone. "I don't chain her up, Max! She's doing what she wants to do, whatever that is."

Harvest came out of her room and poked around in the cabinets. Settling on a box of cookies, she got comfortable on the living room couch, legs draped over the armrest. "Hey,

Mom," she said by way of anemic greeting. Ginger went and gave her a big kiss, which was allowed though not relished.

"So, you still haven't told me what you noticed about the house," Max said.

"Your auntie took me to a haunted house today, I was chased by a ghoul, and she still won't tell me why it's haunted," Ginger said.

Harvest shrugged, chewing.

"Think, Gin. What is missing from that house?"

Ginger squirted some cheese on a Ritz. "The blessed light of Jesus? A cross? Holy water?"

"Yeah, and what else? Pretend you're listing it, which you are—"

"Oh, no, I'm not—"

"You're listing it."

Ginger took a deep breath and let it out. Harvest studied her. "666 Phantom Lane is a stunning example of Queen Anne Victorian architecture. It's a four bedroom...four bedroom...oh dear. I never noticed how many baths it had."

"That's because," Maxie jabbed the air with a bony finger, "it didn't have any!"

"No baths?"

"That's crazy," said Harvest. "Who lived there?"

"The house only ever had one owner, after all these years."

"But how did he take a shower, or a bath?" Ginger asked.

"How the hell should I know? He's dead. What am I supposta do, ask a dead guy?"

"I thought you knew the story!"

"I do. Keep your pants on."

Harvest leaned forward, fascinated.

"Can I get you a drink, honey?" Max asked Harvest. "Some zin?"

"I'm not old enough to drink. Tea is fine," Harvest said, sipping at a ceramic cup.

Maxie cozied up to the breakfast bar. "OK, here it is. Story goes, in the early 1800's, a gentleman by the name of Thadius Banewood contracted for a house to be built so his lady love would want to come join him from Philadelphia and get married and so on. Now this contractor he hired, Ephemius Stout, was a bit of a drunk I guess, and built an entire three thousand square foot house with only one bathroom with a toilet, and no plumbing for a bath."

"Whoops!" Ginger said, sipping her zin.

"It gets worse. Thadius was broke, plus he was getting kind of stinky with no bath in the house, and his lady love was telling him she'd be on the next train the moment a tub was installed. So he ran after the contractor, threatening to sue him if he didn't install the three full bathrooms he had contracted for and paid to have installed. Ephemius ignored him, so Thadius sued him and when Ephemius ignored that, threatened to kill him."

"Wow, what happened then?" Harvest said.

"Well, my dear, Ephemius might have been scum, but he wasn't dumb scum. He was smart enough to take death threats from Thadius seriously. Meanwhile, Thadius had started taking longer and longer sponge baths to the point where they were getting hours and hours long. He'd show up at the tavern afterwards, a broken man, mumbling that he felt unclean and asking to use the baths at the tavern, which had an inn at the back. Thadius was already starting to lose it, but

Ephemius wanted to finish the job. So one night, in the middle of the night, he snuck in to 666 Phantom Lane while Thadius was taking a sponge bath and killed him."

"Yikes!" said Ginger.

"So, the legend goes it's Thadius up there taking a sponge bath, on and on for eternity. The bummer is, he'll stop for a few months and just start up again any old time. Crikey, forty years ago I had the place under agreement with these people who just didn't believe the story, since all the time they'd been in the house nothing happened. Then an hour before the closing, we did the walk through and he started up one of his sponge baths and they were outta there like bats outta hell. Sudsy water, sponges all over the damned place. Thadius was back."

"Wow," Harvest said. "I'd love to see this place."

"What's even spookier is that the town turned off the water to that house decades ago."

The doorbell rang. Everyone jumped, but it was just the delivery boy at the screen door with a couple of steaming pizzas in hand.

Chapter 23

After talking for a good hour around the supper table about ghosts and various supernatural events, Harvest retired to the living room to watch TV.

"I think we need Harvest's help to exorcize this place, don't you Max?"

Harvest lowered the volume on the TV. "Mom, I'm not an exorcist, for crying out loud."

"Can't you sort of fake it this one time?"

Harvest rolled her eyes. "You cannot 'fake' an exorcism. Besides, I don't have that sort of power."

Ginger fell silent as she wiped the counter. "So when am I going to your next Wiccan thing?"

"It's all set. Next week is the Summer Solstice festival. We're meeting down by the lake. But you can't say anything. You can only watch."

"I'm keeping my clothes on."

"We all are, don't worry."

"Can I come?" asked Max.

"You want to come, Auntie Max?" Harvest said. "Sure, I don't see why not."

"I like to see what the young kids are up to these days."

Ginger sat with her wine, swirling it in the glass. "I gotta think of a way to get rid of Thadius. Harvest, what about the Ouija board? Maybe ask it some questions?"

Harvest sighed. "Very strong magic there, Mom. I don't know if you're ready for it."

"Strong magic is just what I need right now, girlie."

Harvest considered this. "You promise you'll do exactly as I say? Not screw around and make jokes?"

"I promise."

"Ooooo," Maxie said, rubbing her hands together, "I love Ouija boards. Scares the crap out of me."

"Well, don't get too scared, Auntie Max," Harvest said, disappearing into her bedroom to find the board. "That will interfere with our reading."

She returned with the board and opened it up on the kitchen table, rummaged around in a drawer for candles and lit them.

"Mom, turn out the lights."

"We're doing this in the dark?"

"Do you want it to work or not?"

"Suck it up, Ginny," Maxie said, going from light to light and switching them off. "We could use some answers here."

Ginger sighed, opened another bottle of wine and brought it to the table where she huddled next to the candles. Harvest directed Maxie to sit across from Ginger, resting the open Ouija board on their knees as they faced each other, then sat next to them. The room was dark and quiet except for their breathing. A soft summer breeze wafted through the screens.

"All right," Harvest said. "Listen up. It's important to be polite to the board, and when it answers your questions, to say thank you. And whatever you do, don't ask for physical signs, like: if you're here, Mr. Ghost, prove it, or anything like that. Too dangerous. Got it?"

Max and Ginger nodded, their eyes glittering in the candlelight.

"Good." She took a deep breath and continued. "I want to announce to the board that we are calling up only good energy today. Negative energy is not welcome. Now, ladies, rest your fingertips on the planchette and just move it around the board a little while."

Maxie pushed the felt-backed triangle toward Ginger, who pushed it back.

"Hey, isn't the board supposed to do this, tell us stuff?" Ginger asked.

"You're warming up. You're getting used to each other's energy, so you can recognize the third party which is the board."

"Holy crap," Max said.

"OK, now both of you stop moving it."

For a few seconds nobody and nothing moved. All stared at the board. Then the triangle jerked to the left.

"Knock it off, Max!"

"I'm not doing it!"

The planchette floated under their fingers to the word Yes.

"Oh my God, we haven't even asked it anything yet," Ginger croaked.

"Were either of you thinking of a question?"

"Well...I was," Ginger said.

"What was the question?"

"'Is Tandy a ho?'"

Maxie cackled.

"Mom. I just said, nothing negative. Don't you ever listen to me?"

"Sorry, honey. I thought it was more like a fact kinda thing."

"OK, another yes or no question. It's a good way to warm up. Max?"

"Is Ginger going to sell a house before the end of the year?"

The planchette vibrated under their fingertips, skimmed by No, and landed once again on Yes.

"I like this thing," Ginger said. "Can I ask it something?"

"Sure."

"Mr. Ouija, will I ever get out of debt?"

The planchette trembled, then moved. It shot over to the D, then to the U, ambled over to A...

"Hey Harvey, you writing this down?"

"Yup."

...then to Y, H, E, W, and X.

Ginger gasped with excitement. "It spells...duayhewx! What is that? Doo-ay Hoox! I got it! Dooay Hoox! That's so exciting!"

"Gin, that doesn't mean anything," Maxie said.

"You're right. It's probably the white zin talking."

A moment of silence was broken by the phone ringing. Nobody moved. Eventually, the outgoing message played and Jim Steele's voice filled the room. "Oh, hi Ginger. This is Jim Steele, um, down at the *Bugle*. I hope you're well, selling lotsa houses. Been seeing your signs all over—good for you! Listen, the reason for my call today is that the Fireman's Ball is going to happen on the first of July and I was thinking, if you're not too busy and you got no other plans, well, I've got two tickets and I thought you might come along. There should be a nice spread and... Anyway, let me know when you can. Uh, thanks. This is Jim." Click.

"He's always liked you, that Jim," Max said, the twin candle flames doubled in her glasses.

"He has?"

"Mom. Duh. Only for like your whole life!" Harvest said.

"Oh," Ginger said. "Who knew."

Max shook her head.

"OK, positions." They put their fingertips on the planchette. "Should Ginger go with Jim Steele to the Fireman's Ball?"

The planchette hovered, then slid over to S, then T, A and G.

"I don't get it. Stag." Harvest said.

"It means no," Ginger said. "Jim should go 'stag' to the party."

"All right, forget this," Max said. "Down to brass tacks. How the hell am I going to sell my overpriced slab ranch with the fifteen cats?"

It spelled S, T, A and G.

"Stag again! That's crazy."

"I know what it means!" said Ginger. "It means 'stage'—you need to stage that place to sell it."

"Maybe I'll give that a shot."

"My turn," Ginger said. "I need to know what to do about the haunting at 666 Phantom Lane."

The candlelight flickered, then grew long and sinewy, as if pulled skyward by an unseen force. The breeze picked up and fluttered the curtains at the window. Harvest shot her mother a warning look. Max's hands trembled as the planchette danced across the board. It spelled, G, O, A, W, A.

They all stared at the board. "Goawa..." Max started. Their hands shot over to Y.

"Go awa...go away!" Harvest yelped. "OK, let's—"

But Ginger persisted. "I need to talk to a certain Thadius Banewood. Thadius, are you here?"

Harvest jumped up and grabbed her mother by the shoulders. "Mom, what are you doing?! I told you not to do this!"

A great thump and bang from upstairs. Everyone froze as they listened to the sound of water coursing through the pipes.

"He's here," Harvest whispered.

"Holy fucking shit," Max said, lifting her hands off the board, which slipped from her lap and onto Ginger's.

"Don't close it!" Lunging to the rescue, Harvest grabbed the board from her mother and opened it up again across their laps. "You called him. Now you have to talk to him, and be respectful! Both of you, put your hands back on the planchette! Now!"

They did so, gaping at each other. Nobody said a word. A metal on metal clang from upstairs.

"For God's sake, Mom, he's here. Now ask him something."

"Um, Mr. Thadius," Ginger stumbled, "do you want me to sell your house?"

The kitchen faucet began to drip.

The planchette moved with such force it nearly yanked Maxie out of her chair. It landed on Yes.

Sweat gathered in Ginger's armpits. Her breath came shallow.

A steadier stream of water from the tap.

"How, Mr. Thadius, can I give you peace?"

The planchette buzzed under their fingers. Water plunged into the sink. Night insects beat themselves against the screens.

S, H, O, W, E, R...

"Shower..." Harvest said.

The planchette moved sharply back and forth under Ginger and Max's fingers, as if the entity were trying to erase something. It hesitated a moment, then jerked from letter to letter.

J, A, K, O, O, Z, E, E

"Oh my God," Ginger said. "He wants a Jacuzzi." She harrumphed. "And don't we all want a Jacuzzi, Mr. Thad—"

Harvest clapped her hand over her mother's mouth. "Thank you, Thadius, for visiting our world. We are honored that you spent time with us." The hard stream of water softened, slowing to a dribble. "And we hope that we can get what you need to put you at peace. Is there anything else you'd like to tell us?"

The pipes banged once more as the last of the water pounded through. The dripping stopped. The house fell silent.

"Then we'd like to say goodnight and goodbye," Harvest said, her hands over Ginger's and Maxie's on the planchette. Gently she eased them over to the word "Goodbye." She lifted off their fingers, removed the planchette, and slowly closed the board.

Chapter 24

Dressed in burlap-colored robes, daisy chains flopping in their hair, Maxie and Ginger ran barefoot through a field of wildflowers. A good hundred yards off, a clot of Wiccans, dressed in identical dingy brown caftans with rope ties, danced in a circle on the niggardly strip of beach that bordered Lake Squamskootnocket. Here we go, Ginger thought, yet another Olympic event, as they trammeled through the long grasses toward the frolicking coven. She and Max gasped at the air which was thick with humidity and the lingering sweet smell from the gummy bear factory, even though it had turned out its last gummy bear a good decade ago.

"Whose idea was this?" Maxie sputtered as she pulled up the rear a few yards behind Ginger. She looked ultra tiny in her robe, the sleeves several inches longer than her arms.

"I thought you wanted to do this," Ginger said, swatting at something buzzing in her ear.

"Why can't we wear shoes, is what I want to know."

"Harvest says we're closer to the earth this way. Something about vibrations. Come on, beats being bare-assed."

They approached the group, who were holding hands and chanting. Harvest, looking like a natural with her flowing robes and hair, turned and held up a stern finger to her lips when she saw them. Similarly cautionary looks were tossed their way by her fellow Wiccans, Frankie, Sheena and Brian. Ginger noticed they all wore the same flowers in their hair, even Brian.

"Mom, Auntie Max, sit over here, OK?" Harvest said, breaking from the group and leading them to a rotting log a few yards away. "You've missed the opening ceremonies so you'll just have to follow along," she added through gritted teeth.

They both nodded solemnly.

The group reformed near the water, walking in a circle one way, then the other, each taking a moment to dip their bare toes in the water.

"Welcome, all, to Litha, the summer solstice," Harvest said. "We have celebrated by collecting herbs and flowers for the coming year: orange, lemon, honeysuckle, and vervain, and by blessing our own gods and goddesses, and asking for their blessings in return. Now let us turn to our spells."

She stepped out of the circle, pulled a candelabra out of a burlap bag and stuck it in the sand. With great ceremony, Sheena placed four red candlesticks in it and lit them. A mirror image of the four flames danced in the lake.

"Sheena has requested a spell for confidence," Harvest said. "She will be taking her cosmetology finals next week, and would like all of our positive energy and thoughts directed toward her at this special time."

The group chanted as Sheena pulled four objects from the bag: a bottle of Wanton Lust nail polish, a blow dryer, a jar of Come Do Me hair gel, and a pair of haircutting shears.

She picked up the nail polish and held it out toward the lake. "This is a symbol of my manicuring skills. I hope that I will remember all the colors. I am confident! I have the power of Earth!"

She closed her eyes in rapture, clutching the little bottle to her heart; with a grand exhale, she placed it on the sand and picked up the blow dryer. "This is a symbol of my blow drying skills. May I never set it too hot! I am confident! I have the power of Air!"

Laying it gently down, she picked up the shears. "These are the symbols of my hair styling skills. May I always remember, over the complaints of my clients: it grows back! I am confident! I have the power of Fire!"

She lay down the shears and picked up the jar of hair gel. "This is the symbol of my ability to sell products for the salon! May I always remember, it helps cover booboos too! I am confident! I have the power of Water!"

Sheena stood in the middle of the circle of objects and began to spin, hands raised high, blond hair fanning out and catching the last rays of orange sunlight. The group chanted louder and louder.

"These people are starting to freak me out," Max whispered to Ginger, who shushed her.

"And now," Harvest said, as the chant died down, "I want to announce Sheena's new Wiccan name. Henceforth in the group she will be known as Dolphin Child. Or, Sheena 'Dolphin Child' Horatzberg."

"Welcome, Dophin Child," the group intoned, tossing herbs at her. She smiled serenely, arms outstretched.

"So, if there are no other items of business, we will disperse for cakes and wine—"

"Excuse me!" Ginger blurted. Harvest glared at her. "Do you have any spells to help sell troubled listings?"

The group turned to her with a Wiccan, hydra-headed scowl of disapproval. Maxie whacked her with a sleeve. "Shut up, stupid."

Harvest turned away from them and raised her arms toward the group. They each took quarter turns, bowing as she said, "I now thank the guardians of the Quarters: oh Mighty Ones of the South, oh Spirit of Fire in the East, oh Keepers of the Flame in the North, and the Red Lions of the West."

The group turned inward again, raised their clasped hands skyward and released them.

With an air of resignation, Harvest said, "All right, everyone meet me back at Sheena's car where we'll have our picnic and fire."

The group dispersed, talking and laughing, except for Harvest, who gathered up wands and bags of herbs and threw them furiously in a shopping bag.

"You're in the doghouse now," Maxie said, getting up from the wet log and picking pieces of bark off the back of her robe.

"I can't win." Ginger's daisy chain drooped across one eye. "I just blurted it out. Don't you ever just blurt anything out?"

"Nobody blurts like you, Gin."

Harvest strode purposefully up to them. "What did I say, Mom? What did I say?"

"You said not to interrupt," Ginger said, still planted on the log. "And I did. And I'm sorry."

"Not only did you interrupt, you asked for us to do a spell and you're not even Wiccan. That is just wrong—"

"I don't want to be Wiccan. I just wondered if there was a spell for—"

"There's a spell for everything under the sun, but you can't just stumble into Sabbat and ask for one! We're all trained! We take turns!"

"OK, OK, don't get your fairy dust all in a twist. I'm your mother and the only reason you're allowed to do this is because I said so."

"Whatever." Harvest turned and marched away toward the waiting gang by Sheena's car, her hair flowing in a dark mass behind her.

* * *

By the time Max and Ginger made it to what turned out to be Frankie's car, the coven had already started a fire in a clearing and was roasting marshmallows for s'mores.

"Did we miss the cakes and wine?" Ginger asked, as Harvest unwrapped chocolate bars and graham crackers.

"No wine, Mom. Iced tea."

"That's OK. I don't need wine."

Sheena pulled a bottle of Carlo Rossi out of her purse. "I brought this..."

"Thank God," Ginger said. "I mean, it's hard breaking the Wiccan ice with just tea."

Brian looked up at her from his cross-legged position on the ground. He still wore the flowers in his dark hair. "We're just people, Mrs. Kanadoo."

"Mom, Max, this is Brian," Harvest said. "And you know Sheena, of course, and Frankie from Shapes."

They all shook hands and said their hellos. Flames wicked up into the night. Brian turned a hot dog on a stick and stared into the fire.

"I thought the energy was great tonight, didn't you?" Brian said dreamily. "I could really feel my gods and goddesses all around me."

"I did get this incredible rush when I held up my blow dryer," Sheena said. "Did anybody else feel it?"

"I thought it was a hot flash, Dolphin Child, but you could be right," Frankie said, leaning against a tree and sipping her wine.

"It was nice to have guests," Brian said, nodding at Ginger and Maxie. "But I hope you both appreciate the secretive nature of these meetings. It's not that we do anything untoward, it's that people think we do. It's a problem."

"Our lips are sealed," Max said. "But tell me, how do you get the names you choose for yourselves? I think I want one."

"It's part of being Wiccan," Harvest said. "It's a sort of spiritual identity."

"Oh." Max gazed up at the stars.

Ginger waved her half-burnt marshmallow in the air. "So let me get this straight. If I was Wiccan, I could make a spell for anything I wanted, and get it, right?"

"It's not that easy, Mom," Harvest started testily, then remembered the group was listening. "First of all, you need to do a lot of work on yourself to become Wiccan—spiritual work—and then when you ask for something, you will get it but almost never in the form you ask for. For example, you might ask for something you think you need or want and get the opposite, because that was what was meant to happen to accomplish your true goal."

"I've always liked unicorns. How about Laughing Unicorn?" Max said.

"I like it." Ginger noshed on her s'more, chocolate gluing up her face.

"Here's an example," Sheena said as she tossed more wood on the fire. "I really want to pass my cosmetology exam. It's a dream of mine. I've been studying for weeks and I really feel like it's going to solve a lot of problems for me. But if I don't pass, then, well, another door will open for me that will lead to something good, because the energy I'm putting into all this studying and wishing is good, positive energy."

Ginger's face screwed up. "You mean you could do all these spells and prancing around the forest in your skivvies and calling up gods and goddesses and still not get what you want?"

"It's not what you think you want," Frankie said, "but in the end, you'll get what you really want."

Ginger sighed and held out her paper cup to Sheena for a refill.

Chapter 25

Humming loudly, Ginger wiped a thick mat of dust off the heavy dining room table and arranged her open house paperwork on it.

She read over her flyer.

Under a photo of the house complete with bats flying out the windows was the text:

> Introducing:
> 666 Phantom Lane, Vandersloot, New York
> offered at $199,999.99
>
> Once in a lifetime opportunity! This stately example of Queen Anne Victorian architecture, featuring flying buttresses, gargoyles and original woodwork and moldings, offers today's buyer a taste of the past along with a big chunk of history and absolutely no tiresome modern conveniences. From the moment you walk in the door and take a look around, you will know what makes this house so special. Original owners are loathe to leave this stately manse. With its four generous bedrooms and half a bath, it can accommodate any growing family who brings a few plumbing plans and a lot of love. Gleaming hardwoods! Super house, won't last!!

Everything was in order and ready for hordes of buyers to come pouring through the door. Ginger sat in a suppurating high-backed chair in the library as she flipped through a deck of tarot cards she had lifted from Harvest's room. There had to be some way to just make a spell happen and not have to get all wrapped up in this spiritual homework nonsense.

She spread out all the cards on an end table and studied them. Lots of pentacles and swords and wands and cups. A whole lot of hooey. And what was this? A hanged man? Nasty. A guy with fifty swords in his back. What was that!? She flipped over a few more cards. The devil...and finally...Death! Yowzer! Not good.

Something creaked, like metal on metal. Her head jerked up, eyes wide. The pipes banged. She jumped to her feet, knocking over the table and scattering the cards. Scrambling to the floor, she gathered them with shaking hands as she listened to water rush through the pipes and thrum to life like blood in cast iron veins.

Taking deep, calming breaths as Harvest had taught her to do, she pulled out the little toxic avenger bell from her purse and rang it. A tiny silence, then the pipes banged louder. She gasped at the screech of the antediluvian taps wrenched open and shut, open and shut, just one floor above her.

She scurried to the foot of the stairs and started up the steps. Halfway up she could no longer think. Her heart drummed in her ears and her knuckles whitened on the banister.

"Thadius? Thadius honey? It's...um, Ginger. We spoke the other day at the uh, Ouija thing. I'm trying to sell your house, like you said you wanted me to—"

The pipes banged louder, water barreling through them. The wrath of the unwashed knew no bounds.

"I put an ad in the *Bugle* and all the agents in my office have buyers who are dying to get in here. Just breaking down my door. Anyhoo, at the moment I'm having an open house and it would be just great if you could not take a sponge bath right now. I mean, I'm done at four and then it's all yours after that, whaddya think—"

Bang, bang, bang, bang...

A stream of water appeared on the second floor landing, just at eye level. It nosed along, and then, as if it could see, took a right hand turn and headed for the stairs and Ginger, who started backing down the steps, never taking her eyes off the water.

"I wish I could afford a Jacuzzi for you, I know how grungy you must feel after all these years of not being able to—"

"Excuse me?" came a timid voice from the bottom of the stairs.

Ginger whipped around, saucer-eyed.

A small, dingy-haired woman with buggy eyes stood at the foot of the stairs, her small, dingy-haired, buggy-eyed husband in tow. "Are you the real estate agent?"

"Yes!" Ginger ran a trembling hand through her hair.

"When you're done with your customers up there, we have a few questions, if that's OK."

Ginger took a few stiff steps down to the foyer. "Oh! Well, we're all set, just wrapping things up."

"I'm Kay," said the woman with a clammy handshake, "and this is my husband Herb."

"I'm Ginger Kanadoo, your kana-doo realtor! Welcome to 666 Phantom Lane! Isn't this a fabulous house?" she nearly shrieked. Behind her, the stream of water dripped down stair after stair, as if aiming toward her.

"We're antique people, and I have to say, we've been admiring this house for quite some time, haven't we, Herb?"

"Hmmm," he said, hands deep in his baggy slacks.

"Let's take a look around, then," Ginger said, grabbing the woman by the arm and directing her toward the great room. "Where are you folks from?"

"East Vandersklee-on-Hudson—" She removed Ginger's hand from her arm. "We've seen the first floor already. We just wanted to have a peek at the bedrooms and so on."

But Herb was already on the stairs. "Good lord, you seem to have some sort of leak up here," he said, watching as the stream reached the first floor, took a left and headed toward Ginger.

Ginger feigned a good gasp. "Oh my goodness! Those buyers must have been checking the faucets and left them running!"

Herb headed up the stairs, with Kay and Ginger right behind him.

"I just love these stairs, don't you, Herb? The way they curve?"

"The details are stunning, aren't they?" Ginger said. "You can't find this kind of quality any more. Just look at these tin ceilings, the wainscoting, this millwork—"

Herb strolled down the hall and disappeared into the bathroom. Ginger held her breath. In a few moments he stepped out, wiping his hands on his pants. "Where did those people go?"

"The people? They probably went out by the fire escape, they said they wanted to check that out."

He just stared at her as Kay walked up and down the hallway, peeking in rooms.

"You've got yourself some real plumbing problems in this place," he said.

"I know, I've already put in a call to the seller—"

"I don't understand," Kay said, joining them. "Where are the bathrooms?"

"Well, here's a half bath right here," Ginger said, gesturing at the open door.

"Half bath? You mean there's no full bath anywhere in the house?"

"That's right!" Ginger said, smiling. "Just another quirky charm here at 666 Phantom Lane."

"Well, how did people..."

"Nothing, in my experience is more thorough than a sponge bath, haven't you found that? And no wrinkling!"

Kay and Herbert looked at each other and back at Ginger. "We need a house with bathrooms. Do you have any of those?"

⁕ ⁕ ⁕

It had been a long, sweltering afternoon with Kay and Herbert in her car when Ginger finally pulled over next to the trailer that sat at the edge of Tandy's subdivision, recently christened Daffodil Court. After showing them twenty-three houses all over Squamskootnocket, Vanderskleet, even Bangerlangersville, Ginger had a pretty good idea what sort of buyers these people were. They were the perpetual dreamer type, the type that held dear an evanescent, almost hallucinogenic fantasy of what their house would be. More than anything tangible, they were looking for a feeling, a certain flood of emotion to overtake them when they walked into the perfect house; something like rapture. They would settle for nothing less than a gauzy-lensed, bodice-ripping house, a house that would send a laser of lust through their aging boomer loins, one that featured hump-able soaring ceilings, youth-revisiting "flow," a lickable view. The search, grueling yet somehow noble, was more important than ever actually finding the house. This lofty pursuit was the Xanax of their lives; the Viagra of their Saturdays, and most certainly the Cialis of their Sundays.

And so it was, with knowing resignation, that Ginger clambered up the rolling hills of Daffodil Court, making small talk with Kay and Herbert about their Quest, about the kids-in-college and the grandbaby on the way, until the moment they crested the last hill, the one that overlooked Lake Squamskootnocket.

A moment of stillness, then Kay gasped, stumbling, and grabbed on to her husband's arm. Ginger feared a stroke and cursed her luck.

"Herbert!" she said. "Look! Just...look..."

He stood still and staring, as if struck by the same disabling awe. All their little buggy eyes did double duty as they scanned the lake, the land behind them facing the town center, and back again to the shore.

Kay's eyes were wet. "How many years, Herb? How many?"

"Dunno, honey. Eight? Ten?"

"—have we been looking for land like this, for a view like this, for a feeling like this..." She rubbed his back lasciviously; he arched back into her hand—Ginger felt a bit ill— "I...I can't even express what this means to us, Ginger—"

"Not that we'll pay full price—" Herbert interjected, spitting slightly in Ginger's eye. She blinked her eye discreetly, absorbing the sputum. For 1.8 million, she would absorb the sputum.

"Don't listen to my husband," Kay said, removing her massaging hand from his back. Chastised, his face registered the loss and he gazed at her adoringly. "He can't help himself."

"Well, I have to say, this is the premiere lot on the subdivision, in terms of size, location and proximity to the lake, and it includes beach rights." Actually, all this was true, Ginger noted with some surprise as she said it. "So all this means that if you want to put a reservation on this lot, I'd have to say the sooner the better. There's been a good deal of interest already. You don't want to be disappointed."

Kay looked with doggy eyes at Herbert.

"Can we draw up our own plans?" he asked, crossing his arms over his small round belly.

"Absolutely. Start from scratch."

"Ohmygod! Ohmygod!" Kay jumped up and down as if struck with fresh paroxysms of joy. "It's too beautiful! Can't you just see it, Herb? The master facing the lake, with French doors out onto a deck?" She ran a little bit down the hill. "The gazebo will go right here, with the Japanese garden sort of just flowing down to the beach..." As if drunk, she stumbled away from them, angling toward the sunset and the narrow strip of sand.

Herb and Ginger walked together down the sloping hill. "You'll have to forgive Kay. She gets awfully emotional sometimes."

"That's no problem. This is an emotional process!"

"I'm sure we'll want to make an offer tonight. Would that be possible?"

"I have the paperwork in my car."

Kay ran back up to them. "Honey, I want this land. The land is speaking to me! It's begging for us to live here!"

"OK, OK, we're doing it!" he said, laughing indulgently. "Ginger said she—"

"I do have one little issue, though," Kay sighed. "I was just down by the water and I noticed it was a tiny bit weedy."

Ginger's heart sank. She literally saw money flying out a window, along with her three in-arrears mortgage payments, new ripped black clothes for Harvest, the celebratory dinner out at the Vanderskleet Meat Rack...

"Have you ever noticed that, Ginger? Weeds in the lake?"

"No, not really."

The truth was, the lake started out pretty well in the spring, but by midsummer it was choked with Moribundt, a nasty Japanese import that choked the life out of it. You could practically walk on it by late August, and it remained that way until winter froze it solid. Spring rains washed away the dead weeds, bringing a few weeks of clear sailing, and the cycle began all over again...

Kay squinted back at the lake. "It's getting dark...it's so hard to tell." She raised her arms. "God, it's so beautiful here! Let's just do it, honey," she said, hugging herself. "Let's write it up tonight, but we won't have Ginger do anything with it till tomorrow. I'll come out first thing in the morning and look at the lake again, just to make sure it's not too weedy. Would that make sense, Ginger? Could we do that?"

"Of course we could," Ginger said, smiling with selected parts of her face. "That sounds like a great plan."

Chapter 26

Ginger, suited up in Harvest's hooded black sweatshirt and sweatpants, huddled at the foot of a dock where she stared up at a log cabin. Framed in a picture window, Old Man Higgins crossed back and forth, talking on the phone, stopping now and then to gesture with one hand. He looked pissed off, as usual. Harvest crept up behind her mother, then passed her and climbed up on the dock.

"For the love of God, get down from there! He can see you!" Ginger hissed.

Harvest crouched down and jumped lightly off the dock. "Well, how are we supposed to get in the boat?"

Crickets chirped, bullfrogs croaked. "Just don't stand up."

"This is insane." Harvest got down on her hands and knees and crawled along the wooden dock. Ginger sank further into the muck as she watched Harvest make her way to the end of the pier, untie a rowboat, and clamber inside. Old Man Higgins never once looked out the window.

"Mom," she whispered. "I don't want to do this. It's wrong."

"My God," Ginger said, shaking her head. "Who raised you?" Remembering, she continued. "Look, do you want to go back to your Wiccan meetings or not? If you do this for me, you can go to as many meetings as you want. Hell, start your own damned coven! And besides, we're not stealing the boat, we're borrowing the boat, remember?"

From her narrow seat, Harvest looked up at the stars and sighed, her slender shoulders stooped forward. The oars creaked as she lifted them in their locks and began rowing toward her mother onshore.

"Hurry up, honey. We have a lot of work to do!" Ginger whispered.

"This is as fast as I can row!" Harvest slapped at the water.

Ginger watched the slow progress. "I can't believe you're wearing white tonight. Have you ever worn white in your entire life?"

Harvest looked down at her white T-shirt with the skull and crossbones. "Sorry, jeez."

The bow of the boat slid into the muddy beach. As soon as Ginger put one foot in, the boat rocked wildly. "Quit it, Harv, you know I have a trick knee!"

"Mom, I'm not even moving!"

After much unsteadiness, Ginger found her center of gravity, took the oars, and pushed off. Lake Squamskootnocket stretched out before them, a vast blackness bordered by the tall pines of Vanderskleet to the west, and the cleared, rolling hills of Tandy's subdivision to the south, a good half mile away. Ginger glanced behind her at Old Man Higgins's log cabin which peered out from a tiny spit of land that jutted into the lake.

"I'll row for a while and then you can take over. How's that for a plan, Harv?" Ginger said, chopping hard into the water.

"You're the boss," said the white T-shirt against the black sky. A triangle of pouty pale face showed between the curtains of dark hair. The night air was cooled only by the wet breath of the fishy lake. Every stroke of the oars brought up a healthy serving of weeds, then dropped them back down again. Black flies buzzed around their ears.

"This is kind of nice, rowing a boat with my daughter," Ginger said. "It's like quality time together, don't you think?"

"Yeah, it's great," Harvest said, shivering, "stealing someone else's property—"

"—borrowing—"

"—so we can do what? Clean out the lake? I still don't get it."

Ginger pictured the offer she had written just hours previous, full price with no contingencies, a squeaky clean pre-approval letter for one p-p-p-point eight million dollars, with a flexible close and fat good-faith check. A more comely offer she could not imagine, and there it was, waiting in the back of her car to present to Tandy first thing in the morning—but only if this pesky weed problem was taken care of...

"Like I told you before, there's an offer on the table for some new construction, but they don't like the weeds," Ginger said, beginning to huff, "so we're going to clear out as much as we can tonight."

"Sounds retarded."

"A commission on one point eight million dollars is not retarded, Harv."

"So you're not going to tell them that this lake is always weedy? That it has that Japanese mutant plant in it that no one's ever been able to get rid of for like twenty years and that it's even cut off the natural spring that feeds it?"

"No! Duh!"

"You know what, Mom? You have no moral compass."

Ginger rowed a bit more, pausing to smack a mosquito on her arm. "Is that bad?"

"Yes, it's bad! You're supposed to tell people the truth!"

"Look, Harv, there's all different levels of truth. You're a little too young to understand all the subtle kinds of truth there are out there, like white lies, or—"

"You're not supposed to lie! It's pretty simple!"

"What, you see a friend wearing an ugly dress and you say, wow, that's one ugly-ass dress?! Is that what you say?"

"No, I just don't talk about the dress—"

"Exactly what I'm saying. Sin of omission."

"Mom, this isn't what a good realtor would do. A good realtor would tell the t—"

"Oh, so now I'm not a good realtor? Me? The woman who, even as she was eight centimeters dilated with YOU, was still showing houses—"

"So what? You almost gave birth to me on some 'gleaming hardwood floor' somewhere? Am I supposed to be proud of that? And that makes you a good realtor?"

"That's pretty damned dedicated, I'd say! Giving birth on the job!"

Harvest shook her head. "If I were a realtor, I'd be an honest one."

"You sound like me thirty-five years ago."

"I'd make a great realtor, though I'd rather be dead than be one."

"OK," Ginger said, hauling up the oars one last time and resting them in the locks, "we can start right about here."

"But we're nowhere near the land!"

"Think: view, OK? We need to clean up *the view*. That crazy bitch has to traipse down here tomorrow morning and think: looks great, no weeds! Where do I sign? So we start here, then work toward the shore."

"But we'll be out here all night!"

"I brought snacks, and look," —she pulled a bottle of Korbel champagne from her bag— "we can toast the stars!"

Harvest rolled her eyes and looked away.

"OK, kid, let's get haulin'." Ginger put the booze away and plunged her hands into the water. She pulled up a good yard of slimy green weeds, spotted with black pods, and flung them into the center of the boat. They made a wet, squelching sound.

"Gross." Harvest reached down tentatively into the velvety dark of the lake.

"Actually, in some cultures, people eat this stuff." Ginger slapped another handful of yech into the pile. "Dutch people, I believe."

"Japanese, Mom, and it's not all edible. Some of it is poisonous." With two fingers she held up a long strand which she let fall with a little plop amongst its brothers and sisters in the belly of the boat.

"Well, I'm not asking you to eat it, dear. But you might want to use both hands, or we're never going to get anywhere."

But after only about a half hour's work, the boat began to fill. After an hour, the pile they had created in the middle of the boat began to flatten out, oozing toward their feet. Soon, no matter how much scooching over they did, the weeds began reaching out for their ankles and legs.

"Mom, this is enough, right?"

"I don't think so, dear."

"But it's all...touching me."

"As soon as we fill the boat we'll go ashore and dump it and come back out again for more."

Harvest made a pitiful whimpering sound but kept at her work. Soon, the sludge had reached the oarlocks and the tops of their knees. Every time they moved, a sea of green oozed around them, and they could no longer ignore the festering odor hovering above the pile of swill.

"Mom, I have to stop. I'm going to throw up."

"Somebody doesn't want to be Wiccan."

"I mean it."

"Squamskootnocket Lake awaits your generous offering. Though I must admit," she added, lifting a slimed sneaker out of the morass, "it smells like payday at a whorehouse in this godforsaken tub—"

"Mom!"

A shot echoed off the lake and up into the hills.

"What was—"

"Harvey, get down!" Ginger yelled, sinking into the pit of ooze until just her head and shoulders bobbed above it in the moonlight.

Another shot skimmed the water close to the boat with a high-pitched whiffling sound.

"Mom, somebody's shooting at us!" Harvest sat frozen in her seat.

"Yes, my little Mensa. Now slide your ass down into the boat!"

"I can't!" she said, eyes squeezed shut, arms straight down at her sides.

Ginger reached deep in the nightmarish bog, searching everywhere for her daughter's Skechers. The moment she felt one, she grabbed it and yanked. Harvest slid like an eel down into the muck, tears gathering in her eyes.

"Who's shooting at us, Mommy?" Her hair melted into the goo.

Ginger poked her head a few inches over the bow of the boat. A shot pinged off the edge of the metal stern. She cursed, dropped her head, and raised it again. On the moonlit shore, the silhouette of a stringy figure jumped about like a coked-out puppet, a hunting rifle in one hand.

"It's Old Man Higgins," she whispered. "He's going to kill us for his yacht here. Stupid fucker."

"Oh my God!"

"We might want to think about swimming home."

"You know I can't swim!"

"Oh, yeah. So that won't work."

The shots kept coming, skimming the surface near them or flying over their heads into the starlit sky.

"The good news is, he's not a very good shot."

Harvest cried soundlessly, her tears falling into the gluey mass at her shoulders.

"I guess this is where we could use a spell or two, my friend," Ginger said.

"I don't know any s-s-spells for th-th-this. What if he c-c-calls the c-cops? We could get arrested!"

"Don't worry about that. He is the cops, in his mind."

"So what do we do now?"

Ginger wiped mud off her forehead. "Guess we'll be here a while, in hangout mode. Good way to bond with each other. Think of it as a mother-daughter camping trip. Or like something we can look back at and laugh about later, or you can pass along to your kids someday." She picked up a handful of green muck. "Hey, this stuff we're sitting in could have exotic powers of regeneration, you know, like that beauty mud they have in France."

Harvest made strange guttural noises.

"Actually, now that I have you here, I'd like to revisit your idea of becoming a realtor. I think you'd be perfect."

"I never said I wanted to be a real—" Harvest said, her voice rising into a shriek as a shot ricocheted off the oarlock.

"You might want to keep your voice down, honey. Anyway, since you don't show any signs of wanting to get a normal job, real estate might be perfect for you. You've seen all the perks I've enjoyed over the years: drinking as much as I want, sleeping late, getting a perm when everyone else is at work—"

"—waiting forever to get paid, buyers getting cold feet, title problems, conservation issues, sellers who want the moon—"

"—see, you know a lot about real estate already, just from me! I don't think you know what you're missing!"

"Mom, I want you look at me. Do you see me?"

"Yes, I do, honey, clear as a bell in this moonlight. In fact, you're kind of like a bullseye with that shirt of yours."

"Read my lips, then. I will never, ever in a million years ever, ever sell real estate. I would rather shove hot coals in my eyes than do what you do."

"But honey, except for this honesty fixation you have, you'd be so good at it! You're a natural! You get yourself a nice haircut and some presentable clothes, hell, you could be Squamskootnocket's next big thing!"

"I don't want to change my clothes or my hair—this is who I am!" Harvest lifted her arms from the muck and brought her fists down with a loud plop.

"OK, then, how do you intend to support yourself? Because, honey, I don't want to scare you, but things aren't going so well for us in the cash department."

"...How bad is it?"

"It's bad. We need this sale tomorrow, or, well, it's bad. Use that fine Wiccan imagination of yours."

"I've started selling spells online," she said in a small voice.

Ginger peered over the lip of the boat at the shore. He'd stopped shooting, but had taken up residence on a rock outcropping. He sat still, as if carved from it, his shotgun pointing up into the night.

"And how's that going?"

"Pretty good. I sold a love spell last week for fifteen dollars. I'm waiting for the check in the mail. I thought you'd be proud of me."

"I'm always proud of you, honey. But you might want to think about upping your prices."

"But I'm new at this."

"People don't know that."

Harvest dared a look at the shore. "Can we go in now? Is he gone?"

"Hate to say this, but you might want to get comfortable where you are—"

Harvest lurched forward with a giant sucking sound. "I'm not staying here one more minute!"

Ginger gently pressed her back into her seat. "Darling, I'm afraid you are. Now, let me see if I can remember one of those bedtime stories I used to tell you. Oh, yeah. Once upon a time, when the radon came in fifteen points higher than the EPA standards, and there was an undisclosed oil tank buried on the property, and the buyer broke her leg on a rotten step during the walk-through, your Mom had to spring into some serious action..."

⁕ ⁕ ⁕

In her dream, Ginger sat in a rowboat buried under hundreds of pounds of heavy, wet vines. She couldn't move anything south of her shoulders. Something buzzed around her forehead, landed, and bit her.

She opened her eyes and took note that the nightmare equaled reality, blow for blow. With a groan, she called on all her strength to break through the sunbaked sea of goo and free one hand to slap at the thing still munching on her face, waking Harvest who opened her eyes and screamed, "Help!!" Her eyes liquid fear. "Get me out of here!"

Ginger looked around. It was morning. They had drifted all the way across the lake to Tandy's land, and were bumping up against the sandy shore. Old Man Higgins was nowhere to be seen.

With a cracking sound, Ginger turned her body, breaking the patina of mossy creme brulee that surrounded her. Monstrously, her other hand emerged from the muck and reached for purchase. Once she'd gotten a grip on the side of the boat she was able to heave her body up to a standing position, instantly hunkering back down as the wee craft rocked wildly in the shallow water. Almost delicately, she crab-stepped out into the bathwater-warm lake and strolled over to the stern where she put a fist through Harvest's murky cocoon, then helped extricate her from the boat.

Harvest whimpered. Shivering, she weakly splashed herself in the knee-deep water.

"Well," Ginger said, stretching, "I slept pretty good. How about you, honey?"

"How did I sleep?? I didn't!"

"Really? I thought it was rather nice. A night under the stars, feeling as one with nature, catching up with my daughter—"

"Mom, it was hell!! Now get me out of here!"

"All right a'ready, Miss Priss Britches! We're on our way. Lucky thing the car is only about a mile away and then we're as good as home!"

Harvest waded out of the lake and stumbled up onshore. "A mile away..."

"What's a mile? Good for us. Nice bracing walk at dawn never hurt anybody."

"But we're covered with—"

"We're a little ripe, yes, but—"

"What are you so cheerful for, anyway?"

"I don't know. I guess I have a real positive feeling today about this deal. I mean look at all the crap we pulled out of the lake last night." They both turned to the rowboat full of gnarled squelch, then beyond to the lake full of same. "It's amazing what a little teamwork will do. As for me, I'm looking forward to some good news back at the office," she said, wringing out her sweatshirt. "I'm so excited, honey. You have no idea what this will mean for us..."

But Harvest had already started walking down the shoreline and toward the access road to the highway.

* * *

By the time they reached Ginger's car, the sun had burned the dew off the grass and was beating down on their heads. Their clothes had baked into stiff olive planes and a dusky green scum clung to their skin. Harvest's hair was green from her shoulders down. She hadn't said a word since they'd gotten out of the boat, and faced away from her mother as she sat in the car.

"I hope you don't mind, honey," Ginger said, firing up the jalopy. "I need to stop by the office on the way home. Very important call to make. Life-changing call. *The* call."

"I want to go home," Harvest said in a dangerous, even tone.

"Well, so do I, hon, but this is important. This call is what last night was all about. What'll make it all worthwhile."

"Take me home, then make the call."

"No can do. You're gonna have to sit tight. I'll take you out for breakfast!" she said brightly.

"Mom, I smell like a dead animal."

"Aw, nobody'll notice." She cruised down Main Street, past the *Bugle*, past the Pit, summer's hot breath shellacking their skin, until they reached Kanadoo Realty's small lot. Ginger parked next to Dickie's car.

"Want to come in and say 'hi' to your Uncle Dickie?"

Harvest stared straight ahead, arms folded.

"I'll take that as a no. Look, I'll just be a minute. Then we can go out for some cinnamon buns at the Pit. See your wikky buddy Sheena."

Chapter 27

Dickie sat at his desk, deep in paperwork. Ginger popped her head in his door.

"Hey, bro, any calls? I'm expecting a verrrry important call this morning—"

He looked up, taking in the sight of her. "No calls. What the hell happened to you?"

She held up a chastening hand. "Just doing a bit of civic duty, a little volunteer work down at the lake. Doing my bit for the environment, you know—"

"Never mind," he said, returning to his work. "Sorry I asked."

Ginger passed Tandy's desk on her way to her own. An issue of *Real Estate Millionaire* peeked out from Tandy's bag. Glancing around for further evidence of Tandy and finding none, Ginger pulled out the magazine. On the cover was a glossy photo of what looked like hundreds of loaves of bread piled into the back of a BMW. The headline read: "Bread Makes Bread: California Realtor Makes Millions Giving Away a Thousand Loaves of Banana Bread!" A Tandy clone with a megawatt smile and crazed eyes held up a loaf of bread in either hand, her backseat brimming with Sold signs.

Ginger opened up to the article and read:

> Geraldine Bixley's real estate career had gone into what felt like permanent 'pause' mode. There was barely enough to supplement her husband's paycheck, never mind take their two kids to Disneyland. She was stymied. She'd tried everything: direct mail, email blasts, attending every town hall meeting religiously, even teaching real estate classes at the local vo-tech high school. Nothing seemed to kickstart her stalled career.
>
> Then one day, her husband Bob, over morning coffee and Geraldine's specialty—banana bread—spoke up. "Hey, honey, what about making a few loaves of your great bread here and taking it to some neighbors, just to introduce yourself?" Geraldine thought the idea was a bit too low tech, but because she had some time, took him up on it, and baked a few loaves for her favorite neighbors, "just because."
>
> The response was overwhelming. Not only did the neighbors love the bread and clamor for the recipe, a few of them decided to list with her that spring, and the rest referred her business!
>
> Encouraged, Geraldine decided she'd bake banana bread for the whole street. Result over the next year: four listings, two sales. Geraldine thought: if one street works, why not the whole town?
>
> This time, her entire family got into the act. Little Timmy looked online and found a place to get the bananas wholesale, while older sister Suzy found a local baker to make the thousand loaves of banana bread. Husband Bob hired a driver to distribute them all over town to every single resident of Backwash, Texas. The result: Geraldine Bixley is now the top broker in Backwash, with two full-time staff and enough income for TWO trips a year to Disneyland!

Ginger slipped the magazine back into Tandy's bag and strolled nonchalantly to her desk, leaving a trail of dried green scum as she went. She stared at her phone. It sat dumbly, like a dead thing. The red light was not lit and blinking. It was ten o'clock in the morning.

She reached for the phone, her sleeve crackling. Her hand hovered there, shaking, then dropped. The answer had to be yes. It simply had to be, or it was over. She was through. They were through. Her bank account was in the negative numbers. Her utilities were about to be shut off. She had the food in her cupboards and no more. Their eviction date had been set for the third week of August. She thought of Carl Kanadoo, and how she had disappointed him, and squeezed her eyes shut, forcing the image from her mind.

She picked up the phone and listened; the dial tone purred low and heavy. She pulled out the listing sheet for 666 Phantom Lane where she'd scrawled the number for Kay and Herbert the day before, and dialed.

"Kay?" she said, stuffing a smile into her voice like frosting in a pastry bag. "Good morning! This is Ginger!"

"Who are...oh yes, Ginger! How are you?"

"I'm doing just great. Such a beautiful day, isn't it?"

"Yes, it is. I'm sorry. I was going to call you, but Herbert and I got a little tied up..."

"Oh. Well, I was just wondering if you'd had a chance to visit our lovely Lake Squamskootnocket this morning."

Pained sigh. "I did have a chance, as a matter of fact, and I hate to say this, but I'm afraid we're a little less excited about that lot today. I mean, Herbert's still gung ho about it, but he never wears his glasses, and I thought it was just a bit too weedy for my taste."

"Oh, but there are a number of other lots, many of them with no view of the lake at all, but with the same char—"

"I'm sure there are, but after I got a better view of the lake, well, it just took the whole feeling out of us wanting to live in Squamskootnocket. It's sort of hard to explain. Anyway, we heard there were some lots available in Bangerlangersville and we're going to—"

"I could take you there today! I—"

"I'm sorry, Ginger, my sister is a broker up there and we're going to use her, I think."

"But—Bangerlangersville—it just doesn't have the—I don't know, the charm that Squamskootnocket has. The old gummy bear factory, the Coffee Pit, Shapes, the—"

"You're right, you're right. The town doesn't have half the appeal, but setting is everything to us and there is the Bangerlangersville Gorge—"

"Oh, that. Lovely spot, though the occasional distraught Bangerlangersvillian has been known to take the plunge now and then—"

"What? Well, Herbert's calling me, so I have to get going—"

"All righty, then, it does sound like you've made your decision." She struggled to keep the smile wrapped around her voice. "If anything changes, you know I'm here for you!"

"Yes. Well. Thanks so much for your help. Goodbye."

"Goodbye and good luck!" Ginger said, dropping the phone back onto its cradle.

For almost a minute, Ginger stared at the phone. Its blackness, its silence, its oneness with itself. She was frozen in space, gripping the back of her chair with white knuckles.

A strident, high-pitched laugh snapped her out of it. Tandy was on her cell phone in the conference room, pacing and looking out at Main Street.

Never taking her eyes off Tandy, Ginger snatched the magazine from her bag and sprinted out of the office into the sweltering heat. Harvest sat like a green statue in her seat; head back, eyes closed.

Ginger started the car, jammed it into reverse and lurched out of the lot, hooking a right back onto Main Street. Harvest braced herself against the dashboard.

"OK, this isn't the way home," Harvest said.

"What I want to know is, what is the big damned deal about Bangerlangersville Gorge versus our very own Lake Squamskootnocket? Huh? Can you tell me that, Harvest?"

"Well, Lake Squamskootnocket sucks, and Bangerlangersville Gorge is beautiful and there's gift shops and rides and stuff and people drive for hundreds of miles to see it."

"And?" Ginger said, laying rubber as she screeched into the left-hand turning lane.

"Why aren't we going home? Where are you taking me?"

"We're going shopping for Squamskootnocket Day. Lots to do to get ready. Thought you'd like to come."

"Yes, but can't we take a shower—"

"Look, we're here!" Ginger said cheerfully, careening into the lot for the Dollar Saver. Mothers in badly fitting shorts with clots of snot-nosed children loaded family-sized cartons of food into trunks. "Wanna come in?"

"Not unless you hose me down first." She promptly slid down again in her seat and closed her eyes.

⁂ ⁂ ⁂

Ginger garnered surprisingly few looks as she headed straight to the fruit and vegetable section. She arrived at the normally overflowing banana bin and gasped. Just three beat-up bananas lay on their sides on the fake grass, upside down as if they were all in a pout. A lanky teenager strolled by with a cart of romaine.

"Hey, Zach," Ginger said.

"Oh, hi, Mrs. Kanadoo," he said, looking her over. "What happened to you?"

"Oh...just doing some gardening and had this sudden urge to make a thousand loaves of banana bread. You know how it is." She gestured at the three lone bananas. "Is there anything else in the back, ya think?"

"I think so. Lemme go check." His eyebrows met in concern as he stared at her a moment longer. Then he turned, disappearing through the produce department's swinging doors. He returned in a minute or two, wiping his hands on a rag. "There's bananas back there—two cases of them—but they're all a mess. All bruised and stuff."

"That sounds fine. I'll take them."

"You sure, Mrs. Kanadoo? I mean they're all nasty and—"

"I said I'll take them, dear. Now, can you go get them for me?"

"Sure, right away. I'll meet you by the registers."

Ginger filled her basket with six dozen eggs, eight pounds of butter, several bags of flour and sugar and multiple gallons of milk, then rushed to join the two crates of bananas which sat waiting for her under a cloud of fruit flies at the checkout counter. A small man with a pinched face looked up at her and over at the bananas.

"I'll charge you five bucks a crate for those. How's that sound, ma'am?"

"Sounds quite generous. Thank you."

He scanned the rest of her items, took her credit card and ran it through his machine, then handed it back to her.

"Denied," he said, not without a note of satisfaction.

"Oh, dear me," Ginger tittered. She returned the card to her wallet and fished out another. "Never could keep up with that one. Give this one a shot."

He swiped it. "Denied. Miss."

"Whoops!" She reddened under the patina of green on her chest. "Here's my last one. Third time's a charm."

The line behind her was growing—an elderly woman holding tight to a bag of grapes and a lottery ticket, a family with four kids crawling over a cart full of diapers and cereal.

He ran it through and handed it back to her. "It's not your day. Sorry."

"Just try that one...one more time. I just used it down the street, I know it's fine..."

Scowling, he ran it through and handed it back to her.

"But I—"

He picked up the intercom. "Zach, I need you at the register."

Ginger squeezed her eyes shut. Her entire life had led her here to this moment: dipped in lake swill and begging for a crate of rotten bananas. Good God, how did she get here?

She forced her eyes open. "Why don't you just let me take the bananas off your hands?" Ginger whispered under her breath. "You were going to throw them away anyway—"

He looked up at her and said in an unnecessarily loud voice, "I don't give away food, ma'am. Never have, never will."

"I'm not asking you to give it away," she hissed. Zach showed up and tossed his boss a questioning look. He gestured at Zach to take the food off the counter and put it back in the cart. "I mean, what difference does it make if you throw it away or if you give it to me?"

The old woman put her bag of grapes on the counter and held a five dollar bill out to the cashier. He took it and rang up her lottery ticket and the grapes, putting them in yet another bag.

"Look, I don't care if you've got a pack of starving baboons out in your car, lady. The bananas stay here." Avoiding Ginger's eye, Zach picked up the cases of bananas and headed to the back of the store.

Ginger squared her shoulders and stalked out of the store straight to her car.

She leaned in the window. "Hey, Harvey, got any money?"

Harvest opened one eye. "Why would I have any money?"

Ginger got in and started up the car.

"Where are we going now?"

"Just hang on tight, little lady. I've got something I need to pick up at the back of this place."

Harvest pushed herself up to a sitting position as they drove down a gravel drive to the back of the store and a loading platform piled high with crates of fruits and vegetables. Ginger put the car in neutral and jumped out, then poked her head back in the window.

"Can you give me a hand?"

Harvest reached for the door handle, then looked out at her mother, narrowing her eyes. "Why are we picking stuff up in the back?"

Ginger shrugged. "Buying a lot of bananas. Said they were in the back and to just swing around and pick 'em up."

Harvest got out and slammed her door. A chunk of rust fell from the handle. She followed her mother to the loading dock where Ginger struggled to pull down one of the crates.

"What are we going to do with all these bananas?" she said, hands on hips.

Ginger glanced around, then heaved the crate into her daughter's arms. "Take bananas now, ask questions later."

Harvest held the crate in her arms, gnats buzzing around her face. "Did you pay for these?"

Ginger threw her arms in the air. "Did I pay for these? Did I pay for these? Is that what you're asking me?"

"Mm hmm."

"Of course I paid for these. Now move it."

Shaking her head, Harvest loaded the two crates of bananas into the trunk and resettled herself sullenly in her seat. In an unholy alliance, the odor of rotting banana conjoined with the swampy stench of Lake Squamskootnocket, creating a yellowish toxic cloud around their car.

"So now will you tell me why we have two crates of crappy bananas in our car?"

Ginger tossed her the magazine. Harvest read the article, groaning.

"Oh, Mom, this isn't going to work!"

"And what is going to work, honey? You tell me! I'm all ears!" She glanced at her fuel tank: a hair away from empty. "We're going to make enough banana bread for all of Squamskootnocket for Squamskootnocket Day, and you're going to help! Or are you too big for your britches to help out your mom in an emergency? Harvest, I hate to say this, but we are in big, big trouble."

"We are?"

"See this gas gauge? Let me say this: we better be home by the time it's empty, because I don't have a dime for gas."

Harvest looked at her with wide eyes.

"So we have to be ready for Sunday, OK? Sunday is it for us. Now, are you with me?"

"Don't we need, like five hundred eggs and twenty pounds of flour, and all of that?"

"We sure do. Which is why we're going to give your Auntie Max a call as soon as we get home."

"Don't we owe her a lot of—"

"She's your Auntie Max. She'll come through."

Chapter 28

It was just past eight in the morning on another blasting hot, middle-of-July day. Crickets were already whining in the long grasses of Daffodil Court, while the one traffic light in town cycled through green, yellow, red as the few and the polite made their way to various commitments or occupations. In the high school gym, sweat gathered on the brow of Sheena Dolphin Child Horatzberg as she pored over the multiple choice questions on her cosmetology exam. Blocking on lipstick colors, she chewed at her pencil and called to her goddesses for answers. Not half a block away, Frankie went to open Shapes for the day but stopped short with her key in midair as she read the sign: "Closed: Rent Past Due." Brian, still in his pajamas, stood at his screen door as he opened the final letter from the twenty schools he'd applied to, the last one to turn him down. Harvest, as she cracked the hundredth egg of the morning into a mammoth bowl, swore to herself she would never email Shelley again.

At that moment, Jim Steele drove down Ginger's street as he had every day for thirty-five years, and just like every day for thirty-five years, he slowed a bit just before he reached her bungalow so he could rest his eyes there a few moments before picking up speed and finally making his way to the *Bugle*.

But this time, he didn't speed up. He turned into her unpaved drive and stared.

There, parked on the lawn at a jaunty angle, was Ginger's baby-poop colored 1966 Pontiac with a For Sale sign taped to the window. Jim got out of his car and walked around it, admiring it for all the years it had held Ginger in its cracked leather seats. He turned and headed up the walk.

Harvest was the first at the door, wiping her hands on a towel. "Mom, Mr. Steele is here!"

"Call me Jim, Harvest," he said, leaning in slightly, his arms folded across his short-sleeved checked shirt.

"Mom, Jim is here!"

Max gave Ginger a look as she plunged a spoon into a giant bowl of batter. "Your boyfriend's here," she said, stirring the mixture ineffectually and staring into space. A fat black fly circled her head, too dazed with the heat to land.

"Oh, shush," Ginger said. "I don't need any damned boyfriends right now." Her face dripped with sweat as she pulled loaves of banana bread out of the oven and set them on racks on the dining room table. The floor was covered with bread; only a narrow path of carpet remained. Banana bread crammed every corner, lined every windowsill, and marched in threes up the stairs and out of sight. Harvest, otherworldly white under a patina of flour, returned to her post at the sink where she reached in with her hands to smush a vat of bananas.

"Mom, he's—"

"I know, I'm coming," Ginger said, rushing past her and tossing down a ratty pair of potholders.

"Come in, come in," she said, holding the screen door open.

"I didn't mean to disturb you, Gin." He took a tentative step into the living room. His face lit up. "It smells wonderful in here. I didn't know you could bake."

"I can't, but Harvey can, thank God. We've got a little banana bread project going for Squamskootnocket Day tomorrow. Here, take one," she said, reaching for a loaf on the stairs.

"Take three," Max said from the other room.

"Oh, no, one is plenty! One is great! I can't remember the last time I had homemade banana bread. The guys at the *Bugle* are gonna love this—"

"So, what brings you here this fine morning, Jim?"

"Well, I confess, I was driving by and couldn't help noticing your car was for sale. 'Bout time you got rid of that old heap. It's great that you're finally upgrading—you must be doing OK?"

"Uh...Jim?" Ginger glanced back at the kitchen. "Why don't you and I step outside a sec? It's kinda stuffy in here."

They walked out to the yard in silence, the air around them heavy with banana.

"The thing is, Jim, I'm not exactly upgrading. You could almost say I'm downsizing. A bit. It's like a lateral move, only with a downward slant. Hard to explain."

"I guess I don't understand, Gin. I—I'm sorry."

"I'm selling the car cause I need the cash, to put it bluntly," she said, not meeting his eye.

"But Gin, how will you...get around? Sell houses?"

"Now, there's a question with an answer shrouded in mystery, at the moment. You know, I've got a lot going on. I've got listings—"

"I know. I see the signs—"

"I've got buyers banging down my door, but I just don't have the liquidity right now to...to...buy a pack of Wrigley's."

"Oh, Gin, why didn't you tell me? I can lend you some—"

Ginger put up her hand. "I just couldn't, Jim. I can't add one more person to the list of people in this town I owe money to." Actually, it never occurred to her to borrow from Jim. Hmm.

"Don't be foolish. I know you're good for it, Gin! How much do you need?"

Ginger looked good and hard at Jim, and it hit her that he really was in love with her. She'd been hearing it for years and never really believed it or even paid attention to it, but finally, watching him shuffle the banana bread to his other hand so he could fish out his wallet from his back pocket, she got it. She also got that she didn't feel the same, and probably never would, but at the same time hadn't given herself the chance to feel anything for any man since Carl died, and had let her life become all about work and raising Harvest, and nothing else. And as she watched him reach for a clump of bills in his wallet—all the bills, in fact—she thought: how must I look to him? Sort of frumpy and dumpy and thick through the middle, hair frizzed out to a ball in the heat, covered with banana goo as well as the traces of rankness from her dabblings in Lake Squamskootnocket the day before. She shifted uncomfortably in her slippers and sweat pants on her beat up lawn, trying to remember the last time she had sex and having no luck at all, just not a dram of memory re: that, and how she could probably tap into this Jim thing indefinitely if she wanted to, since he lived alone and had no kids and probably had a good chunk of savings by now...

"Here, Gin, take it. And I can get more this afternoon..."

She stuffed her hands in her pockets. "No, I can't take that. But I thank you, Jim. I do."

"But Gin, we're friends, aren't we? All these years..."

"We are friends. And Jim, I have a car to sell, if you're interested."

He shook his head and put his money away. "Ginger Kanadoo, you are something." He walked around the car, peered inside, kicked a tire, opened it up, and got in. "Can I take it for a spin?"

Smiling, she handed him the keys. He disappeared around the block and was back in under a minute.

"I'll give you five hundred for it."

"It's not worth two fifty."

"It is to me."

"I don't feel right—"

"I want the damned car, Gin. I'll pick it up in the morning. So take the sign off and put her in the garage. I don't want anybody else buying it out from under me." He patted the dashboard. "I'll put some work into'er and she'll run like a dream."

* * *

The next morning, Ginger woke to the sound of a motor revving outside her window.

"Goddamned Harley assholes!" She rolled over and jammed a pillow over her head. But soon the motor sound was replaced by a rapping at her door which wouldn't go away. Finally, Ginger got up and looked out her window.

Someone sat in her driveway on a vintage Vespa with a sidecar. Ginger ran downstairs and opened the door. "May I help you?"

The man took his helmet off and smiled. It was Jim.

"I couldn't leave you without wheels," he said, getting off the bike. "It's old but it runs down the road." He held the bike out to her. "Look, I put your plates on the back." The plates, which read K-DOO RLTY, were wired on to the wheel rim.

Ginger ran her hand over the bottle green metal. "I've always wanted one of these. Damn, it's sporty!"

Jim stood grinning as she started it up. Belches of yellow smoke billowed out but the motor caught and she got on in her robe and slippers.

"It's a '66, just like your car."

"Sweet," she said, revving the tiny motor. "With the side-car for Maxie and everything."

"I was thinking more for taking Harvest around town, but, whatever you like."

"I mean, sure, it'll get a bit nippy by September but I'll bundle up, and look, there's first gear for the snow..."

"Oh, you'll be into something better by then, Gin."

Ginger sighed and got off the bike. "I just can't pay you for it now, Jim, is the problem. As I said I'm very low on—"

He held up his hands. "No, no, it's a gift. A temporary gift if you like, a loaner, till you get back on your feet."

"Thanks, Jim. This is, well, I just don't know what to say—"

"Hey, what are friends for?" He handed her a check for five hundred dollars, then fingered a wad of bills in his wallet.

"Are you sure you won't let me just lend you some money and you can hold on to your car—"

"Nope, I can't do that. You're driving away with the ole K-doo roadster this very morning."

"Come on, Gin, you need this—"

She held out the car keys and tinkled them together. Reluctantly, he took them and got in.

"See you later?" he said. "At the fair?"

"With bells on," she said, waving as he drove away.

Chapter 29

Ginger, behelmeted, with Harvest hunkered down in the sidecar, putt-putted under the street-wide "Squamskootnocket Day" banner at the entrance to the town common. She waved like the queen to the local farmers and their vegetables, the basket weaver at the basket weaving booth, the olde English metalsmith as he banged away at an orange-hot piece of iron, the quilt lady surrounded by her comforters and potholders, handbags and crocheted vests. Many sweated under colonial attire, especially those working the booths, but most visitors wore shorts and sundresses. Ginger was decked out in a short-sleeved tangerine pants suit covered with buttons that read, "Realtors Are People Too," "Kiss Me I'm a Realtor," and "Hug a Realtor Today."

Harvest, in a black sundress, cowered as more and more people recognized them first, gave them odd looks second. "Mom, get me out of this thing, now."

"We're almost at the booth, honey. Now keep smiling."

Harvest dipped her head low, her hair cascading over her face. Soon they pulled up to the Realtor Appreciation Booth, which was just a table spilling over with loaves of banana bread. Maxie sat behind it under a wide-brimmed hat, smoking a cigarette and sipping at something from a thermos.

She got to her feet when she saw them pull up. "I thought you'd never get here! I'm bored shitless!"

Ginger and Harvest de-biked.

Maxie tossed away her cigarette and made her way around the booth to gape at the new set of wheels. "What in the world...?"

"Jim gave it to me, or loaned it to me. Is she beautiful or what?" Ginger stroked the cracked leather seat.

Max shook her head. "You've gotta sell some houses, my friend."

"Don't I know it. How's the bread going over?"

"Everybody's at the war thing, so I don't know. That should break up soon though."

On a grassy field in the middle of the fair, American soldiers in colonial gear fired muskets at Native Americans who scattered, howling, into a thicket of bushes. In a moment they emerged, firing bows with suction-cupped arrows at the soldiers, who feigned an occasional over the top death, but in the end it was the Native Americans who all caught the bad end of a musket. They lay on the ground a few seconds, then got up, brushed themselves off, and headed toward the barbeque pit, laughing and talking with the soldiers.

Three of the soldiers broke off from the group and headed toward Ginger's booth. Two were heavy set. One was thin and nervous looking, his tights hanging off his scrawny thighs.

"Holy crap, it's Old Man Higgins. Hide me!" Ginger cowered next to a mountain of bread.

"Just be cool, Gin, just be cool," Max said from behind her shades.

Ginger recognized the other soldiers by their gait: her rotund brother Dickie under his three-cornered hat, and Jim, with his slightly pigeon-toed walk.

"Hey, Gin," Dickie said, approaching the booth. "How's business?"

"Great! Lotta interest in all my listings. It's been crazy!"

"Yeah, 'cept for my listing," Old Man Higgins said, waving his musket. "Not a whole lotta interest there. More like zero! Nuthin'!"

"Hey, it's in the *Bugle* again this week," Jim interjected. "It'll happen."

"I don't know how you're sellin' my place with banana bread, is all I can say," he said, arms folded over his tight ball of a stomach.

"Here, have some." Maxie handed him a loaf.

"Ya tryin' ta kill me? I'm allergic to bananas."

"I just hope you're ready for this afternoon's announcement," Dickie said, eyeing Ginger.

"I'm always ready for the Realtor of the Year Award announcement, Dickie." Ginger beamed.

He gave her a dark look. "I'll be making it in a couple of minutes." He broke off the end of a loaf and stuffed it in his mouth.

"I'll be right here."

Dickie and Old Man Higgins wandered away together toward the blacksmithing booth, but Jim held back.

"Allergic to bananas," Max muttered. "Nobody's allergic to bananas."

"He's an ass," Ginger said. "Hasn't he ever heard of the bubble? Jeez!"

"Hey, look," Jim said. "I just wanted to apologize for being a soldier again this year."

"What are you talking about?" Ginger fussed over the rows of bread.

"Well, I'm sure it's a problem for you, you know, you being a descendant of the proud Kanadoo tribe and all."

"Hey, it was an important battle they re-enacted. Or that's what everyone says, anyway."

"You're right," Jim said, "if it weren't for that battle, this town would probably have been called Kanadoo, instead of Squamskootnocket—"

"Which is an old Indian word for...what's it an old Indian word for, again?"

"It means 'hideous death of a thousand innocents,' I think."

"That's it. I always forget."

"Anyway, it's practically a celebration of how your ancestors got killed and stuff." He shifted his musket over to his other shoulder. "And that's not right."

Ginger sighed. "That's OK. In life, some of us get slaughtered, and some of us go on to eat turkey. It's kind of a crapshoot."

"Still, next year I'm gonna be a Kanadoo Indian."

"Well, thanks, Jim, I appreciate—"

Feedback shrieked from a mic on the back of a pickup truck. Dickie, still in full citizen soldier regalia, stood in the bed of the truck, a beer in one hand and mic in the other.

"Hello and good morning! I want to welcome all of you to the tenth annual Squamskootnocket Day! What a great turn-out!"

A tepid spatter of clapping, a couple of catcalls.

"We've all got a lot of booths to visit and a lot of old friends to catch up with, but I wanted to announce the lucky winners of our yearly awards."

A few people gathered closer to the truck.

"The first award goes to the Journalist of the Year, and this year it goes to...Jim Steele!"

Jim broke away from Ginger and stepped through the crowd. Dickie leaned over, gave him a blue ribbon and shook his hand. Jim held up the ribbon briefly, reddened, and headed back toward Ginger's booth.

"Next up is the award for Realtor of the Year."

Sweat prickled on Ginger's brow. She couldn't stop smiling, and had even taken a few steps toward the truck. Her breathing was shallow and quick.

"This year it goes to...Tandy Brickenhausen!"

Ginger's smile froze on her face like a funhouse mask. Her ears could not process the noise they had just heard. She stumbled forward and stopped short as if an invisible wall kept her from taking another step.

"Looks like Tandy's not here...probably out selling houses!" Dickie quipped when no one came forward to accept the ribbon. The crowd tittered. "I'll get this to her later," he mumbled, stashing the ribbon back in his bag and pulling out another. "And now, the award for Homemaker of the Year goes to..."

Ginger broke through the wall for a moment and stumbled a few steps forward. She reached out her hand, then let it drop. "But it can't...she isn't..."

As she mumbled more nonsense words, her peripheral vision began to darken and fade, as if curtains were slowly being drawn, until only Dickie in the bed of the truck existed in a beam of otherworldly light, though she had long stopped being able to understand his words. They seemed to pull out long and drippy like warm taffy. She dropped her head in her hands, eyes shut tight. Why couldn't she comprehend what he was saying...?

From some distant part of her brain, she felt a comforting hand on one shoulder and another around her waist, as if holding her up. She heard the faint sound of other voices as well.

"Ginger, it's OK," Jim said, wiping her brow with a handkerchief. "This doesn't mean anything. You'll always be realtor of the year to me..."

"Hey Gin," Max said, her tiny claw clutching at Ginger's elbow. "Keep your shit together. You win a few, you lose a few."

"Mom," Harvest said, attempting to lead her back to the booth. "Are you all right? Jim, go get her some water!"

Ginger let herself be turned around and led to a folding chair. "Tandy Brickenhausen? Realtor of the Year? It's...it's..." Her eyes welled up.

"Mom, it's OK. Just sit," Harvest said, giving her a little shove. Ginger plopped down in the seat.

"Thirty-five years. Thirty-five years I've been Squamskootnocket's Realtor of the Year. And now it's over, just like that?! Because: why? Because she listed a subdivision. Big whoop! I could have done that in my sleep if she hadn't beat me to it! And has she sold anything there? I don't think so!"

"Don't worry, Gin," Max said, settling back in her lawn chair. "These damned awards are all a crock of shit. You know that!"

"They're not if you win them."

Jim rushed back with a cold glass of ginger ale. "Here, Gin, drink this down." Ginger did so without acknowledging him.

"Where is she?" Ginger, eyes wide and spooky, let the plastic cup drop to the grass.

"Dickie said she was at the subdivision today," Max said. "Hey, look, we'll get back at her. Before her open house next week we'll douse her Mocha Chai Machiatto with ex-lax. She'll be in the woods the whole time, mucking up the wetlands! Or maybe she'll try to go to your outhouse listing, which isn't even an outhouse any more! Don't worry, Gin," she patted Ginger's hand, "we'll get her."

Harvest gave Max a harsh look. "Mom, everything happens for a reason."

"Did you really just say that?" Ginger looked at Harvest as if she'd never slapped eyes on her before. "I try to raise you right, and then you come up with this regurgitated hooey—"

"Just try to relax," Jim said. "There's always next year."

Ginger's hands tightened on the chair. She drew in a deep breath and parsed it out slowly and evenly. Her eyes grew hard, her shoulders set. She pushed herself out of the seat, sprinted to the Vespa and leapt on it, kick-starting the motor. It sputtered to life on the first try. Without a word, she spun out and carved a wide circle in the lot, one Weejun dragging the dirt for purchase.

"No, Mom, don't go!" Harvest yelled, running after her.

"I don't like this," Max muttered, sipping at her thermos.

Ginger, wild eyed and helmetless, jammed it into gear and roared away from the booth, ripping up the gravel path that crossed the common as she zoomed out to Main Street.

⁂ ⁂ ⁂

Much later, Ginger would try to reconstruct just what was going through her mind as she hurtled down Main Street leaving behind the lights and sounds of Squamskootnocket Day; the wind in her hair, the sun in her eyes, her past in her past, her future in the future, her present a numbing buzz of rage and forward motion. At that moment there was only here, now, this bump and turn in the road, this red light to run, this speed limit to break, this side road to veer onto, nearly flipping over into a ditch...

All Ginger felt as she raced along was a burning need to set eyes on Tandy again, to see just what it was this woman had that could destroy her, annihilate her, wipe out over thirty years of hard work in the blink of an IM. She needed to comprehend what anorexic tale there was to tell, what innovative e-presence strategy, what big-city cunning, what thinking outside the box, what flip and tease of upmarket fifties-hair-worn-in-irony, what Beemer logic, what blinding newest of the new that could erase her, Ginger Kanadoo, your kana-doo realtor, from the face of the earth.

That was her only plan: just to look at her.

Ginger careened into the subdivision, stopping inches from Tandy's car after fishtailing so hard she nearly slammed into the construction trailer. She paused, gasping for breath as if she'd been running. A relentless white noise roared in her ears.

"Tandy!" she yelled. "Are you in there? Tandy!" She beeped her little roadrunner horn. "Come out, now!"

Nothing. She revved the whining insect motor again, looking all around for signs of her. At the very top of the hill, directly blocking the blistering sun, sat a tractor. She squinted at it, then gunned the scooter up the hill, leaning her weight forward. The Vespa crawled steadily upward, throwing clumps of dirt and gravel behind it, until Ginger reached the crest of the subdivision and a circle of level ground.

She turned off the bike and peered down the embankment. There, at the bottom of the hill, just a few feet from the narrow beach at Squamskootnocket Lake, stood Tandy alongside Danny Ezerstadt. Motionless, they both looked up at her, shading their eyes from the sun.

Ginger dismounted the Vespa and gazed up at the looming excavating machine. 'Caterpillar' was written along the arm that elbowed to a fifteen-foot section with a shovel on the end as big as her scooter, its teeth caked with mud. She climbed up the giant rollers and pulled herself into the cabin of the thing. It smelled like Camels and rye whiskey. After settling into the hard mylar seat, she looked out and down the hill. The plastic-sheeted windows of the cabin distorted the silhouettes of Tandy and Danny, who had begun waving their arms. Their mouths moved—as if they were shouting—but still Ginger heard only the oceanic roar in her ears.

She studied the gears, fascinated. A key stuck out of the ignition, a filthy plastic nude dangling from it with a piece of twine. Ginger turned the key and started up the earth mover.

The guts of the thing rumbled to life with a voluptuous grinding and chug, like a dinosaur digesting a meal. For a moment she sat back, gazing out at the rolling hills of Squamskootnocket, the trees in bloom at the base of the hill, the newly framed houses with their four car garages in various stages of construction, and she imagined herself hearing her name called at the fair..."and the Realtor of the Year...well, who else could it be but our own Ginger Kanadoo!" and she ran up to the podium in slow motion, showered with rose petals and kisses, champagne popping and spraying in her hair...she saw herself driving through Squamskootnocket, her grinning, sporty thumbs-up For Sale sign outside every house on every street as far as the eye could see...she pranced through an orchard of trees with hundred dollar bills for leaves; they rained down on her as she gaily gathered them in a festive basket...she was naked except for a thong, rolling in piles and piles of money, laughing, throwing the bills up in the air and kissing them, tossing them coquettishly at all her debtors...she threw open the doors of a stunning fifteen-room mansion for Harvest who wandered from room to room, unable to speak...

Meanwhile, the part of her brain that was only casually observing reality saw that Tandy and Danny had begun to run up the hill toward her, an event that until this day she doesn't remember associating with her hand reaching down and releasing the emergency brake on the tractor, sending it lurching into motion down the hill, first at an almost leisurely pace, then rolling faster and faster, its fantastic heft sending it gobbling up yard after yard of ruptured earth until all Ginger saw was Tandy, closer and closer and clearer and clearer through the fogged plastic, a slip of black with a white face and her hands framing her cheeks just like The Scream; Tandy who had frozen in place in shock and fear, her death-by-flattening-via-tractor only seconds away, until—at the very last millisecond—Ginger lunged at the wheel and wrenched it to the right, erasing Tandy from her field of vision but revealing the quickly approaching Squamskootnocket Lake, its blackness like the maw of hell opening up to devour her, and her eyes grew wide and she screamed as the dark water came at her full throttle—

Chapter 30

Harvest's face melted and re-formed, then melted again in front of Ginger's eyes. With all her will she lifted her arm, which seemed to weigh a thousand pounds, to reach out and stroke her daughter's sweet pale cheek, her daughter who could speak to ghosts but who refused to find a way to make a living...but after a few moments she could no longer hold it up, and dropped it again.

"Oh my God, did I die?" Ginger asked. "Am I dead? Is this—are you an angel?"

"No, Mom, you're OK. You're alive, and I'm not an angel."

"But...where am I?" she said hoarsely. The room's dimensions drunkenly swam into focus: the narrow hospital bed with its thin, coarse blanket tucked around her, the beep and purr of machines on either side, the tray of untouched food at the foot of the bed, the uniformed officer standing in the doorway—

"Who's...who's that?"

"That's Officer Lumley, Mom. You remember Officer Lumley, from all your speeding tickets?"

A beefy cop with sloping shoulders and an officious air stood rocking on his heels in the doorway.

"Was I speeding?" she whispered to Harvest.

"In a way."

"Yes, but what—"

She looked her mother in the eyes. "Mom, listen to me. This is important. We're in Vanderskleet General Hospital. You went to Tandy's subdivision this afternoon and stole a tractor and drove it into Lake Squamskootnocket."

"Wow." She pushed herself all the way to a sitting position and reached down for her lime jell-o cubes. "I'll never do that again." She pulled her arm back. "My God, am I hurt?" she asked, her face whitening. "Concussion? Internal bleeding? Spinal fracture? Massive head trauma?"

"Nothing. Except you broke your pinkie." Harvest picked up Ginger's left hand from the bed.

Ginger stared at it like it was someone else's hand. "My God, will I be OK? Were there multiple fractures? Will this even heal properly? Will I be able to drive again? I could sue for loss of income—"

Harvest turned her hand over and showed her the tiny splint. "The littlest bone broke on your little finger, here, at the tip. They used a piece of a popsicle stick to set it, because they didn't have anything small enough."

Ginger glanced around at the equipment hovering near her head. "Then what's all this stuff for?"

"That was for the lady who was here before you. She just passed away, which is why you have this bed, you were in the hallway for hours—"

Ginger threw back the covers and jumped out of bed. Cold air rushed up her spine, and she realized for the first time she was in a hospital johnny. "Get me out of here! Get me my clothes! I need to get out of here!"

Officer Lumley took a step forward. He towered over them. Harvest held up her hand to him, then gripped her mother by the shoulder. "Mom, you can't leave, OK?"

"Whaddya mean I can't leave? I'm leaving! You can stay here if you want, but I'm...I'm—"

"Mom, you can't leave because you're under arrest."

Ginger put her hands on her hips. "Of all the cockamamie bullshit—"

"It's true, Mrs. Kanadoo," Officer Lumley said as he straightened up even taller, his implements of peacekeeping clanking together. "You are under arrest for the attempted murder of one Tandy Brickenhausen, as well as grand larceny. As soon as you're discharged here, I'll be escorting you to the county jail."

"What?" she said to Officer Lumley. Then to Harvest, "What?"

Harvest shrugged. "It's true."

Ginger cocked her head at the cop. "Could you excuse us for just a few minutes? My daughter and I would like to go get a little dinner at the cafeteria together. Would that be OK?"

"But Mom, I already had din—"

"Well, I'm starving." Everyone looked at her full dinner tray at the foot of the bed. "And I need some hot food in me. Is that OK, Officer Lumley? Is that OK, having some decent food, or is that against some local, obscure, no-hot-meals-after-false-arrest Vanderskleet law?"

Officer Lumley stood aside and made a lead-the-way gesture.

Ginger harrumphed, straightened her shoulders, and thanked Harvest as she slipped a robe over her johnny. She shuffled out into the hall in her one-size-fits all slippers, Harvest at her heels.

"Slow down, Ma. It's not a race."

She kept moving. "Just trying to lose the old galoot."

"You're not going to 'lose' him, Ma. He's going to follow us wherever we go."

"That's all you know, little missy."

Officer Lumley hovered at the entrance of the cafeteria. The room stank of old cheese and antiseptic. Ginger got in line behind a doctor in scrubs and a patient in a wheelchair. When it was her turn she squinted up at the menu, then down at the miserable little person in a hairnet. She couldn't make out the gender.

"Excuse me, Missss-ter, but do you have any white zinfandel? Or if you don't have an expansive wine list, any alcohol at all of any kind?"

"We're a hospital, ma'am," came a squirty little voice. "We don't serve alcohol."

"Nothing medicinal in a place full of medicines? Hard to believe!"

"No, ma'am. I got coffee, decaf, tea, and cocoa. Plus pop, a' course." It gestured with a horrible little forearm to a Coke machine in the corner.

"We'll have two cocoas, please," Harvest said, fishing for her change purse.

They carried their instant cocoas to the farthest corner of the cafeteria by the window. Officer Lumley kept his distance but watched their every move.

"Harvey," Ginger whispered. "You have to get me out of here. I'm not guilty, OK? I mean, were there witnesses?"

"Tandy, for one. And Danny. And Jim followed you and said he saw the whole thing."

"Oh my God, it's not going to be in the *Bugle*, is it?"

"Jim said he'd do his best to keep it out."

Ginger clasped her hands together as in prayer. "Oh, thank you, Jimmy, thank you thank you. Does Dickie know?"

"Well, yeah."

"Shit. Fucking hell." She sipped at her cocoa. "So is Tandy...mad?"

"She's pressing charges."

"I had no intention of killing anyone, Harv, you have to believe me. That's just silliness. I got in that tractor because I felt like it. Because your grandad used to drive one of those, and I always wanted to see what it was like, but he would never let me, and so here was my big chance—"

"Grandpa was a lawyer. He never had a tractor."

"Or maybe it was your Uncle Matt. In any case—"

"Mom, tell the truth. You need to tell me the truth."

Ginger swirled her cocoa, glanced behind her at Officer Lumley, turned back to Harvest. "Killing that woman was the farthest thing from my mind. I wish I could tell you why I did what I did with the tractor. I was kind of in a haze. I didn't have a goal. I just did one thing, then the next, then the next and the last thing I remember was seeing Tandy in front of me and I grabbed the wheel and turned it so I wouldn't hurt her. Don't I get any points for that?"

Harvest looked out the window at the gathering clouds. "I don't know, Mom, I just don't know."

"Look, I have to go to the bathroom. You think our man in blue will allow that?"

⁂ ⁂ ⁂

Ginger brushed by Officer Lumley on her way to the woman's room. Six stalls were lined up against one wall. Ginger entered one of them. Harvest stood at the sink, staring at herself in the mirror. Eventually she splashed some cold water on her face and washed her hands, drying them thoughtfully. She heard a crash and whipped around.

Her mother was halfway out one of the casement windows, her bottom half wriggling, her legs kicking at the wall. Harvest ran over to the stall door and yanked at it but it was locked. She got down on her hands and knees, crawled under the door, climbed up on the toilet, grabbed hold of her mother's ample waist, and pulled. Ginger popped back in like a cork from a bottle, sending them both tumbling to the floor of the stall.

Ginger moaned, holding her pinkie. "I think I broke it again."

"Mom, why do you do these stupid things?"

"I saw this once on Dragnet. Shit, I was almost out until you grabbed me!"

"You were stuck, Ma."

Ginger got teary-eyed. "Harvey, I can't go to jail. My career...you...what will happen to you? Oh God, I'm a big, fat failure. You have to help me escape."

"That isn't the way, Mom. They'll find you."

"You're right," she said, wiping her eyes. "They'll hunt me down and shoot me like a dog. There's no place to hide. Or...how long can I live on the lam? I suppose I could live off the land, making zin from grapes I find in fields, hopping on trains for points west..." Her eyes got misty again.

"Mom, you're going to jail."

Ginger looked at her. "You mean that, don't you."

"I do. I can't help you if you run off."

Ginger snuffled up again. "So you'll help me, Harv? You won't abandon your old ma?"

Harvest put her arms around her as Ginger began to bawl. "No, Mom, I would never do that."

Chapter 31

Ginger still wore the clothes she'd been arrested in, the tangerine short-sleeved summer pantsuit and sensible white wedgie sandals, her suit jacket covered with the big bright buttons that said: "I Heart My Realtor," "Realtors Need Love Too," and "Happy Realtor Day!" She mindlessly played with them as she lay sprawled on her cot watching with glazed eyes *The Price is Right* on a tiny black and white TV which sat on the cement floor of her eight-by-ten-foot jail cell. A filthy commode was the only other object in the room. Daylight filtered down weakly from a narrow window high up the wall.

The clang of a door opening and closing, voices male and female. She jumped up, turned off the TV and hunkered there, listening.

It was Harvest! Finally!

She straightened herself in her filthy clothes and jumped at the bars, shrieking, "Let me out of here! I didn't do it! Helllllpp!"

The voices stopped, replaced by the sound of footsteps coming toward her. One set she was sure belonged to Joe Lumley, the other was unmistakably her daughter's.

Joe gave Ginger a look as she rattled the bars, fumbling with his keys until he found the correct one. Harvest, in black jeans and a black halter top, waited patiently.

"Harvest, what took you so long?" Ginger stepped back as the door opened and Joe locked them both in.

Harvest set an oversized shopping bag on the bed. "I had a little trouble with the Vespa, OK? Plus I met with your attorney—"

"—who's retarded—"

"—he's not retarded. He's doing the best he can. He serves the whole Squamskootnocket Valley, he said, so he's a little busy."

Ginger plopped down on her cot, eyes cast down, then lifted them enough to look at the bag Harvest had brought.

"So what did you bring me?" Without waiting for an answer, Ginger reached in and pulled out sweatpants, T-shirts, underwear, socks, a Snickers bar and a little book. "Oh good, something to read!" She opened the book and thumbed through the pages. "But this is blank!"

Harvest sat down next to her on the bed. "It's a book to write in, Ma. You know, your thoughts and stuff."

"Like a diary?" She turned it over in her hands. "I've never written one before, and I never will, but thanks anyway, hon." She gamboled about a bit more in the bag, realized she'd reached the bottom, then sat back against the cinderblock wall and sighed.

"I thought it would be good for you to try to process everything that's happened. You'd be amazed at what you discover."

Ginger thought back to reading Harvest's diaries, before she'd been caught and Harvest started hiding them better. They were a pretty cool read.

"Mom, I'm going to ask you one more time. You just gotta come clean with me. Did you try to kill Tandy?"

Ginger tossed aside the Snickers bar she had just unwrapped and started to pace the length of the tiny cell.

"Honey, you are really starting to bug me with this stuff. Actually, it's not just you—that stupid lawyer keeps asking me too. Even Jim asked me yesterday when he brought me an Elvis from the Pit, and now you again and I—"

"Well, what have you been telling everybody?"

"You know, different stuff—"

"Different stuff?" Harvest slapped the palms of her hands down hard on the mattress.

Ginger paused under the window. "OK, OK, just listen. The truth is: I don't know. The truth is, I sort of blanked out. I just don't remember much about that day. I mean, maybe I did want to kill her, maybe I lusted in my heart, like Cheney or whoever, but I didn't kill her, bottom line, OK? She's still freakin' breathing, isn't she?"

Harvest shook her head and turned away.

"Well, is she?"

Harvest looked up at the window. "Mom, do you have any money? I'm getting a little sick of banana bread."

Ginger rushed over to her and took her hand. "Oh, no, honey, I don't! I've got some rice pudding I saved from lunch—"

"Didn't Jim give you money for the car?"

"I sent it right off to the bank...not that it'll make much difference. We're still going to be evicted in three weeks."

"I know. I've been thinking about that."

Ginger sat back down with her on the bed. They both stared up at the amber evening light framed in the window.

"Harvey, I was wondering. If I were Wiccan, do you think I could get out of jail?"

"It could be easier, yes, but not necessarily. There's no easy fix with anything, Mom, even with magick on your side."

"But there is a chance that it would help?"

"Well, yeah."

"Then that's it. I wanna be Wiccan."

Harvest sat up straight. "Mom, becoming Wiccan has to come from your heart, not just because you want to get out of jail."

"But I wanna be Wiccan! Just make me Wiccan! And stop being such a fuddy-duddy witch and get me out of here!"

Harvest got her to her feet and went to the jail cell door. "If you don't stop acting like an infant, I'm going to leave you here to rot. Now, if you were really serious about being Wiccan, you'd spend some time thinking about what you did. And how you can make it right."

A range of emotions washed over Ginger. She wasn't sure which to grab onto: terror, wonderment at who her daughter was, confusion, or a tiny smidgen of hope. She settled on terror.

"You do realize that I'm going to the big house tomorrow in East Packasquantskunt unless someone comes up with five grand to spring me."

Harvest looked away, her hand on the door.

"Will you visit me there, sweetie?

She nodded, her eyes wet.

"And thanks for coming to see me today and bringing me this stuff. And I will think about what you said, I really will. I'll write in this book," she said, holding it up.

"Joe," Harvest called down the echoing hallway. "We're finished!"

Joe soon appeared and unlocked the door. Harvest pushed it opened with a screech.

"I'll start right now." Ginger grabbed a pen and held that up too, then started scribbling in the book. "See? I'm writing down all my thoughts and feelings—"

"Bye, Mom," Harvest said with a finger wave, and walked slowly down the long hallway and into the light.

⁂ ⁂ ⁂

A few hours later, after a dinner of spaghetti and canned pineapple chunks, Ginger opened her eyes in her dark cell as the beams of a flashlight played off the walls and ceiling above her. She had changed into her sweatpants outfit, transferring her pin-on buttons to it to keep her cheered up, though it wasn't easy catching much shuteye the way they poked at her through the clothing.

Through the ooze of semi-consciousness she watched the lumbering shadow of Joe Lumley fill the hall, inhaling the cloud of tobacco smoke that always preceded him. This fortuitous nocturnal visit could only mean one thing. She jumped from the cot and opened her arms.

"I'm free!"

"Not exactly." He handed her a phone through the bars. "But you do have a phone call." She gave him a questioning look, as in, what fresh hell could this be... "It's Dickie."

"Dickie!" She grabbed the phone from Joe and turned away. "Are you gonna come get me? This is great! You're just in time—"

"No, sorry, I'm not coming to get you. In fact, I have some bad news for you."

"How is that possible?"

"I just got an email from Big Jean."

"An email—"

"Yeah, she's online now. She didn't tell you? She thinks it's great shit, the internet. Guess her roommate got into it and she took off from there. Even started her own blog, www.whymydaughtersucks.com. Gettin' tons of hits. Anyway, long story short, you're fired."

"But...why?" Ginger said, tearing up.

"No offense, Gin, but you are wanted for murder—"

"Attempted murder, and I musta not wanted to murder her too bad because I didn't do a very good job, now did I—"

"Oh, don't get all bent. Actually, I don't think that was why, anyway."

"Well, why?"

"To be honest, I think it's cuz you missed her birthday. She turned ninety on Sunday."

"Shitshitshit!" Ginger said, stomping around her cell. "I totally forgot. First time ever. And this had to be the time." She sighed. "So what'd you get her?"

"An iPod and an X-Box. Christ, she has everything else, a new PC, a laser printer—"

"I can't believe she fired me. Her own daughter!"

"Says she doesn't need you for your 'shopping abilities' any more, whatever that means."

She gripped a cold bar of her cell. "You know what, Dick, I gotta go."

"Sorry about all this, Gin."

She sniffled.

"Were you really gonna kill her and all that? Man, things weren't going your way, but I didn't think ya had it in ya."

"Goodnight, Dick," she said, and clicked off the phone.

She slid the phone out into the hallway and crawled back into bed. The moon shone down bright on her face as she lay on the thin pillow, blinking, wide awake, craving a spot of zin to take the edge off of things. With one hand she reached under the pillow and pulled out the little blank book and opened to the first page. Illuminated by the moonlight, she sat up with the book in her lap.

Oh Gods of Wiccanity, she thought, I need a miracle! I am no longer a Kanadoo Realtor. Banished from the business, forgotten by family, cut off from the world and on my way to the pokie at first light. She wrote, "I will be a good realtor. I will be a good realtor. I will be a good realtor." She stared at the scrawled sentences. She thought of Harvest's pale face, her earnest words. She squeezed her eyes shut and took herself back to Squamskootnocket Day, conjuring everything about that afternoon, looking for the moment when she had the thought, "I am going to kill Tandy Brickenhausen," but she couldn't find it. She relived the rage she felt at hearing the announcement, the out-of-control thoughts and strange behavior up to starting that tractor, and then she remembered: she only realized Tandy was in her sites after she had released the brake and started rolling down the hill...she sighed with relief.

She looked down at the little book, now wet with her tears. She took her pen, crossed out the word 'realtor' and replaced it with 'person.' With a wave of exhaustion, she lay down and slept like a baby.

* * *

Two weeks passed. Ginger was almost getting used to the routine of prison: the harsh orange jumpsuits and harsher overhead lights, the five a.m. wake up calls and nine p.m. lights out, the grits and government cheese, the one hour of recreation a day where she tried to make friends with anyone who didn't scare the shit out of her. She eventually got a roommate, a three-hundred-pound woman named Sam with four teeth who was in love with Meg Ryan, and who one day remarked that if she squinted at Ginger just so, she could almost see Meg's perky, lopsided grin. Ginger was quick to volunteer at times like these that Jim Steele (who visited her daily) was her husband and that he was going to bail her out at any moment, a moment which had not yet arrived for various reasons. Even though Ginger swore up and down she was in jail for an unfounded attempted murder charge, she became known as "That Crazy Tractor Bitch" by the inmates, and was treated with a strange brand of respect. She asked Sam what she was in for, and Sam told her that she had started her own meth lab, but even though Ginger let out a low whistle, she didn't see why people should be punished for teaching math.

One afternoon, right after lunch, Ginger was told she had a visitor and that she would be taken to a visitation booth. She thought for sure it was Jim, but as she was led into the small room with a table, phone, and bulletproof partition, she was overjoyed to see Maxie seated on the other side.

She grabbed the phone and sat down. Max picked up her phone. "I thought you'd never come to see me, Max. I thought you hated me."

"Don't be an idiot. I've been busy. We've all been busy. How are you? You look good. Thinner." She pushed over a small white cake. "I baked you a cake."

"Thanks, Max. Is there a file in it?" she whispered.

"Why would there be a file in it? It's coconut cream, your favorite. So, how's life in the slammer?"

"Let me tell you, I've really been bettering myself here. Writing in my little book. I'm even thinking of writing a memoir, calling it something like, *Radon in the Well: Deep Thoughts of a Realtor in Jail.* Anyway, I've been doing some hard thinking. You know, having thoughts. I've been going to these AA meetings here just for something to do. It's that or pump iron. I mean, I like my Taylor Country but I'm no alky. Anyway, people talk about their feelings and stuff, which, I don't know if you've ever thought about feelings—I certainly haven't spent much time on that—but I realized this, Max: I've been to Squamskootnocket, I've been to Vanderskleet, I've been to Bangerlangersville, I've even been to Saskawee-gee-on-Lake, but you know, I've never been to me."

"We have to get you out of here."

"Do you have any money? You know I'll pay you back the minute I—"

"Please. I'm still paying off the dachshund and the five hundred eggs and fifty pounds of flour and the—"

"No more royalties from the Guinness Book of World Records? I mean, you're still the oldest realtor in the world, right?"

"Sure, but it's not enough to get you out of here. Look, Ginger, I've got some really good news, but when I tell you, you have to promise me you won't be jealous."

"Of course not. This is the new me, Max. Everything bad that can happen has already happened to me. It's over. I'm zen. I'm one with the universe. Nowhere to go but up."

"I'm Wiccan."

"You bitch! How can you be Wiccan?"

Max sat up taller in her chair. "My name is Maxie Laughing Unicorn Kanadoo."

"How did you—"

"Keep your voice down, I've got a lot more to tell you—"

At that moment the door opened behind Max. Harvest shyly entered the room, followed by Sheena, Brian, and Frankie. They all smiled and waved at Ginger through the glass. Max handed Harvest the phone.

"Hi, Mom."

"Hi, honey! It's so good to see you!"

"Sorry it's been so long since I've come by. We've all been really busy. We just had our August first full moon celebration where we welcomed Maxie here," she put a hand on Maxie's birdlike shoulder—Maxie beamed— "and since this month's celebration is about grains, breads, the continuation of the harvest and sacrifices—not literally—the group has decided to come together to help me out. And each other as well." Everyone smiled big. "So what we did was, well, we all got our real estate licenses. Online."

Sheena took the phone from Harvest. "I failed my cosmotology exam, so I took that as a sign that it just wasn't my calling."

Brian took the phone from her. "You probably know that Shapes went out of business," he said, as Frankie nodded, "and actually, I didn't get any financial aid so I can't go to college right now, so we thought we'd start our own real estate company." He handed the phone back to Harvest.

"Are you OK, Mom? Don't cry."

"I'm just...I'm just so happy..."

"And we think we can get you out of here pretty soon, right?" Everyone nodded. "I've sold a few more spells, Frankie's been teaching some yogalates out of her home, and Jim's offered to pitch in too, so we're talking about some time next week..."

"I can do our website," Brian said. "I'm thinking: black and blood red."

"You guys...you're all behind me. I'm overcome." Ginger wiped her eyes.

"So listen, Mom, I thought we'd call ourselves Coven Real Estate."

"I love it! We'll have a 'hire the Wiccan' policy."

"That's perfect, Mom. So now you need to think of a name. You know, a Wiccan name."

"How about: Ginger 'Dragon Wind' Kanadoo?"

"Welcome, Dragon Wind!" The Wiccans clasped hands, smiled and raised their arms high behind the glass partition.

Chapter 32

TWO WEEKS LATER

Late on a crisp fall afternoon, Ginger stood at the foot of the subdivision next to her moped, staring at the construction trailer. A light burned in the tiny window. Every cell in her body wanted to jump back on her ride and toot toot on outta there, but instead she draped her helmet over the seat, partially covering her new COVN RLTRS license plate and "Support Your Local Wiccan" bumper sticker, brushed off her chaps, strode up the three plastic steps and knocked on the aluminum door.

"Come in!" came Tandy's voice. Its tenor was that of a realtor expecting a buyer: full of sugar.

Tandy sat at a metal desk covered in builder's plans. The smell of sawdust and freshly turned dirt filled the trailer. Her face, frozen in a smile of welcoming, stayed that way except for one eyebrow which arched superciliously the moment she saw Ginger, then settled into: inscrutable. She gestured at a folding chair. Ginger stayed standing.

"To what do I owe this honor?" Tandy said, her smile well on the fade.

"I guess I came to let you know that I'm not mad any more about what happened—"

Tandy barked out a laugh. "You! Not mad at me?" She tapped a pencil quick and hard on the table. "I'm sorry, but I was under the impression that you were trying to kill me."

Ginger rubbed sweaty hands on her pants. "Well, that's just the thing. I wasn't trying to kill you."

"Oh, were you trying to kill Danny?"

"I wasn't trying to kill anybody. I was just screwing around with the tractor. I didn't even realize you were in the way until after I released the brake. And then, well, then I had to do something about it."

Tandy gazed out the window at the multimillion dollar monoliths rising up all around her. "Do you really expect me to believe you? I was one second—a heartbeat—from death. Because of you. I mean, think about it: there's me, meeting with Danny, then there's you, hurtling down the hill in that monster machine, coming straight at me."

"You have a point. It would have been better if I'd gone to a matinee or something. But instead I, well—"

"—instead you tried to kill off the competition."

Ginger cleared her throat. "You can think what you want. I can't change that. I only have power over myself."

Tandy gave her a funny look. "Is that some kind of witch thing?"

"The fact is, I came here to apologize for putting you through all this. I'm sorry." Ginger gasped. "OK, I said it."

"Well, I don't accept your apology. I don't believe a word you're saying."

Ginger shrugged. "That's too bad. That's your choice, I guess."

"Yes, it is my choice. Now please leave."

"Do you, um, have a restroom in this place?"

Tandy turned her back to Ginger and filed something. "There's a Sanican outside." Slam of drawer.

"Okee dokee."

Ginger opened the soup-can door and stepped down to the hard-packed dirt outside. She took a deep breath and let it out. Her head felt clear and light, and she was shocked to discover that, as much as she had been dreading the last three minutes of her life, now she felt ready to face anything.

The door of the Sanican squeaked open and snapped shut behind her. Just as she was finishing up and reaching blindly somewhere to the right for a scrap of toilet paper, she saw something move on the inside of the door. A striped thing that wriggled a few inches diagonally down in front of her. She froze. It froze. Her heart thudded in her ears. With aching slowness, she turned her head and looked to the right for the toilet paper holder. A tiny set of beady eyes looked back at her from that wall. A second something! She set her eyes front again. The original something had moved and was now on the floor at her feet.

Then she heard a sound—ftttzzzzzz—like tiny wings beating hard. Almost never a good sound, she thought. She gasped, then shrieked as something bit into the back of her neck, tiny leathery wings beating her head as it sunk its teeth deeper into her.

She burst out of the Sanican, hiking up her pants with one hand, with the other swatting madly at the thing embedded in her neck. She hurled herself on the Vespa and kicked it to life. After a few agonizing moments she got hold of the slimy thing and lobbed it into the bushes.

It wasn't until she reached Main Street that she noticed a stabbing pain in her ankle. The other one, the one on the floor, had lodged there. Wailing, she roared down the road as fast as she could to Jim's office.

⁂ ⁂ ⁂

Ginger sat on the toilet in the bathroom at the Squamskootnocket *Bugle*. Jim sat on the floor, her ankle resting on his lap.

Gently, he rolled up her pant leg. "Good lord," he said in an almost reverent tone.

"What? Can't you get it off me?"

"Oh, don't worry. These little suckers'll pop right off if you hold an ice cube on 'em."

"Well, get one, then!" Ginger said hoarsely, her face stained with tears.

He tenderly set her foot down on a towel and ran out. She tried not to look at the thing but couldn't help it. It was a long, froggy amphibian of some sort with green webby wings and fangs that were mostly sunk into her flesh. Jim rushed back into the room. He pressed a cube on the thing's head, and in moments it unlocked its jaws and opened its mouth, dislodging inch-long teeth. Jim threw it in a shoebox and covered it, snapping several rubber bands around the box.

"What the hell is that thing, Jim?"

He was quiet as he washed her ankle with warm, soapy water. "I can't tell you what a find this is. I actually believe that thing in that box is a very rare Winged Saber-Toothed Salamander. They're extremely endangered. Their breeding grounds are protected." She winced as he poured disinfectant on her foot. "You, my dear, have made an amazing discovery.

I'm going to call the Squamskootnocket Conservation Commission about this first thing in the morning. Believe me, they'll be very interested in what we've found here today."

"They will?"

"I promise you they will. So tell me, Gin, where were you exactly when you came upon these marvelous creatures?"

Chapter 33

SIX MONTHS LATER

A brisk winter wind whistled through the partially constructed homes at Daffodil Court; some framed, some just a foundation, others only a giant hole in the dirt. One was actually finished, complete with HouseAlive! technology, just waiting to tell someone it was time to replace the sour milk in the fridge or track down that AWOL teen.

The wind rattled the half open door of the abandoned construction trailer, scattering plans to the floor. A fine snow sifted through a screened window leaving a powdery dusting on the desk, file cabinet, and phone. Tandy's signs, once everywhere on the subdivision, had been taken down or simply abandoned, buried under the snow.

Even the Sanican was gone.

The moment the Conservation Commission of Squamskootnocket Valley determined that the thing that attacked Ginger was indeed the rare and endangered Winged Saber-Toothed Salamander, and that its breeding ground was all of

Old Man Higgins's land except Ginger's outhouse listing's tenth of an acre, all construction at the subdivision was called to a halt. Indefinitely.

Not long after that, Tandy packed her bags and headed out to the Pacific Northwest, or that was the rumor. No one ever heard from her again, although when Harvest googled her a year later she learned Tandy was currently serving time for extortion from her former company, Stoops of Manhattan.

With no one else left at his shop, Dickie sold out to a Dollar General and retired in Florida, rather than gather a new crew of agents and "go against a gaggle of witches." No one missed him.

Regina Freenspeet's house eventually sold to a young couple who had no sense of smell, a condition known as anosmia. Harvest recruited them by researching online "people with anosmia looking for a home in Squamskoot-nocket Valley, New York." She got one match. So in the end, Ginger never had to tell Regina that her house smelled like shit; however Harvest insisted that in order to be a good Wiccan, Ginger had to come clean and let her know the truth. So Ginger took Regina to the Coffee Pit and ordered her her favorite club sandwich. She started out with, "Well, the good news, Regina, is that you don't smell like shit. Your house, on the other hand..." and so on. There were tears, there were hugs. Anyway, it worked out, and finally Regina was able to sell her house and run into the waiting arms of DeeShaun and his five kids at Dallas/Fort Worth International Airport.

Brian scored one when he sold Ginger's outhouse listing to an outhouse collector from South Dakota who nearly faint-ed with love when he saw it, saying, "Do you have any idea who crapped here? *Any*? Sammy Davis Junior, Bella Lugosi, Cher, Mel Torme. All the big names!" He offered full price, cash, immediate close. Offer: accepted.

Danny Ezerstadt was interested in buying 666 Phantom Lane, but just as with Regina, Harvest insisted Ginger get real about the home's special features, as in: Thadius. Turned out Danny wasn't fazed in the least. He bought it, gutted the place, put in four full baths (one with a Jacuzzi) and relisted it with Ginger who sold it in days. Except for the discovery of one hell of a bathtub ring one morning soon after reconstruction, there were no problems at all.

But beyond the jubilance around soaring sales for Coven Realty, there was love in the air. Over Elvises at the Coffee Pit, Jim proposed to Ginger and she accepted, confessing to Maxie later that "ever since he removed that slimy monster from my ankle, I couldn't get him out of my head." Harvest wasn't alone too much longer either. Listing new construction in Saskaweegee-on-Lake, she met and fell head over heels for a young Wiccan carpenter named Sally "Raven Thunder" Frankenspiel.

In fact, all was fruitful and peaceful until one Friday night in the middle of February when Ginger got the call from Max: Big Jean had died. Beyond the sadness around her death, they realized the reason her loss seemed especially painful. Nobody had had a chance to say goodbye. No one in the family had reconciled with her after she'd fired Ginger. After some discussion, Max and Ginger decided that the only solution was to get out the Ouija board, have a séance and try to get in touch with her that way.

* * *

Late that night, Harvest lit six heavy beeswax candles and set them in the center of the kitchen table. Outside, a nor'easter was blowing in, piling snow in drifts that almost reached the windowsills of their tiny bungalow. Ginger sat at the table, teary-eyed, while Max took a seat across from her.

"Yah gotta remember, Gin," Maxie said, tucking in to the table, "she died where she was happiest. Online."

"She did look peaceful, Mom," Harvest said, laying out a plate of Raisinettes and a glass of Sutter Home, Big Jean's favorite food and drink. "The way they found her, she looked like she just fell asleep on her keyboard. They told me she was IMing some guy in Columbia, something like that." She sighed, appraising the layout of her offerings. "Anyway, are we ready for this?"

"I am," Maxie said, cracking her knuckles. "My sister. What a piece of work."

"No negative thoughts, Auntie Max, only respectful ones. Or she may just not bother showing up."

Max nodded somberly.

"Mom, you ready?"

Ginger nodded.

"OK. Let's start by holding hands." They did so and all took a deep breath. Harvest raised her chin. Her voice was full and resonant. "Our beloved Big Jean, we bring you gifts from life into death. Commune with us, Big Jean, and move among us."

Ginger trembled as she held her daughter and Max's hands, but beyond its usual fifty-year-old draftiness, the house was silent and still.

"Grandma," Harvest said softly, as if she really were in the room, "all three of us here—your daughter, granddaughter, and sister—feel that we missed saying goodbye to you. We wish you peace in your new world, but, if you are able, would like your company for just a few minutes in this one."

Maxie started to snore.

"Auntie, wake up!" Harvest hissed, squeezing her hand. Max blinked and looked around, the candles reflected twice in her huge glasses.

"Right," Maxie said. "...right. Come on, Big Jean, show us what you've got."

A cool draft pooled around Ginger's feet. She shivered and gripped everyone's hands a little tighter. Harvest looked at her.

"If you're with us, Grandma, give us a sign."

A familiar, sweet smell rose up from the floor. The odor grew stronger as swirls of ashy smoke escaped from under the table and curled up to the ceiling. They all began to cough.

"It's weed!" Maxie said, smiling. "She's here!"

"Hi, Mom!" Ginger sat forward in her chair.

"OK, let's get out the board," Harvest said, opening it between Max and Ginger. "Big Jean, welcome! Please stay. We'd like to ask you some questions..."

She pointed at Ginger, who cleared her throat and said, "Mom, it's Ginger." A thick coil of smoke twirled like a lasso up to the rafters. "I just wanted to say I'm sorry I didn't get to visit you very much toward the end. Things got...busy. I just want to know, do you forgive me for forgetting your birthday? Because I forgive you for firing me..."

The planchette lifted slightly, then dropped. Max and Ginger gasped, then rode the thing over to Yes. Ginger smiled.

"Big Jean? This is your sister, Max. I just wanted to say goodbye, and good luck. I learned a lot from you, and even though you were kind of mean, we sure had a lot of fun, didn't we?"

The planchette drifted to the other side of the board, then flew back to Yes. Max smiled, her eyes wet.

"I wanted to say goodbye to you too, Grandma," Harvest said. "We all love you and wish you—"

Drip, drip, PLOP. Never had a drop of water in a metal sink sounded so loud. Everyone turned their heads toward the noise. The drops quickened, morphing into a stream which soon blasted full force from the faucet into the basin, sending up a fine spray. Harvest jumped to her feet, turned off the faucets and froze, listening. Nobody moved.

Upstairs, the pipes began to bang, water coursing through them. Harvest rushed back to Max and Ginger who sat transfixed. She rested one hand on each of their shoulders.

"Is someone else here?"

Max and Ginger gasped as the planchette sprung to life under their fingers. It leapt to the letters T, H, A, D, I, U, S.

"Thadius is here! Welcome!"

Again, the planchette was on the move. Harvest read off the letters. "T, H, A, N, X...F, O, R..." And then it stopped.

"Thanks for what, Thadius?" Harvest asked breathlessly.

Off it went. "J, A, K, O, O, Z, I."

Everyone laughed as Thadius continued. "F, I, N, A, L,Y...C, L, E, A, N."

"You're welcome!" Ginger said. "It was a pleasure."

But the planchette wouldn't stop. "B, I, G...J, E, A, N...I, S...D, A...B, O, M, B." It hovered, then shot to the W and spelled, "W, E, R, E...I, N...L, O, V, E."

As if completely spent, the planchette fell to the board and stayed there. Something, or somethings, had left. The electricity that had buzzed so strongly through Ginger's and Max's fingers was gone.

"Big Jean, Thadius, is there anything more you'd like to tell us?" Harvest asked.

Already, the pot smell was beginning to dissipate. The pipes knocked one more time, then fell silent.

Harvest motioned for all of them to once again take each other's hands. "Big Jean, Thadius, we want to thank you for joining us tonight. It meant a lot to all of us. Go in peace."

The draftiness around their feet disappeared, replaced by a cozy warmth. For a few moments, they all sat motionless just looking at each other, as the wind stopped its howling and the snow fell soft and silent outside the kitchen window, sparkling with the light of the full winter moon.

⁂ ⁂ ⁂

Acknowledgments

I am indebted to the following people
for their contributions to this work:

To my first readers: Kathleen Kotwica, Anne McGrail, Elaine Courtney, Nina Huber, Marguerite McGrail, Steve Drouin, Cynthia Kimball, Kate Carney, Joan Donner, Ray Bachand, Elise and Stephen Smith, Susan and Jon Abrahamson, Hugh Kennedy, and Katrin Schumann for their love and support and for talking me off the bridge at regular intervals.

To my editor, map-creator and dear friend Valerie Spain, to my cover copy genius and lifelong friend Mary McGrail, from the bottom of my heart, thank you.

For their unflagging enthusiasm and general cheering on: Aaron Zimmerman, Julie "Giulietta" Nardone, Linda Werbner, Gail Shobin, Cat Strahan, Susan Gonnella, Beth Byrne, Mike Hunter, Judy Leerer, Barbara Epstein, Judy Blomquist, Lee Griffin, Marisa Bachand, Gary Mott and Tony Kahn from WGBH, illustrator Victor Juhasz, cover designer Henry Sene Yee, and artists/writers/publishers and generally wonderful people Nancy Grossman and John Grossman of Back Channel Press.

And finally, deep gratitude to my husband, George, my love and greatest champion.

Erica Ferencik is a realtor living in Framingham, Massachusetts, as well as a prize-winning writer of fiction and nonfiction including novels, screenplays, and essays. Catch her on NPR via WGBH's "Morning Stories" or go to www.CracksintheFoundation.com where you can "Ask Ginger!" all your burning real estate questions.

Interior design by Nancy Grossman of Back Channel Press. Text set in Scala Regular, with headings and footers in Lydian. Layout performed in Serif PagePlus. ⁕